THE
BRIDE
WHO RODE
IN WITH THE
STORM

Kitty-Lydia Dye

THE BRIDE WHO RODE IN WITH THE STORM
Copyright © 2021 by Kitty-Lydia Dye

ISBN: 978-1-955784-09-2

Published by Satin Romance
An Imprint of Melange Books, LLC
White Bear Lake, MN 55110
www.satinromance.com

Published in the United States of America.

Cover Design by Caroline Andrus

Dedicated to my mother and Bramble.

CHAPTER 1

January 912 – Heimer's Settlement, East Anglia

More enemies than friends went to the feast honouring Grimulf's return. The Varangian Guard had put down his axe, finally sated on the war and bloodshed his youth had craved. Most anticipated him claiming a wife and a great many hoped their daughters might catch his attention tonight.

The guest of honour had yet to be sighted. They blamed the storm. Not because it might have delayed Grimulf, but because he would have turned back to ride through it just for the thrill. His father, had he still lived, would have boomed with laughter along with the thunder if someone was foolish enough to warn him to rein in his son.

"It'd be the same as trying to tame the winds. It's not my job to stifle his lust for adventure. That's for his wife to do, if she wants him home long enough to net a few sons!"

Rain harried the land, striking the dunes and rattling the coarse bracken bushes. Night approached, the lightning only

1

a faint eyelash-like flutter of white against the whorls of magenta and poppy-red entwined with the clouds.

The mead hall blazed from the fires of the feast, fearlessly built on the edges of sand cliffs overlooking the sea. Timbers were carved into snarling dog creatures with lizard flesh instead of fur.

The guests ignored the whistle like wail of the wind. Their ale, a sharp, nettle sting needling their throats warm, sloshed into held out drinking horns. Trickles spiderwebbed down the sides as serving maids served up their smiles, too occupied with watching interest glisten in the men's eyes.

Grimulf's men caroused, exchanging stories from their battles. None seemed to care their master was missing. One man was too busy showing off the scar from his throat to his belly to any maid willing to trace her fingers along the raised flesh, still tanned from a Syrian sun.

Those who had come to report to their own chieftains sullenly licked the mead from their lips, eyeing the hall doors. They were not so trusting of the sudden truce brokered by the young man. He had absconded with many an enemy cursing his name. This night could lead to years of peace and unity against the Lady of the Mercians or the continuation of bloodshed.

Hunting dogs roamed beneath the tables, hungering for fallen scraps. Grimulf's favoured dog was amongst them. Shuck snuffled at a boot, tail thumping. The man's hand came down to scratch him on the ear, then gently nudged him lest he gave the game away.

Grimulf hid amongst his own people, hunched over like an old man with a cloak wrapped around him and a gnarled stick in his hand. He deeply breathed in the nutty aroma of the fires and the marsh mud damp and clinging to people's shoes.

This must be what home smells of, he thought, *warmth,*

comfort, the promise of a bed to soon tumble into, and not alone either.

This land was his to shelter and command. He wanted to settle. He must after what had occurred in Byzantium. Instead of battle, his blood now burned for that other conquest—the begetting of heirs.

Upon disembarking from his boat, Grimulf had sent a scout ahead to gauge the welcome awaiting them. Rudolf did not return at the appointed time. His party found him face down in the waterlogged sands.

Amazingly, Rudolf lived. As they dragged him, his hand went around Grimulf's throat, fighting even when his sword had been swept off by the sea.

"What's the sea belched up, then?" Grimulf had joked even as thick fingers dug in tighter. "Something a fisherman would throw back in!"

Rudolf's warning roared with the blood in Grimulf's ears. It had been his own kinfolk who had ambushed him. Those once loyal to his family had turned to another chieftain.

With three sons, there should have been no threat to Heimer's line. Grimulf had never expected to be foisted with the duty of their farmstead and the surrounding lands.

He looked to the throne, where the true heir should have been sitting. Instead, it was as barren as a shell picked clean by the gulls. Harald and his wife perished in the shipwreck that had also ferried off their father.

He'd been a boy then, desperate to escape the fury bubbling inside, unable to rage against the taking of their lives when there was no one to blame save the Gods. His brother Ragnar had thought it best he was out of the way, rather than interfering with his running of things.

A messenger had arrived with news Ragnar had been slain by an unknown enemy. Whoever killed him knew the new chieftain's hold would be weak, after so long being absent. Grimulf must quickly shore up support amongst his people.

If Grimulf claimed a bride, it must be now. No one here truly knew him, thinking him the reckless youth who had run off to be a soldier. Depending on his choice of wife, his bed might be warmed by an ally or remain frigid from the viper he invited between the sheets.

He eyed the daughters of his enemies as a wolf did a deer. Hungry, but cautious. They were all beautiful, whether it be their bundles of honey-hued hair, the daring quirk of their smile or throaty laughter. They were certainly strong in their haunches: a sure sign of healthy bearing and something soft to embrace in bed.

No matter his concerns, a decision must be made. He had considered this throughout his voyage. Rudolf's revelation had only spiced it with danger.

Whatever came at him, he would have the pleasure of bending it to his will.

Night swathed its damask across the sky. Each time lightning struck it shot across like an arrow aflame. The dogs lifted their heads, staring at the shadows dancing in the rafters.

Grimulf thrust aside his stick. It was time to announce his arrival and make his choice. He mounted the steps leading to the empty throne, curved back straightening to reveal the tall, rigid form of the true man beneath.

The hall doors burst open. In strode a horse, white as the frost coating the grasses. Seaweed dragged behind one of its legs. Sand encrusted the hooves.

Draped across it was the long skirt of a dress dyed the vibrant hue of sea, delicate silk detailing resembling spider's gossamer. A woman clung to the thick neck. No more could be discerned of her, not her hair or eyes or whether she was maid or crone, for a veil engulfed her face and breasts. Bone hair pins held the veil in place, so it could not even suggest the contours of her face, shielding her from their gaze.

Guards hurried after her, snatching at the horse's reins,

but the creature had none. She had ridden here without a saddle, simply clinging on.

Women and men stared in awe. One old farmhand shuddered, muttering *phantom* under his breath. She was a gust of winter wind turned corporeal. Common sense warned not to meddle with those from the other world, for it might be Loki up to his tricks.

"Where is Grimulf?" the woman cried, and at least Grimulf now knew she was young. "I must speak with him!"

Murmurs of apprehension. This woman was not a Dane. She was a *Saxon*. Most likely a Christian. Not even a Saxon man would dare come to these pagan lands, what would lure a woman here? One youth too far into his cups clumsily mounted the table, helped by his friends, to proudly declare he was the mighty chieftain and more than ready to welcome her.

The actual Grimulf, sneering in distaste at the runt, pulled down his hood.

"I am who you seek."

The woman made no response. Though her face might be covered he felt the heavy weight of her stare. She was assessing him. His curiosity hungered to see what colour those eyes were, whether they were wide with fear, bright with interest or narrowed in disdain.

The horse shifted, snorting and heaving after its furious ride.

"Come now," Grimulf urged, voice rough. "You've made this perilous journey—speak!"

She did not flinch, instead her hands slowly rose, scooping up the veil. This simple action transfixed him.

First, she revealed her slender throat, then her thin, pointed chin, petal shaped lips half-parted, red from the bite of the cold and slightly trembling as she panted. The veil did not go any higher.

"My name is Rosamund Thorne. I come from the nunnery ten miles from here. I have ridden without rest."

"And why would you be so foolish—"

"I had to come. My God commanded me."

Now she threw back the veil. Curls of her dark hair cradled her face, as clinging as water weeds, so only one eye could be seen. Her eyelashes were dark and heavily fringed, the arched eyebrow thick and imposing. She stared down at him, the pale blue eye oddly unsettling and stark. She looked like a soldier given her orders, and no one would get in her way.

He thought she might throw herself weeping into his arms, but she was not miserable. Instead, anger flushed her cheeks. The barely held in fury animated her pale features.

By Odin, she was stunning. He felt a stir within him. And yet she was a nun, a woman wed to her Christian God, forbidden and untouchable.

It made her even more appealing.

"When I was at prayers," she told him, "a vision came to me. I must come to this heathen place and offer myself as your bride. And convert you to the true faith."

A held breath of silence, then the hall roared with outrage.

Grimulf hoped desperately she spoke the truth. His curse hungered within him, snarling and pacing, whispering all were out to get him. One night he might snap and kill them all.

This woman offered salvation. If she spoke true, he would get on his knees and worship her.

The bride surveyed the men closing in around her. They were like baited bears who had dragged off their furs to reveal facsimiles of human creatures.

In her opinion, the one called Grimulf kept his pelt on.

His wind thrashed hair was red as the amber found along these coasts. His beard had not seen a knife for some time, the face beneath hidden.

Her mouth curled with aversion. She doubted he had touched scent or water, instead stinking of the road. The musk of hard work on a man might be appealing, but too much and they were no better than common beasts.

His eyes shone through the fire and bracken of his hair. They were completely black and easily mistaken for shadows, yet at that moment they reflected every light in the hall, engulfed in white flame.

She could not tell his expression. Normally she was adept at reading men. Perhaps it was because she herself had changed. When she wore a habit, pilgrims had often spoken their secrets to her, simply unable to mistrust a nun.

All that had been stolen from her, leaving only Rosa.

Exhaustion clawed at her. It had hunted her as endlessly as the dogs had done, but now she might finally give in. She dearly wanted to rest. But in this place, she must bargain her flesh to gain a marriage bed.

She was amongst pagans. *Vikings*. In raids she had seen men carried off to be thralls, women left behind, ravaged and weeping. She came to this willingly.

She watched Grimulf, awaiting his answer. He cracked a smile at her, which barely showed through his beard. His otherworldly eyes looked to the Heavens.

"What a task your God has set you! I am afraid his powers do not extend as far as here. You are on your own."

There came a shout, one of the warriors calling he'd have her instead. Grimulf held up his hand. In an instant there was silence. Even as dirt-weary as he was, he still commanded these men.

"I admire your gall. Most of you women must be led by the hand like a lamb to the axe." His grin turned sharp as she bristled. "A Viking woman chooses her husband and brings to the marriage her wisdom and dowry. Well, nun, what do you have to offer if I am to be your choice?"

Rosa faltered. She should have expected this. Had she been arrogant enough to assume he would accept her without incentive?

Thunder boomed again. The double doors gaped open, slathering rain pelting over the stones. Lightning swept its white cape across, then whipped it back to reveal the night sky.

If he rejected her, she would be thrown out. Left to fend for herself.

The wolves were out there. She would be devoured.

At the threat of this fate, Rosa's hands began to tremble. Her grip around the horse slackened. Shadows ringed her vision.

She must not faint!

Only Grimulf saw her face. The others could only see her from behind, and it was an enticing view. None of them knew of the fear spilling out.

Grimulf's mocking smile dropped. He took a step forward, the horse shying, but with one stroke to its nose it calmed.

He held out his hand. There were no words to reassure her, only that offered hand. He wore no glove. His flesh was slightly darker, the tan ending at the wrist. The smallest finger was crooked from a long-ago break and on it was a chunky silver ring of a snarling wolf's head.

His hands were as large as paws. He could break her fingers as one would crack a nut.

Rosa grasped his hand just as a dying man would snatch for land. His eyebrows rose at her ferocity and he seemed... pleased.

Grimulf pulled her into his arms. She expected stale sweat and the stink of horses. She smelt a trace of the road, the heady scent of masculinity alongside something dark and feral but tinged with it a fresher smell. As rough as he looked, he had bathed recently.

As her feet touched the ground, her limbs went limp. She had ridden without rest. The insides of her thighs were red raw, thickened and puffy from going without a saddle. To feel the chafing of her legs made her flinch, the sensation akin to needles being pulled in and out. Her eyes flicked down, expecting her gown to be drenched in blood. It remained as dark as the seas.

Sensing her weakness, his arm came around her waist to support her, the broad forearm resting beneath her rump. It forced her to look at him, past the great bush of beard. Their chests pressed tightly together, his heartbeat a steady thumping sound resounding inside of her. If she felt his lifeforce penetrating her, he must have her sparrow flutter of a pulse tucked within him.

"Now, little bird," he whispered lowly, the heat of his breath caressing her ear, "tell me why I should choose you, besides this?"

His hand passed over her buttocks, firmly squeezing. A small gasp made her mouth fall open, shocked at herself. There had been a sharp sensation that could not quite rightly be called displeasure.

It was just as the other nuns had warned; the flesh was weak.

"I will bring you the true faith," she began.

"I am quite happy with the Gods I serve," he replied.

"My father, Edward Thorne, is a distant relation to the Queen of the Saxons. There will be a great dowry for the man who marries me."

"That is promising, Rosa." She liked the way her name rumbled over his tongue. "But a smaller dowry is a better exchange for a sensible woman. Your people have soft, pale hands as delicate as milk." He still held her hand. His thumb ran over her palm. "What work can these hands do?"

Rosa straightened. These were her strengths. She should have offered them from the start, rather than a wife she was like a servant bartering over her wage.

"I can cook. Sew. I ran my brothers' households for several years before they were wed. At the nunnery, I was renowned for my skills in healing."

He was appraising her, seeing if she spoke the truth. Rosa held steady. She was not some weak wisp of a thing who only sat around, beautiful and bored. She was of use. One more push was needed. He was wavering, she was certain.

"I am only twenty-three, with many years to bear you healthy sons. None have touched me—" Her throat went tight. She was untouched through sheer luck and her own hare-like stamina. "I am a virgin. My brothers are dead. My father is far from these lands. No one will come to reclaim me."

Her muscles went taut. Slowly, she pushed herself onto her tiptoes.

"I am a stranger here. As my husband, you will be my guide. I have no ties to any who might be your enemy. The only ally I have will be you."

Rosa pushed herself the rest of the way, dragging her body against his. Their mouths crushed together.

Her first kiss had been stolen from her two nights ago. That one had been rough and sloppy, like being smothered. This was different. She assumed because she had initiated it. She braced herself, preparing for him to wrench back control.

Grimulf's mouth remained soft upon hers. His gentleness surprised her.

Gone was the rest of the hall. She heard a rushing noise akin to the lapping of waves, her blood running quick. This moment became the same as a held breath.

The scrape of his beard was a strange sensation. She was not certain whether she liked it much, though supposed she would have to get used to it. Delicately, his teeth scraped over her lip and, curious, she opened her mouth. His tongue entered, so sudden and strange her lips clamped shut.

She remembered. When the man who hunted her had forced his foul breath upon her, their teeth had crashed together.

Grimulf stilled, thinking she meant to bite him. When she did not he chuckled, the sound travelling between them, vibrating into her core. Her lips were wet and burning when he withdrew.

"Well, I'll certainly enjoy showing you how to properly kiss," he murmured, just to her.

"Then…?"

He turned to look upon his people. His arm remained draped around her waist.

"Welcome to my new bride Rosamund, daughter of Edward Thorne, sent by the Nailed God himself! We will be wed—"

"Tonight," Rosa interrupted. "I must be your bride before sunrise."

He looked at her curiously but did not rebuke her.

"Then tonight it shall be. We will celebrate with the dawn!"

His men were slow to cheer, but they did. Feet stamped. Horns rapped against the table, the spray of ale cresting the air like seafoam.

The storm faded, whimpering, while the people within the mead hall roared louder than the thunder.

Grimulf led Rosa away from the noise and heat. They left the hall and entered one of the many longhouses that surrounded the area. An old woman broke from the crowd, but she kept a few steps behind them.

Oil lamps were lit as Grimulf made his way around the

main room. Shadows rose and dipped like waves. Rosa stood to the side, watching the journey of a spider clinging to a curtain overhead, its long, thin legs slowly stretching as it moved from tassel to tassel.

"Give me a moment," he told her, unclipping the cloak's brooch at his shoulder and allowing it to tumble at his feet. "I will make myself presentable for my bride."

He watched her, gauging her reaction. Was she meant to pick up after him? This was to be her house, she supposed, and she must keep it clean. Rather than swooping down in a panic to serve him, Rosa casually knelt and took the cloak. She shook it out, a few broken brambles coming free, then folded the cloak and laid it aside.

"Surely it is better to wed now and tend to ourselves after?" she suggested baldly, though within her breast her heart thudded.

She had a head start from her pursuers, but she had wasted a good deal of time swaying Grimulf into taking her. They might kick down the door at any moment. She gave him a tight smile.

"Why must we be in a hurry? Is the world about to end and I do not know?" he joked.

He leant down, pressing his nose to her throat. She tensed at the sudden intrusion. He made a small noise, meaning what she did not know, though perhaps something had been answered for him.

"You should bathe. You've been without rest for several nights, according to the state of your horse. This may be your only chance to pause and think on what you are about to embark on." He pulled away, face so close their noses brushed, and his eyes were narrowed, the lights in them gone. The expression the same as a snake considering whether to eat the mouse. "My servant will draw you a bath and find you a suitable dress."

Rosa had made her choice. "This is to be my bridal gown," she told him. "But thank you, I will have that bath."

"Good. You reek of the road."

Grimulf boomed with laughter at her scandalised expression. After all, she had believed him to be stinking of sweat and dirt when they first met, and instead he was the cleanest out of them.

Rosa flushed, ducking her head. "Do not tarry long... husband." She clutched bundles of her skirt in her hands and went into what turned out to be the bedroom.

The old woman who had followed them was already there. She smiled fondly at Rosa, and the young nun found herself relaxing slightly. There might be some allies to be found here. Once she was clean and comfortable, and married, she might finally feel safe.

"I am Gunhild," the old woman told her in a slow, drawn out voice, each word perfectly spoken. "I have held house for Grimulf's father and brothers. Now it is time for me to watch over you both."

Already, a bath had been drawn. While Rosa had been bartering herself in the hall, Gunhild must have decided on Grimulf's choice and slipped off to prepare.

Rosa glanced around the room that would be shared by herself and her soon to be husband. It was sparse, though finely furnished with an ornately carved box-bed and stools. There was no life, no weapons or signs someone lived here, not even a tapestry. Her arms drew closer to her chest, not quite an embrace but an urge to hold herself.

"Grimulf has been gone for some time. It will look homelier soon, once his possessions have been moved in. You are sure to make it cheerful, just by being in here."

Rosa almost wanted to laugh, quick and nervous, and say it made her sound a part of his collection. She had lost her tongue. Instead, she stood there while the old woman pulled free the pins keeping her veil in place, allowing her arms to be manoeuvred and her dress and shift to slip down to pool around her.

Then she was naked and standing before the wooden tub. A tiny trail of steam arose from the water. She wavered, unable to take the first step.

"Is there anything else you need?" Gunhild asked.

Rosa looked over her shoulder. She must have revealed too much of her distress, for there was a faint widening of alarm on the other woman's face.

"Might I be alone for a little while?"

Soon Rosa was by herself, left to face her decision. If only she had been married in an instant, then she would not have to let reality sink in.

She had to go through with this, it was her only path to survival. If not, she would die. No one would protect her. The only person she could rely on was a Viking, a stranger, and she did not know how far his benevolence extended, considering she had foisted herself on him.

She was astounded the man had even accepted her. It had been the last attempt of a desperate woman. She wondered why he had. There must have been plenty of other women, Danish women, willing to share his bed.

At the nunnery, the other nuns had often commented on her beauty, though in warning rather than admiration. A woman's face, even the exposure of her hair, could lead men into a great many sins. Now, Rosa knew too well the perils of a man fuelled by lust.

Nothing could pause time, not even prayers. Rosa stepped into the bath. Heat crawled up her leg. She had been so wind whipped and wet from her ride it felt as if talons were raking across. She forced herself further in and sat down. Ripples trembled over the surface.

Her head dipped under the water. When she resurfaced, black fronds of her hair covered her face, her breasts, as clinging as seaweed. She shuddered, suddenly icy cold, as she recalled the sensation. Had she not clung on to her horse and been dragged free, she might have remained under the waves, drowned and lost forever.

She must never tell Grimulf what had brought her here. That it was far from God sending her on a worthy mission, but instead the devil pursuing her. If he knew the truth, he would abandon her or even worse turn her over to her hunter. He was to become her husband, yet she could not trust him.

There was a white bar on the side. Curious, she sniffed it. A slight greasy film smeared over her palm and she was met with a distinctly nutty scent. She put it down but could see no rosemary to freshen herself with. Rosa did the best she could, scrubbing her skin clean with only the water and her bare hands.

Rosa had not been raised as a Viking wife would be expected. She knew nothing of their ways. What if he wanted her to fight? Or he might quickly tire of her fumbling about, having to learn everything as a child might.

Her only plausible theory as to why he was marrying her was because he needed someone who was a stranger. He had just returned to these lands. Perhaps he thought the other women were loyal to his enemies.

Unless, and she smiled derisively as she considered the ridiculous notion, he truly was considering converting to Christianity?

Rosa leaned back, lifting her leg to better reach her calf. Her head ducked down again, washing out the rest of the tiny fragments of leaves caught there. She remained under the water, watching the ceiling overhead undulate. There came a distant thudding noise. A shadow appeared over her.

Terrified, she jolted up. She spluttered on her scream for help, began choking. A large hand pounded on her back as she hunched over.

Rosa had expected to see green eyes, narrowed with stark

crow scratches, overburdened from the weight of heavy grey eyebrows. Thin lips twisted in hunger for cruelty.

Instead, all she got was laughter and Grimulf's fond black eyes. "It won't do to perish before your wedding!"

"You…You startled me!" she managed to force out.

Her arms went around her chest and her legs crossed together. She did not miss the disappointment on his face as she hid herself.

"What were you doing, floating beneath like a mermaid?" He leaned over, so they were face to face. "Unless you are Melusine? You're not going to sprout wings and scurry off now I've seen you bathing?"

"I'm what?"

"Did your mother not tell you these stories?"

"My family did not hold with children's tales," she told him stiffly.

No, her brothers had always been quick to mock her interest in wisps and goblins when she had been a girl. Any sign of dreaminess and her mother had quickly given her something practical to do: needlework, reading, prayers. Her father pushing her into the nunnery had been more to do with stopping her from wandering off and causing scandal for their good name, rather than a bid to please God.

"But they are the best kind!"

Grimulf moved back and she shivered, suddenly feeling cold again. She found herself unable to move, for doing so would mean uncrossing her legs. Common sense told her not to be ridiculous. He would be her husband, what was the point of hiding herself before the marriage when all would soon be revealed?

He had changed into a bright red shirt, short-sleeved even in this weather to reveal his muscular arms. There was a slight slit at the front, revealing hair much darker than that on his head. Water glistened in rivulets on his throat as he dried himself.

There were marks upon his arms. Rosa carefully examined them, curious as to what they were. She had never seen such things before and thought they were scars or some sort of birthmark. The colours were much too dark and resembled familiar shapes: a wolf mid-chase encircled the shoulder of his right arm, on his left wrist was a swirling, thorn like design of an eel.

"What are they?" she asked, expecting him to mock her for her lack of knowledge. He glanced at the thorns.

"I was marked with them in the East. Inks are pricked into the flesh and they remain with you until death. I had the wolf done as a boy, after my first kill. It is of Fenrir, the wolf-child of Loki." For some reason, his lips tightened into a scowl, but it was aimed at his flesh rather than her.

None of this was familiar, yet she wanted to know more. Rosa pressed her lips together. From her mother's teachings, men did not want women who talked too much. She needed to marry him before she became a nuisance.

Rosa returned to scooping water and splashing it on her shoulder, still using her other arm to cover herself.

Grimulf watched her struggle a few moments, before saying, "Do you not plan to use the soap?"

At her incomprehension, he glanced at the bar on the side. "Soap, girl."

"But it is a hard bar of...something."

"And quite good at cleaning you." His smile grew wider. Grimulf knelt and before she could take the soap he had it in his hand. It seemed as small as a pebble in his grip. "Let me help. You'll not be able to reach here."

Grimulf dipped the soap into the water, between her hip and the tub. She remained still but he could see the way her cheeks darkened. Lathering the soap, he began spreading it across her back and shoulders.

"I... I can do it myself," Rosa protested.

His large fingers gently encircled her throat, not to hold

her in place but to caress and massage the knot of muscles there. At the touch, she found her body oddly relaxing when she should be tense.

"Perhaps I am inspecting what I will soon be acquiring, as a good merchant should." His voice rumbled behind her, like an encroaching storm. His hands smoothed over the planes of her shoulder blades.

"You make me sound like a horse about to be bought," she complained half-heartedly, leaning into his palm. Instead of a groan, a hiss of surprise escaped her.

"What's this?"

Gone were his teasing words, instead replaced with concern. His touch, tender and uncertain, began probing her side. Rosa panickily tried to think what he saw, whether she had been injured and not realised. It must be a bruise from when she had been thrown to the ground. She had hoped it would not show.

"It is nothing," she said. Rosa shifted, her wet hair coming down, covering the bruise. "Many of the nuns were quite old, and so they set me to perform laborious tasks. Sometimes I was not careful enough."

"A nun seems a more dangerous occupation than a knight if you become so battered and bruised. Is that why you wear your habits, to hide your battle scars?"

She knew he wanted to demand what she hid from him. Strangely enough, though he had every right, he did not. Instead, he held out a small pot.

Rosa twisted off the lid. Within was a black paste and a small stick. Grimulf took them from her.

"When we go into battle, we must resemble monsters. We strike fear into men's hearts before dispatching them with our blades."

"But we are not going into battle. We are to be married."

He smiled then, a small quirk of his lips. "Is that not the greatest battle? Tilt your head."

Rosa leaned forward for him. Her eyelid widened and remained open as he sailed the stick through the kohl and coated the line of her eye. The water surrounding her waist curled over her hip, droplets spilling down her lower back. Her eyelashes tremored, wishing to blink.

Her eye was beginning to water, yet she kept watching him. His attention was completely focused upon her. Eyes narrowed, like a hunter with his arrow, watching for the flick of the rabbit's ear. She should be afraid, being bare and vulnerable.

His other hand cupped her cheek as he guided the stick. A slight furrow appeared between his eyebrows from concentration. One finger traced the shell of her ear and her shudder was not from fear. His lips cracked apart in a teasing grin.

She thought a Viking unable to smile. Throughout this night Grimulf was proving her wrong. She wanted to hear him laugh again.

"Keep still," he ordered, moving on to the other eye.

He switched hands, mimicking what he had done before. The water had begun to cool and she shivered slightly. His warm hand stroked over her shoulders, pulling some of her wet hair aside to spill over, clinging to her breasts and concealing her from him.

Was he attempting to give her some decency? Most husbands would take pleasure in what was theirs. Unless he believed he would not be able to hold himself back. She let out the breath she hadn't realised she had been holding.

"I believe I have invited a cat into my home," he teased gently, showing her in the water's reflection.

The undersides of her eyes had been coated in this strange kohl. She felt the slight weight of it upon them, having to resist rubbing. Two flicks covered the corners and two spikes stroked down.

It made her appear as if her eyes narrowed in rising fury,

bleeding darkness. The colour was the same black as her pupils, the whites even starker than before. She had the strange urge to... Her face tightened, nose scrunching and cheeks twitching. A slight hiss escaped. Then she realised what she was doing and cleared her throat, flushing. Grimulf laughed and now she did not mind being foolish. She loved that sound. It was like the boom of thunder, yet safe and tucked away.

"Do you wish me to...?"

"Aye, let us see what you can do."

Rosa took the stick and pot from him. She rose to her knees in the bathtub to loom over. He craned his neck, as though he gazed in appreciation of the moon. His hands came over to steady her, fingers kneading into her buttocks.

He might wish to conceal her, but he seemed incapable of resisting touching her.

Rosa applied the kohl lightly, figuring out what she wanted to do before adding a much darker layer. She swayed slightly, all her senses honed in on the soft drag of his fingertips across her naked flesh, so near but achingly far from the gate of her inner self.

As she did this, she imagined all the times he would have done this to himself before being thrust into battle. She had yet to see him roar in fury but knew she would at some point.

She saw him in her mind's eye, charging through a spray of seafoam to emerge from the waves, wild and furious, shield on one arm, sword raised in the other hand. Even the very stones would want to turn and run.

She licked her lips when she caught his eye. He knew how much he affected her, radiating a quiet smugness which infuriated and yet made her want to laugh. *Not quite so smug*, she thought, *if he doesn't want to rise up and satisfy us both*.

Rosa was not happy with what she had done, her hand had wavered too much from her unsteady seat, but she was never happy with what she did. Her heart was calming now, yet she must hurry.

The kohl just barely ringed his eyes. At the corners she had done harsh, rough jerks, knowing she had been thinking of the storm. Hesitantly, she moved aside for him to look at his reflection. He was silent a moment. Her arms came around herself as she shivered.

"Are you certain it was not Thor who sent you?" Grimulf wondered.

"Are we to be married now?" She hated how like a child she sounded, anticipating the arrival of something pleasant, when all she was doing was dreading this.

"In a moment. Dry yourself off and get dressed. I want your help with something first."

She did as he commanded. "With what?"

Grimulf tilted his head to the side, revealing the thick cords of his throat. From his boot he slipped out a knife, gleaming and sharp as a claw. Rosa cringed, then straightened, forcing her fear down.

With a single twist, Grimulf now held the blade. He offered the handle to Rosa.

"Be a good wife and shave this bracken from my face. You'll finally be able to see your husband, then."

Grimulf had not planned to offer this stranger a weapon the moment they were alone.

Most men would have bound her to the bed. Threatened or bled her until the truth came out. Now she was the one with power.

He thought it a subtler way of discerning her true purpose. If she wanted to run him through, he could easily subdue her and turn to more brutal methods of interrogation. Honeyed water lured butterflies closer.

Rosa hesitated. She seemed unable to comprehend.

"But you will be exposed."

"And?" He cocked his head, smiled conspiratorially. "A man should be able to trust his wife. I'll be the very first one willing to let his woman wield a dagger near his throat."

Slowly, she took the knife from him. At least she was willing to accept the test. Grimulf opened the vial he had brought with him, pouring over his hands the oil. The strong scent of spices and honey thickened the room as he slathered it on his face, the curls of his beard glistening.

"Make the first one here," he suggested, stroking the side of his cheek. "You'll not kill me if you slip."

"I'd rather not hurt you at all," she revealed, disquiet making her honest. She pursed her lips when she realised how open she was and surged forward, quick to have this over with.

Grimulf shut his eyes as he felt the coolness of the knife press against his cheek. A moment's hesitation, then the blade was scraping over, his beard cloven away. It was not near as he usually liked it, but perhaps she was being cautious. Good. She at least had not been sent as a pretty-faced assassin.

But why had she come here? A sensible man would not believe the amusing fiction God had sent her on this arduous quest, to wed herself to a heathen devil and lure him to the good and right path.

He had brought riches with him. The emperor had gifted him generously for his years of service, even if things had soured. Many would want to tie themselves to the beginning of such a prosperous lineage. However, those who wanted him would be Danes. Rosa's own kin would be offering her lords as suitable husbands.

Out of his many theories, the strongest one that stood out was she had been running from something. Most women did that by joining a nunnery. She had even run from being a nun. What had chased her and, he wondered darkly, did it continue to pursue her?

At the gentle press of her fingers, he turned for her to shave his other cheek. Her next stroke did not shake, steady with growing confidence.

He was curious as to why he had accepted her ludicrous proposal. He certainly admired her bravery, and was amused by her gall, but there had also been fear trembling up her legs. She was no shield maiden.

There had been promise there. She had held herself against the taunts, remained strong enough to speak her mind, even while fighting exhaustion. Most of her kind would have fell weeping and begging at his feet.

Even when she had wavered, her show of weakness had not disgusted him. A part of him had wanted to carry her off and tend to her. It had stirred protective instincts he had never had the chance to satisfy. This was an indulgent desire; he could not base his entire future on it.

She might be a slight thing, but her hips were curved and thick, tempting a man to wrap his arm around, and perfect for childbearing. Once their offerings to Freyja were made, their union would be blessed with strong sons.

And the activities of achieving such a thing? Grimulf's gaze travelled down while she was distracted with her work. Parts of her body were damp, her wedding gown clinging to her flesh. Her breasts reared, the material dragging down against the swell, pressing close to the thin stretch of her stomach.

There was something about flesh just barely revealed that was too enticing. It urged a man to tear the rest of it off and find what was hidden beneath. Not that he needed to, already he knew how slender she was, the pale, milky hue of her skin, the way her hair, wet and trailing, had clung to her naked shoulder. At the resurgence of the memory, he was hard again, not that she would be able to tell. He widened his legs slightly to make himself comfortable and crossed his arms. This would be a test of perseverance.

He wanted her a great deal. Any man would. It was a shame for her to be wed to her God. At least now she had realised such a folly and was willing to have a true, hot blooded man.

She might have let him in the bath with her if he had pushed. But Grimulf had known she would not have been completely willing. Where was the fun in forcing a woman, when there was pleasure to be had when she was the one crooking her finger?

It had been the look in her eyes as she had glanced at him. Plenty of desire there, but also a wary anticipation that had brought about a tenderness in his breast.

She nudged his chin with her knuckles, he followed her movements and the knife went to his throat, slowly scraping the underside. The oil trickled down his neck, caught by the hairs emerging from under his shirt.

He had chosen her because they were both strangers to this land. There were enemies closing in on him. He needed someone who had no other allies. She might be hiding something from him, but he would soon have the truth from her. The only people they could rely on were one another. Just as it should be between man and wife. He would be her sword and she his shield.

He smiled grimly. Would they have to put their weapons to the test?

He opened his eyes. Rosa wavered before him, holding his knife awkwardly, uncertain what to do next. He held out his hand and, relieved, she gave it back to him. He cleaned off the blade with a cloth and stuck it into his boot.

Grimulf ran his knuckles over his face. "Not a bad job at all," he mused, "considering how rushed we are."

"Thank you."

She had returned to being meek and dutiful. It irked him.

What were these Christians thinking, teaching their daughters to be so subservient? Rather than anger, he wanted to tease her into reacting.

"We'll have to strip you, of course," he told her. "You might have worn a dress in church, but we'll have none of that. It'll be bare in the fields, together with a priest and bonfire. We'll say our vows before Odin, leap across the fire to ensure the children are all hale, then I'll take you with the others cheering us on."

He gritted his teeth to hold back his laugh as her eyes widened in horror. Her mouth formed an O of outrage, cheeks flushed, and she would have argued had he been able to dampen his smile.

"This is a jest, is it not?"

"Unfortunately, yes."

The winds whipped about, splattering them with rain. The tree they stood before, old and with gnarled, rotted roots, had once been struck with lightning. It had split the tree in twain and the people had named it Thor's tree.

Grimulf and Rosa stood before one another. With her hurrying him, all Grimulf could do was comb his unruly hair and tie it from his face. He wore the finest clothes in his possession, which meant they were from his brothers' chests, as what he had brought with him had been well used battle armour, discoloured and scarred from the sands. A torque of silver encircled his throat.

Rosa at first meant to wear only her wedding dress. Shivering and wind pinched, as if ensuring the ceremony would finish quickly so he must carry her into the warmth of the hall. Grimulf had placed his cloak around her, her shoulders dipping at the weight. Her lips pursed, thwarted, and yet she nuzzled into the fur collar in relief. She was a perplexing, yet curious woman.

When she had leaned forward, clinging slightly to the edge of the bathtub, baring herself to him as he applied her kohl, he might have pulled her to him then and there. Water glistened on the swell of her breasts, nipples slightly reddened from the heat. She had wanted him as well.

He could not touch her. One day he might, but while he was afflicted he would not dare. A single mark might curse her as well.

The softness of her flesh beneath his lips as he had smelt her could still be faintly felt. He had not broken the skin, though. The hunger that controlled him kept him teetering over the edge.

He should have never agreed to this. She was not safe. But it was too late now. She was his. Willing and lovely and exactly who he needed.

She would most certainly be the death of him.

There was holly pinned to his shirt and ivy draped over her skirt. Some of the bright red berries broke free when he moved forward. He caught them, then clasped her hand as the vows were called.

The villagers watched, hunched against the elements. The eldest of their people, a woodcarver known as Thorstein, would act as their priest.

Grimulf had meant to speak with Rosa when they were alone. He needed to warn her, even if she blindly followed her God's orders. It would be monstrous to bind her to him when she did not know what he had become.

When he had entered his room, the sight of her naked back had stolen his words. He had stroked, kissed, bitten another's flesh before, and yet she had transfixed him. There had been no scars to mar her, only the slight mottling of bruises which concerned him. She had a story to tell, perhaps one even more terrible than his own.

She was slender and pale, naked and defenceless in his den. His wife. She would be his and with it came the responsibility of her protection, the pleasures of her flesh.

There was the promise of children, warmth on cold, lonely nights. He was not a lone creature.

With what he kept secret, all this should be forbidden.

Had he truly not had the chance to tell her? Might he have simply held his tongue because he did not want to lose her as quickly as she had arrived?

"I will honour you with my body, it will be your sword and shield. None shall trespass against you," he intoned.

He withdrew his sword from its sheath. A man and woman exchanged swords, yet Rosa had none to offer. She only had herself to trade. He took her hands, urging her to wrap them around the hilt.

Rosa, pale and uncertain, stiffly clinging to his sword, stammered what he had said. There were soft groans from some of the women; these were not the wife's words, they were for the husband to speak.

Grimulf did not mind. Grinning at her, he whispered, "Now, this is what we say together."

Slowly, he spoke the words and Rosa shortly followed. Her wedding dress and loose hair whipped about her. The waves surged. A few straggling gulls soared over them, heading inland.

"Our blood shall merge upon this night. Our children will be strong. Sons brave and daughters fair. Bless this union, Freyja."

There was no sow to sacrifice and offer to the Goddess. Some looked in search of another offering.

Grimulf held out his wrist. "Take this as my due."

Thorstein approached and cut him with his knife, a stream of blood falling amongst the roots of the tree. Rosa blanched, yet she also raised her hand.

"You do not have to do this," Grimulf told her, but she kept her arm raised expectantly.

Reluctantly, Grimulf nodded. Thorstein cut her wrist faintly, a few droplets emerging. She barely flinched, Grimulf noticed with approval.

"With this vow our fates are tied."

Grimulf took from his hand the wolf shaped ring and set it on Rosa's finger. It did not sit properly and only fit upon her thumb.

He made his own ring. He took his knife and grasped one of her dark locks and sliced it free. He curled it around his finger, tying it until it resembled the intricate design of his people's knotwork, snugly fitting above his knuckle.

The dogs had begun howling. They were wed. Let nothing, not even death, tear them from one another.

Grimulf pulled her into the mead hall, the sword dragging between them. She felt cold, just like the first waters broken from the washbowl on a winter's morning, even though her face was red. He noticed the glimmer of sweat beading on her neck.

No one truly watched them anymore. They raced over to the overladen tables, eager for another excuse to continue celebrating into the night. They could express their doubts over his choice when morning and the hangovers came.

"Are you all right?" Grimulf whispered to her.

Almost, she shook her head. His grip tightened. Then she smiled widely at him.

"I am. I swear."

Her eyes were scrunched up, wetness peppering the dark eyelashes. His thumb settled on her cheek to brush away any tears that might escape. She pulled free to take his hand, pressing her lips to the rough scars on his knuckles.

There was relief in her gaze, shining bright along with the dew in her eyes. Why? She should be wary of him, of this stranger who would soon carry her to his bed. He cupped her face and found the flesh there burning hot.

"You need rest," he realised.

"Will I not get it soon?" She laughed, a snapping sound. "Is it not the wedding night?"

"Calm yourself. I will not hurt you. You are *my wife*."

Even if he barely knew her, if he only felt lust and some concern when he looked upon her, it meant he was her protector.

"Will you be a better husband?" Fever had loosened her tongue.

"What—?"

The hall doors burst open a second time that night. Men still bearing their swords swarmed inside. Grimulf's guards were quick to respond.

The new arrivals lowered their weapons, hands held out in peace. Rainwater streamed from their cloaks, hissing and turning to steam from the nearby fires. Their furs were matted and mud clagged their boots. Hunting dogs panting from the chase slithered from the men's sides to join the other hounds hunting for scraps.

"I hardly expected such a welcome from my kin!" a voice boomed, and the strangers parted to allow a familiar figure to heave his way to the front.

Grimulf felt his spirits lift. He knew the man leading them, even if he was grizzled and clawed at by some creature. He had timed it well to arrive so soon after his return.

"Uncle!" Grimulf breathed out. "I thought you'd be dead by now."

"Hah! Death does not want me," Olaf Blacktongue retorted. "I'll wander for as long as I fancy."

It had been Jutland's storms that had chiselled the old man's face. The winds had raked its nails, giving his flesh a cracked look, like a piece of flint struck and beginning to split.

He grimaced a smile, revealing chipped rows of yellowing teeth. His knuckles, bloodied in places from the chafing of the brittle night, rubbed at his lip, crooked fingers uncurling to scratch at his stained beard. He saw no point in looking presentable. He had once asked Grimulf why he should bother when the only ones to gaze upon him were his men.

He was amassed in furs, little could be discerned of his actual frame, a woollen cloak trailing behind. Beneath this the metal of his armour clicked. He looked the same as always, rough and ready to go hunting whatever the elements brewed.

"I am sorry to hear of Ragnar," Olaf went on, "but at least he is now in Valhalla, by your father's side no doubt. I would have been happy to keep an eye on your lands. You must be hungering to return to the sea."

"I have had my fill. For now. My brother was a great leader here and I will continue his work. It is time for me to settle."

Grimulf took Rosa's hand, pulling her through the crowd. He wanted to introduce her to the last of his family, as his parents were no longer here to give their approval.

Even though she had offered her blood, the villagers watched as one might examine an exotic creature trapped under the point of a knife, avidly seeing it squirm. It might have been a story from one of their sagas, yet when it walked amongst them they were suspicious.

"What is this?" Olaf wondered, frowning. "What else are we celebrating?"

"My marriage. I am lucky indeed. A beautiful woman chased me down and threw herself at my feet."

Rosa's fingers curled into Grimulf's shirt. Reassuringly, his arm went around her waist. Grimulf took that chance to glance at his wife and smile at her. What he saw made him pause.

She was not frightened by the arrival of more Vikings. When she looked at Olaf, her eyes burned with triumph. The redness of her cheeks deepened. She needed to be carried off, some peace and quiet would help her.

"And what a beautiful woman she is," Olaf mused. "I'd call her one of those Christian angels."

His uncle's green eyes brightened as they roved over his bride. Grimulf was tempted to snap at him, but the older man was most likely shocked at his choice of wife. Anyone would be surprised. He could not begin quarrelling with his kin the moment he returned. With a traitor in his midst, he needed plenty of allies.

"You are welcome to join in the celebration," Grimulf said. "I will have rooms prepared for you. I would greatly appreciate your knowledge of these lands, as I have been gone for so long."

"You wish to go raiding already?"

"No. Farming and fish is what I will focus on. I want to have a good supply for my people."

Olaf grinned, revealing his broken teeth. The fresh scar on his cheek lurched.

"I'll be pleased for a good bed to rest on," he said. "I've been travelling these last few nights."

"You were dragging your leg when you came in. Is the injury recent?"

"It'll mend," Olaf told him. "I fell from my horse while hunting a doe."

"Ah, of course! Did you manage to catch your prey?"

"No, it slipped away in the night. But I'll taste its meat yet if I see it stumble by again. First, though, introduce me to your wife."

"Rosamund Thorne... sir," it was Rosa who spoke, voice harsh. Grimulf's hold around her squeezed in warning.

"Please, you must call me uncle as well."

Olaf surged forward. Grimulf reached for his knife, but there was no need for that. The old Viking only meant to hold Rosa's shoulders and lay a kiss upon her forehead. Olaf let go and there was something besides the disgust on Rosa's face that made the hackles rise in Grimulf. Before he could work out what had set him on edge, she staggered, perhaps to get some distance, but kept falling.

Grimulf caught her with a shout. Her eyes rolled into her head, breath shallow. The sword crashed to the ground. He felt her forehead, almost scalding himself.

On her arm and shoulder were smears of red. Shocked, he checked her for any wounds he might have missed. The stain came from the holly berries he had caught during the ceremony, which had burst in his hand, and in touching her he had spread the stain.

It boded ill to him.

He heaved her up, carrying her as a bride should be held. However, he would not be taking her to their marriage bed but instead the sick bed.

Olaf looked on with some concern, but muttered, "A shame. It won't be binding until she's been bled."

CHAPTER 2

There were no remnants of the storm the next morning. The sky had turned the colour of glass, brittle and close to shattering with only the faintest hues of blue. Sunlight tucked itself behind woollen clouds.

Rosa lay in Grimulf's bed. Her hair spread out, lank with sweat. Her expression twisted in a grimace as she faced whatever nightmare plagued her.

Gunhild had removed her wedding dress, changing her instead into a simple linen shift. The furs were thrown to the ground, where they waited for her shivering to renew to be wrapped around her again.

Shards of the day came through the half-shuttered smokehole overhead, touching her cheek, her furrowed brow. The flesh was paler than it should be, when already she was the colour of fresh milk from her years of being shut away in the nunnery.

"What brought you here, child?" the old woman wondered, as she bathed Rosa's face and throat. "What devil hounded you?"

The celebration had perished, crumbling like an untended fire. The people were solemn as they left their homes, set on their daily task of tilling the fields and caring for their livestock.

It was great misfortune for a bride to sicken on her wedding night. She might not even survive this day. One of many ill lucks to trouble the chieftain and his family.

Some whispered this was justified, as the wedding had not been done properly. The wedding had been rushed, no sow sacrificed, it wasn't even on Freyja's day. What had Grimulf expected? His lust for the nun had blown away his reasoning.

Rosa's cry of pain was stifled as her head thrashed. Her body wrenched and her hand lifted, fingers trembling, as though begging for someone to take it and lead her to safety.

Grimulf made to hold her, but he hesitated. Gunhild took her hand. Rosa did not wake, instead falling back with a great groan of misery.

He could not stand it. Grimulf ran from the house.

Days passed. No change appeared in the young bride. Some now whispered she was a changeling wife, not of this world and too weak to remain in it. The moment Grimulf had claimed her she had sickened.

Just as suddenly as she resembled the snows, her cheeks went as red as burst berries and her forehead became drenched in sweat. No matter how many times her brow was wiped clean it soon glistened with droplets. No food would pass her lips. It was a great effort to slip water into her mouth.

Grimulf could not bear to see her like this. Instead, he went out, chopped wood to keep her fire stoked, hunted for the fattest hares for when she could manage to eat.

He wavered before the bedroom each time, offered his kindling or cooking as a worshipper might do at a temple. Gunhild would always thank him profusely, leaping and taking the things. There was never hope in her face, though.

Grimulf had not slept. He would rather sit outside, anxiously mouthing his pipe, away from the cloying scent of sickness or the pitiful groans that did escape Rosa.

Because it took him to another doorway from long ago: his mother's bed while she had lain sickened from birth-fever and his younger sister stillborn. Ingrid had beckoned him in, but he had been too afraid of the blood and the smell. He had recognised it too well from when he went hunting. The boy never expected his mother to smell the same as a fallen doe. Instead, he ran.

And he was still acting the coward. Had he not learned? Even though the boy he once was had hidden and covered his ears, he had heard her. His mother had not wanted to be alone. All she had wanted was his father by her side, but he had been on a voyage with her eldest sons. Only Grimulf remained and he'd been of no use.

Grimulf went to their room. They had not even slept in each other's arms. Rosa had barely been his wife, yet would she be taken from him so quickly? He would not have this. There must be some way to cure her.

Gunhild looked up as he entered. It seemed, from the darkness around her eyes, she had not slept either.

"We have plenty of wood for the moment, my lord."

"Does she still refuse to eat?"

"It has become worse. She will not even drink now."

Grimulf's throat lurched. Something must be done. All he knew was brute force, but he would make her drink. She would survive.

"Fetch me a pitcher of water. Find any honey in the stores, go begging to one of the other houses if we have none."

Gunhild bowed her head and rushed to do this task. Grimulf took her stool, sitting vigil by Rosa's bed.

She no longer resembled the passionate young woman who had burst into his hall. All that remained was the trembling fear she had failed to hide. The flesh of her cheeks had sunken in. Her hair lay about her head, lifeless and unwashed. The shadows beneath her eyes ringed them like bruises. It was as though she had been beaten, rather than simply wasted away.

Grimulf was hesitant to take her hand. He thought she might shatter if he was too rough. Her flesh held together at his touch but seemed tiny in his. Limp and lax when all he wanted was for her to squeeze back.

"Do not leave me so soon," Grimulf murmured. "I thought your God had some great plan for us? I am still a pagan... still accursed."

She was a Christian woman lost amongst enemies. Might she pass on before he even had the chance to unravel her mysteries? She had pushed herself a great deal to reach him, and it did not sit right for her to stumble at the very last moment.

Gunhild returned, bearing what he had asked for. "Drink," he urged his wife. However, instead of bringing the cup to her lips he brought it to his own.

Grimulf lifted Rosa into his arms. Supporting her head, he pressed their lips together. There was a gasp behind him from his serving woman. None knew what sickness possessed Rosa. A kiss could pass it over to Grimulf and their leader would perish.

He would take the risk.

He passed the water to Rosa. Some trickled from between their lips, trailing down their chins, but a good amount was taken in by her. He did this again, until he thought it enough.

Next was the honey. He dipped in a spoon, barely covering the tip, and slowly fed it to her. While he did this, he massaged her throat with his thumb, willing her to swallow so at least her belly would not be empty.

Yet her eyes would not open. Grimulf sat with her hand in his.

"Rest, Gunhild, you have done well," he said. "I will be here when she wakes."

With Rosa caught in the fever's grip, she could not protect herself. The nightmares came.

There was a fire crackling in the distance, wood smoke creeping over her face. She did not think of a comfortable fire in the pit, but an inferno raging through her hallways and seeking her.

An owl shrieked as it plummeted on its prey. To her, this was no animal. She heard the screams of her fellow novices instead.

The darkness coating her eyes flashed. Red surged.

She had returned to the nunnery, and it was aflame. Shadows passed over the windows, nuns racing from the fire and running towards the swords of the raiders. Glass shattered and fell over the grasses, shimmering just as rainfall did.

Tears coursed down Rosa's face. The night air was cold and clawing at her. She wanted to go and save the old women who had taken her in. Her family were dying in there and she could do nothing.

She ran, a younger novice's hand clasped in her own. They staggered through the graveyard, hunting for somewhere to hide. Rosa kept on looking back, seeing the terror on the girl's face and the nunnery transformed into something else, something twisted and blackened with flames dancing on its crown. Another sob tore from her.

Horses were thundering through the darkness. Rosa threw herself and the other nun down, concealed by the stone carving of an angel. They held one another, trembling as their burning hot skin was cooled by the winds, lips wordlessly moving in prayer.

They were praying the riders would not stop, that they

would carry on with the silver plates and crucifixes they had stolen. Most did. Then a single horse slowed. Rosa heard the snort of its breath, the mist scuttling over their heads, the scrape of hooves against the ground.

"I know you are there."

Her heart had clenched because she recognised the voice. Nausea coated her throat. She had to run. She needed to escape. She still held the other novice's hand. Rosa took a steadying breath.

"Run, Mildritha!" she cried, and forced the nun from her.

Rosa lurched not away from the horse and its rider but towards them. Mildritha ran on ahead, vanishing in the darkness where they could hear screaming.

Hands grasped Rosa, holding her tight. She struggled, but all it earned her was a vile chuckle of amusement.

"And here I was, thinking you would welcome my return as promised."

"I did not realise the monster that hid beneath your flesh!" she spat back.

Her hair was grasped, stopping her thrashing. The rider dismounted so they were face to face.

He was a squat man advanced in years, thickened by the furs and armour he had swaddled himself in. His grizzled grey and white beard had curled in on itself and did not conceal his mouth, which seemed oddly separate. The lips were pink-hued from the winds, with a droplet glimmer of spittle. A small pair of eyes, the wrinkles around them long and stark, and the green colour so pale the only thing noticeable was the black pupils.

Olaf, a Viking from one of the nearby camps settled here. He had come to their nunnery a month ago, professing he had heard of their Christian faith and was considering converting. They had welcomed him, offering all the comforts they would their pilgrim travellers. None had suspected. He had been hearty and rough, but kind.

Rosa had thought his attentions that of an uncle, during those nights she had brought meals to his room and spoken with him when he bade her wait a moment. She had even prayed beside him! During that time, he had been secretly planning to bring his men to rob and slaughter them.

And what else? she thought, as he pressed himself close to her from behind. When she had felt his eyes upon her, what else might he have kept hidden? She shuddered in revulsion. He grinned in the shadowy darkness while before them her home burned.

"A fine little creature," he said. "It took a great deal of patience to hold myself back when you would come into my room, like a doe nuzzling against its hunter, but there was a greater prize at stake."

The hairs on the nape of her neck tore free from the punishing grip he had on her. Her fingers went stiff and she scratched across. Red marks glimmered on his cheek. At the slight sting he laughed.

"Aye, go on. Shall I let you go and we'll have a hunt across the lands, with all my men chasing you?"

She froze at the threat. His bloated palm sloppily wiped over her cheek to smear her tears.

"You are too pretty to waste on them, and young as well," he told himself, as if he was all the counsel he needed. "You look just as Aethelflaed did before she grew haggard with spite. I'll get a son or two out of you, before you're worn and sucked dry. Another prize for my stores, once I claim what I'm due."

The back of his hand struck the side of her head, the sudden blow causing a ringing in her ears, a bright light in one eye. She did not succumb. Her teeth gritted together while all around her the world spun.

"God will punish you for this," she warned. "If you touch me, all that you are will shrivel and burn, just as you have torched this nunnery!"

He said something in response, but she could not remember. He struck her again and this time the darkness took her.

When she awoke, she was somewhere else entirely. A shadow loomed over. Something large and warm gripped her hand.

"Rosa?" the voice sounded distant, as if submerged in water. She tried to focus her eyes but somehow that made everything else blur. Gentle caresses combed through her hair.

"It's all right now, you're safe."

She could not believe that. She was not in the nunnery; that had been consigned to the flames. Where was she, then?

There was only one person that shadow could be. Olaf. Rosa thrashed, desperate to save herself. Her nails blindly scratched, even as the shadow surged forward and tried to hold her still. Hands gripped her wrists; her arms were pressed down upon a bed.

A bed—! Rosa screamed.

There were sounds of panic. Something scraped and crashed to the floor while footsteps hurried over. A woman's soothing noises joined the man's worried voice.

"I must get away," she heaved. "I have to get away from him. I'm not safe."

"You are, Rosa. I swear," the stranger told her. "I will always protect you, even from death."

"He is coming for me."

She was spiralling faster into the dark depths. Her body slackened.

Rosa woke again. She was in another bed and wearing her singed nun's habit. What was happening to her? She could no longer tell what was real.

A shadow loomed above. Olaf. She cringed.

He threw a dress at her. Barked at her to change.

She knew she had spent a week in his camp, she knew this, yet the days had woven themselves into a tapestry. The memories were foggy and rippling. Olaf's screwed up eyes watched her all through them: when she ate, bathed, slept. Others' faces smeared into a blur.

Then the final night reared, bright and terrible, the same colours as the fire she had been stolen from. The tapestry consumed her vision.

The wedding dress shone like a jewel plucked from the waves, but it was too blinding. A contrast to Olaf's dirty, fumbling hands forcing her into the dress. The blood of the sow they had sacrificed to Freyja, to seed her with many sons, stained the floor she walked across.

Vows were made in words she did not know. Olaf had dragged her to his tent by her hair and she had cursed him all the way. He had not touched her all that week. Had he believed in her threat? Did he think it no longer applied now he had wed her and made her pagan?

His hunting dogs had been sloping around his bed, lean and ravenous. Somehow, she was feeling in her dress and the meat was there, as if magic had placed it, yet she had a distorted memory of taking some from the wedding feast, tucking it away.

At the scent of food long denied to them, the dogs lunged forward. They circled her, barking and snapping, until she was pressed against one of the tent walls. Olaf cursed them, but their stomachs were their masters now. He might have her trapped, but he could not get to her.

Olaf stormed out, the tent flapping about as though he had sliced through. Then all that remained were the dogs and she thought, *perhaps death at their fangs would be better than life as Olaf's unwilling bride.* She was lifting the meat to press to her throat when another figure slipped in.

The woman's face was smoky, insubstantial, for she was one of the Viking's thralls, a captured slave from somewhere far off. Her belly full with child, as though she had eaten the moon.

"Adelina," a voice echoed, distant in the shadows. Rosa thought it was her name.

The thrall threw more scraps to the side and the dogs chased after them, abandoning Rosa. Her hand crooked for her.

"Come quickly, before my master returns."

The tent flap lifted. She had pulled at Adelina, begging her to join her. The thrall had shaken her head, stroked her stomach.

"We would not get far. There is word that Grimulf has returned. I have seen Olaf tremble and start awake at the thought of this man. Only he will protect you."

Rosa ran out, engulfed in the light that promised freedom.

Her eyes were cracking open, crusted with her nightmares. She tried to rub the irritation, but her arms were too weak to rise. Every little part of her body ached and there was a great gnawing pain in her stomach, as though she had swallowed a little wolf and it was ravenous.

She smelt the familiar nauseatingly sweet scent of sickness rising from her, yet only slightly. She had to press her nose to her skin to catch it. Her hair, though clammy and damp with her sweat, had been brushed. The clothes she wore were fresh, a comfortable linen shift left unlaced around the throat to let her breathe.

She forced herself up, letting out a shaky gasp of relief. The dream and her jumbled memories slunk somewhere deep inside of her. Not forgotten but put aside for now.

This was not Olaf's tent. She was safe. She was with Grimulf. A stranger, yes, but the fond look he had given her as she held a knife to his cheek had been proof she did not need to fear him.

The rest of the night surged back to her. The wedding, the warmth of his hands clasped around hers, the sudden frisson as he claimed her mouth.

And the new arrival.

Her fingers dug into the sheets as she clung to them. How long had she been abed? Her heart started pounding in fright, shudders vibrating through her already pained body. Plenty of time for Olaf to tell Grimulf his side of the story.

She had not suspected the two men were related. They might as well be water and fire considering how different they were. And yet they were uncle and nephew.

She turned her head, trying to make out the rest of the room, but it was too dark. Maybe she was not safe in her marriage bed. Outside, there might be a guard stationed.

No, if Olaf had revealed who she was they would have killed her to be rid of the dilemma.

Rosa tried to leave her bed. She had to find out what was happening. Her limbs could barely respond, tremors running along her arms as she braced herself. A soft whine of dismay came out. *Useless, hopeless flesh!* she thought.

One of the shadows righted itself and leaned forward. Hands steadied her, but also gently pushed her on to the bed. She flinched, uncertain if she was still hallucinating.

"Calm yourself, my little deer, no one will harm you."

The cover over the smokehole was pulled aside to let the dawn in. Her husband smiled down at her.

"Do you know me now, Rosa?" he asked.

"Grimulf!" she gasped and embraced him.

"Good," he teased softly, almost strained. "I'd not know what to do if you said another's name."

"How long?"

"A few very long nights," Grimulf answered.

He removed her arms from around himself. Then she heard the splash of water hitting the bottom of a vessel. A cup was held to her lips. Gratefully, she drank.

She reached to feel his cheek. The rough emergence of his beard met her fingers. Even after all this, it was this which made her chuckle.

"I will need to shave this again."

"In a while. First you must recover your strength."

Was Olaf nearby? She doubted he would leave her alone, even when she was another's wife. Rosa paled with terror: Olaf had married her first. In truth, he was her husband rather than Grimulf.

That marriage had not been consummated. The church would annul it for such a reason. But, until she let Grimulf taste her flesh, this joining was just as tenuous.

"I will get better once I am up and moving," she argued. "I've been here too long. The sisters once had to tie me to the bed when I sprained my ankle."

"And I will do the same thing if you are disobedient," he growled lightly, a threat as well as a promise.

The sensation Rosa felt flickering within was completely different to how she'd felt when Sisters Mildritha and Eawynn had to bind her hands. This was new, frightening, but somehow enticing as well.

His hands stroked her arms, palm brushing over her stomach, the other hand just barely missing the curve of her buttocks. She flushed. Perhaps she need not worry about Olaf if Grimulf satisfied himself.

He certainly thought she was strong enough for *that*. Though from what she had heard and been warned about there was not much the woman did, save lie there and make herself at least somewhat comfortable.

"You'll not be leaving this bed until you're fattened up again. I daren't lift you, for fear you'll blow far off across the seas from a northernly wind!" Rather than climb in, he kissed her and stood. "I'll get something for the grumbling in your belly."

The redness of her face now came from embarrassment. She hadn't even realised her stomach was making such noises. Too focused upon the smoky scent of Grimulf, the barest brush of his mouth and the comforting heaviness of his caress. When he was not close enough to touch her, she felt almost hollow, as though needing him to ground her.

What she said was not a demand to return, though.

"Thank you for tending to me."

Grimulf made a rough sound of surprise, now it was he who sounded uncertain. "It was mainly Gunhild. I did not do much."

"You were here with me."

"I am your husband. I would never abandon you." His fingers curled around one of the timber posts, agitatedly tapping against it as she looked at him expectantly. "Gunhild will bring you another bath."

"Are you going to help me bathe again?"

He made a choked sound. His forehead rested against his hand, but he was chuckling.

"Best not," he told her. "As I said, you're not yet strong enough... and a wolf can only be tempted so long by the flash of the rabbit's tail."

Grimulf ducked out. Rosa settled, clutching her arms, as though she might mimic the touch of her husband.

She'd never experienced conflict before, at least, not from within. In her youth she had rebelled against her parents, but always known what she desired. At the nunnery all she had felt was peace. Not once had she doubted.

And now? She was a woman of God, his bride, and yet she had tied herself to a mortal man. A pagan.

She had done this to save her flesh and beating heart, but what of her immortal soul? Her fingers interlocked, clasped in prayer.

She was uncertain if she would receive an answer. Many women would have martyred themselves. She had only thought of her survival. If she had died or remained with Olaf, the man would have won. At least she had some control over what happened with her life. The man who was her husband now certainly did not make her regret...

Olaf could ruin everything. At any moment, if she dared to relax, he could contest the marriage. She had no idea if a Viking union was considered as sacred as a Christian one, or if they could easily be broken.

Before she could worry even further, the curtain lifted. This time Grimulf carried a trencher of meats and bread. He helped her sit up.

"Meat to put upon my bones?" she said and wondered if perhaps she was a little delirious.

"If only it was that easy."

He held a piece of bacon out to her. She certainly wasn't weak enough to need to be fed like a kitten, but her lips brushed his fingertip.

Perhaps it was not her who was weak, but him. Unable to withhold himself completely and needing the touch of her.

She took each mouthful, tongue flicking out once or twice. Each time he stiffened.

It was as if she bewitched him, but it was not enough to tempt him to crawl over and take what she offered. She would have to be stronger in her attack if she wanted this marriage consummated.

"Who was that man who arrived?" she asked as he picked another rasher of bacon. "Before I fainted? I do not remember much."

"That was my uncle. Olaf is greatly concerned for you."

"Is that all?"

"What else would he say?"

"I am not your typical Viking wife."

"You'll get the chance to show him why I made such a choice."

Rosa's teeth caught upon his thumb.

"He's still here?"

Grimulf licked the slight graze.

"I have only just arrived and know nothing of running a farm. My uncle offered his guidance."

"What did you do before?" As much as she enjoyed his caresses, she knew nothing of this man. He might even be another marauder, just like Olaf.

"I was a trader and explorer, that is all you need to know. My brother passed recently, a fall from his horse. As I am the last one left, it passes on to me."

"I am sorry."

"We all have our stories to weave," was his cryptic response, and as he looked upon her it seemed as if his eyes impressed themselves on her cheeks, for she would not meet his gaze.

She remained silent. Sighing, he stood.

"I will call for Gunhild and let you have your bath in peace."

"Wait." She made to speak further but found her mouth had gone dry. Grimulf paused, cocking his head, his back to her.

Her pulse fluttered in her throat. Could she tell her new husband all that had befallen her?

Olaf was Grimulf's uncle and Rosa was only his wife. One he hardly knew. He might not believe her. He might even, and her throat lurched in misery, agree with his uncle's methods. He was a Viking.

What she said instead was, "I find myself unable to stand for long. Please, will you not stay and help me?"

Rosa was careful when leaving her bed, not because of the pounding in her head or the shakiness of her legs, though she felt them, but because Grimulf would not let her push herself.

Her husband now, she realised. She must obey him. Somehow it seemed another one of her dreams.

He fed her more honey. She wanted to snatch the bowl

47

and spoon from him to prove she was not weak. There would be future battles. He seemed content to tend to her.

The bath was drawn. He took her hands, carefully pulling her. Each step was as trembling as a fawn newly woken from the womb. It would have made her laugh if she hadn't been dizzy. Asking him to stay had been a ruse to tempt him, yet she found she had spoken the truth about her weakness.

This time, as his hands passed over her sides, mapping her again, it was not the sensuality of a soon to be lover, but a protector tracing her wounds. She found herself leaning in to his touch, lapping up his comfort. The gentleness felt more intimate than a first kiss.

Rosa wondered what he saw now. Before, she might have been windswept, feverish, but she had been hale. Rosa looked at herself, disquieted by the chalky pallor and thinness of her legs. No wonder he treated her as tenderly as a seashell. As emaciated as she was, she doubted she sparked much desire.

And she must make him burn if she was to survive here. Nothing could break apart their marriage.

As warm water sloshed down her back, she shivered. Olaf's foul features seemed to ripple over her mind's eye. She wished she could banish him alongside her nightmares.

The thought of him was what sent her rushing out of the bath. Grimulf caught her about the waist.

"Easy now. Where are you hurrying off to?"

"I'm not a horse who's lost her shoe," she argued, afraid her thoughts were much too easy to tell. "I have been abed too long. I wish to go outside."

He must be able to see the heady state she was in. Any sensible man would have her in bed and ensure she stayed there. Any husband would want his new wife bound there, at least until she was with child.

He knew he'd have no peace if he did.

Grimulf, after much arguing, let her dress herself. He draped one of his cloaks over her, made of thick layers of wool and ringed with a collar of rabbit's fur, pale and speckled brown. After he clipped the silver brooch, his thumb pressed under her chin. Rosa's eyes flicked up to look at him.

"You are the chieftain's woman now," he told her. "But it does not mean you can wander as you please. You are a stranger... I myself am considered one. There are things you must be alert for." His lips pursed. For a moment he did not go on.

"For what?" she pressed.

Grimulf shook his head. He gently nudged her chin and pulled her hair free from under the cloak. She took it from him, weaving it over her shoulder into a braid.

"Promise you'll not leave this place without me as your guard."

He made it sound as if she had become his prisoner. This did not anger her, life at the nunnery was much the same, and having a companion meant less chance of Olaf getting close.

"I promise."

Then Grimulf took her arm and led her out of the house. She raised her hand at the sudden shards of daylight, even though the sky was as dull as a pebble in a river. The clouds had a sooty tinge, coated in the smoke from the old men's pipes.

Those they passed looked upon her with wide eyes bright with surprise. *Had they thought me dead?* she wondered. She pressed closer to Grimulf's side. The villagers watched her as children watched a grave, anticipating ghosts.

Once the initial shock subsided, then she saw their true intent. Men tilling the fields pulled their caps off, soon going back to their work. The women were welcoming, reaching out and taking her hand, as though feeling she still had a pulse. They offered hopes and charms for a fertile future.

These women sat outside their homes, clustered together gutting buckets of fishes or weaving wool. Rosa wished she could sit amongst them, submerge herself in their gossip. Her face was going stiff from her smile. She'd rather be doing something of use rather than be under this much scrutiny. She had hoped it would be over once she had escaped the mead hall.

It was comforting to have Grimulf beside her, even if it was mostly due to the sheer warmth radiating from him. The man was like a bonfire.

There was a rigidness from him as well. They might as well be two carvings put next to one another; not quite comfortable while others watched them, preferring to be by themselves.

It was the old men who set her on edge most. They sat there, sharpening their sons' tools or watching over their beasts, and their eyes were narrowed. Like a pack of wolves that had a noticed a fox creep past. Not quite prey, but not an equal either. None of them trusted her.

The village was comprised of several longhouses and byres. Areas were fenced off to keep the cows and pigs apart, the chickens left to roam and peck at what remained that wasn't frost bitten. What could be grown in this weather were at the backs of homes, struggling rows of cabbages, oats and beans. Smoke crept from the roof of a shack, where the herring were kept.

The mead hall was a distance away, stood upon the dunes, whereas the village was further from the seas. They could not see the waves, only hear the crash of them and watch the shudder of the tall, sparse marram grass.

There were no churches, only the lightning cleft tree belonging to Thor. No other life for miles.

"The horse I came with," she said, as Grimulf made to turn home, deeming she'd had enough fresh air, "what happened to him?" Her heart twisted at the thought of the creature collapsing and dying because she had pushed him too hard. He had saved her.

"The stallion? He's fine." He took her to where the stables

were. "I've claimed him as part of your dowry, but you may ride him whenever you please."

"I have no desire to ride from here."

"Then we will have to go together, though with saddles this time. There is only one reason your thighs should be aching."

His voice had gone husky and his hip brushed against her intentionally. Something that felt like tangling thread writhed deep within her.

Was he to claim her on a bed of straw? *Good. Get it over with,* she thought. Olaf had yet to make his presence known, but he must be close.

However, when they entered they found they were not alone. There was a man about Grimulf's age, with his blond beard knotted into a complicated plait and a scar covering the bridge of his nose. He leaned heavily against the spear he used as a walking stick, a flagon of something knotted around the shaft for him to easily drink from. Horses, tall and regal, the white stallion amongst them, nosed against his hand as he offered them a mound of oats.

"Rudolf!" Grimulf called joyously, releasing Rosa's arm and striding over to clap his hand on the other man's shoulder. "So, the healer managed to stitch you back together."

Rudolf grimaced, reaching for the drinking vessel. "Most of me. I had to get out of the old man's clutches. He's making me drink this swill." He pulled off the cork with his teeth, taking a swift, pained drag of the contents. "I'll be poisoned before I've recovered."

Rosa moved to one of the horses, not wanting to appear as if she was awkwardly wavering alone. She comforted herself with stroking the horse's neck.

Rudolf eyed her. "Who's this?"

Rosa forced another smile and returned to fussing the horse.

"My wife."

"What! I was only gone for a few nights. Has she bewitched you, then? She has the look of the fey."

"Then be sure not to look into my eyes," she said, voice light, not knowing if this was how a wife acted with other men.

As if remembering she was there, Grimulf reached over and took her hand. "Perhaps she has. Rosa, this man has been my friend since the cradle. We fought together in Byzantium for the emperor. Know that you can trust him."

"A pleasure, my lady." The man bowed his head. Quite quickly he dismissed her from his thoughts, his eyes flicking back to his friend. "Your uncle wishes to speak with you. No doubt wanting to impart his wisdom."

"Then I will see you later. There is much we have to discuss."

"Do not hurry yourself. I would not want to be the person who gets between a man and his woman while their passions still burn."

Grimulf returned her home. Rosa delayed him awhile, for he wanted to see her eat. While she was distracted with spooning broth, he questioned her. It was gentle, curious, focusing on her youth, her brothers, life in the nunnery.

She was thankful she did not have to lie about this. So long as she avoided the last month, she could not trip up.

Once or twice, her gaze trailed over to the bedroom, only covered by a thin curtain for privacy. He noticed, but he made no move to acknowledge her confusion. His hand settled upon her knee, warm and heavy, but would not move further.

When Grimulf spoke of his own youth, before he sailed overseas, he made it sound like a story. A gentle rhythm came from his words, as if she could shut her eyes and truly see the picture he spun for her.

Suddenly his hand withdrew. Grimulf stood, leaning to kiss her. He stole her breath and then left her. No doubt off to see Rudolf or even Olaf. Her skin now prickled.

Rosa went searching for anything to distract her. There were some of his clothes, gloves, shirts, that had felt the rigours of the road. She sat and stitched by the fire.

As if sensing her need for company, Gunhild appeared. The old woman was like a house spirit. She did not ask how Rosa felt; the dark circles under her eyes were answer enough. She sat beside her, watching.

"He will do well with you." The old woman did not wait for her reaction. She'd stated her opinion and did not care what others thought. "What are you able to do? I can see you're strong enough to sew, is that all?"

"I'll do whatever you set me to."

"Good. Come with me and I'll show you how to make skause."

As they stood by the bubbling stew, a knock came on the door. Rosa, after looking to Gunhild and having the woman jerk her head at her, went to answer.

One of the old men stood there. This one had a bare crown, wisps of grey and white hair surrounding his skull, like waves around a stone island. Old he might be, but he was broad enough to fill the doorway as Grimulf did.

After a short, worried pause of staring, she recognised him as being the man who had overseen their wedding: the craftsman, Thorstein. His arm curled towards his chest, concealing something she swore she saw squirm. His cracked lips spread into a grin.

"Good evening, my lady. I am pleased you are up and about now."

"Thank you." At least someone was pleased to see her. "Would you like to come in?"

"I'm afraid not. Dear Gunhild in there is not fond of me. I tracked blood and mud in here ten years ago and she's not forgiven me yet. My beast had a litter before you arrived. I think she was meant for you."

He shifted his arm, revealing what he held.

"What...What creature is this?"

Thorstein boomed with laughter and the thing in his hands began scratching to be released. No such luck, though, as the tiny claws did little to dent the man's calloused fingers.

"Do you not recognise a mouser, little one?"

"That is a cat?"

Rosa peered at the thing but did not get too close. Especially when its fur stood on end and it hissed threateningly.

"A Norwegian one. The granddaughter of the old Tom I brought with me the first time I came here," he told her, lumping the creature into her arms.

Rosa supposed it did look like a cat, though it might also be a bear cub. The cats she had cared for as a child, and the feral mouser that had roamed the nunnery, were more furball kittens compared to this one.

It was meant to be young, but it was the same size as a human baby. Her wrists were beginning to ache from the strain. How could a kitten be this heavy? But she couldn't let it drop to the ground.

Its fur was brown streaked with black, absolutely unruly. The long tail flicked lazily and the cat stared at her with an insolent look.

Rosa tucked the cat under her arm, cradling it as one would an infant. It got itself comfy, lolling its head petulantly, but made no move to squirm free.

Thorstein continued telling her, "They're crafty little beasts with a lot of courage. They pull Freyja's chariot. I've even seen one take on a bear. It is tradition to bring a mouser for the new household. You cannot complain at that?"

There were many things she had rejected. A lot of women were aghast she had refused to sacrifice anything besides some of her blood to their Goddess of Fertility. She needed to be approachable to Grimulf's people, at least willing to accept some of their ways, even if they held little meaning to her. A cat was not an unpleasant gift. She would be grateful for the company.

"Thank you," she said, and he was pleased at her smile. "I have always loved cats. Does she have a name?"

"I thought you'd want to name her."

"Then... I will call her Morgana." It had been her grandmother's name and the cat's pinched, frowning expression reminded her of the old woman.

"The witch?" She knew she had chosen wrong. Thorstein's open face closed off.

They believed in magic. They saw no wrong in a woman practicing it, yet she was not one of their women. If they thought her skilled in such things, they would assume she meant to harm them with it.

"Thank you again, Thorstein," she said, trying to be cheerful. "I must go help Gunhild with the cooking."

She carried the cat with her. Not once did she look back, afraid she would see his mistrust. She would have to be careful.

"What is it you wished to speak to me about, Uncle?"

Grimulf had spent little time with his uncle, even if they had not seen one another in seven years. His attentions had been focused on Rosa and her recovery.

The Viking had called him from the mead hall, into the night and cold. The seas were stretched before them as they crouched amongst the dune grasses. The tide had come in, devouring the sands. Waves lazily lapped against their vantage point, dark pieces of flotsam bobbing along, easily mistaken for macabre shapes.

Even though he saw the sea before him, he might think the sky and land had been exchanged: the stars had a dull gleam that night and the moon rippled as if it was an insubstantial reflection. Clouds textured the dark sky, grey plumes trailing across like seafoam. Then the smoke from his uncle's pipe drifted across.

Grimulf gave the man his full attention. He half raised his hand to slap him on the back, but paused and instead pulled out his flint and knife. He started sharpening his blade.

"Well?" he demanded.

"You've got a great many years of exploring," Olaf began. "Before he was taken your father kept sailing, even when his beard went white and his teeth started to drop out!"

"I've had my time. My brothers never travelled as much, and now I must take on their responsibilities."

He should be warmer towards his kin. He had been when he was a youth.

As the youngest of three sons, Grimulf had been left to his own devices while his father prepared his elder brothers for succession. Most of the time, if he was not earning the old man's ire, he was ignored. Only his uncle had spared him any effort. The man had taught him how to fight, told him tales of Scandinavia, stoked the flames hungering for exploration.

When Grimulf had been in mourning for his father and brother, it had been Olaf who suggested he travel to the East. They had meant to sail together, but the warrior had changed his mind, preferring conquering this land.

Since his father's death it seemed bad luck had spread through the family. Now that Grimulf had returned, would he see a change in their fortunes?

Olaf reached over. His fingers gripped his bicep, squeezing the muscle there and causing it to flex.

"There's adventure in you yet. Don't let your strength be wasted on the fields."

"And who will tend to these fields in my absence? Collect taxes and ensure my people's houses remain standing?" The scraping of the flint quickened.

"Assign me as overseer. When your brother had to be elsewhere, he called me to assist. I would not have suggested this if I thought you happy with your decision. I saw it in your eyes. The haziness of your thoughts clouds them. You are thinking of the seas and the voyages in your future. All this will be here when you truly wish to return."

Grimulf might lie to himself, but his uncle saw the truth. He had accepted the duty he had inherited yet doing so did not change who he was. He was an explorer.

This land was unfamiliar, uncomfortable territory, no matter how much he wished to feel a sense of home. Even though he lived as close as he could to the waves, it did not compare to the salt winds buffeting his ship's sails or watching shimmering scales as fishes swam past. Now all that awaited him was tilling the soil and the excitement of a thunderstorm to quell what sparked in his blood.

It would be childish to run off. A man shouldered his responsibilities.

"I have a wife. Hopefully children will follow."

"And why should that stop you? Plenty of women have joined their husbands. Why not take Rosa with you?"

Grimulf considered the notion. He pictured the young woman on deck, clutching her shawl, hair whipping in the winds... He shook his head.

"No, she is too weak for now. I will not risk her life."

"That is the problem with buying a horse without testing it. You're now stuck with a lame beast. When will she be strong enough, then? She is not like us. Beautiful, but weak just like a flower."

The flint paused. Grimulf's fingers tightened around the knife.

"You know nothing of my wife."

"And neither do you, nephew."

Grimulf wanted to lunge, strike him, beat the smug, twisting sneer from his face. The younger him would have, then Olaf would have dealt him a few retaliatory blows. The tussle would descend into laughter, with the pair staggering off for drinks. It burned in Grimulf to give in. Olaf wanted him to.

No longer could he rein himself in. There was something deep inside that wanted to bite and instead of playfully wounding—kill.

Grimulf tucked away his knife. "Good night, Uncle. Thank you for your concern, but I am no longer the boy you knew. For once in my life, it is time for me to do something that would please my father."

He arose, slowly walking home. The cold had begun to bother him; he desired his wife's company instead.

Rudolf caught up. He must have been watching and waiting for him and Olaf to finish speaking.

Their breaths misted in the night. Grimulf glanced at the shadows, spying for those who should not be near. They stood by the smokehouse, the crackle of flames coming within while the scent of wood and salt crawled out.

"What happened to the hoard?" Rudolf asked. "Was your uncle asking after it?"

"He doesn't know. And no one else will. The winters have been getting harsher and I've been told not as many fish have been caught. I'll see them through this rough patch."

"So, we'll definitely be staying."

"I've made my choice. You and the rest of the fellowship are free to go with the winds. I know you left a pretty dancer behind."

Rudolf considered the prospect for a moment, tugging at

his beard. "No, my life is by your side. You need all the allies you can muster. Those who know you are the man you were and not a…"

"Is everything prepared?" Grimulf demanded, not wanting the thing he dreaded to be named.

"I found somewhere far enough. I will go with you when the change occurs."

"Thank you, my friend. I'm afraid I have more tasks for you, and not the kind you are fond of."

"Give me a man to run through or a woman to pry secrets from. I cannot bear to smile sweetly as a fat priest would and try to worm my way into anyone's good graces."

Grimulf chuckled, picturing his friend as how he described. "Must you always gripe, man? For some reason people like to tell you things. They must think your head so empty you wouldn't remember half of it!"

"Give me my orders, then. I want to get in the warmth."

"I need to know what Ragnar was doing before he perished. I cannot start questioning my people, or else they will start to wonder if all is well. Do not let my uncle know of this. I do not want him starting a fight with anyone before we have proof."

They parted. Rudolf went towards the mead hall alone, when before the two would spend moon and dawn together. Now, Grimulf went to his wife.

His step was quick. The mystery of his woman awaited him.

Grimulf stepped inside to find his wife sitting by the fireside, wrapped in one of his cloaks and with a cat upon her lap. She dozed, chin upon the palm of her hand while she idly ran her fingers through the cat's fur. Gunhild must have gone to sleep already.

Grimulf knelt, watching her. She had a slight flush, a remnant of the fever, but at least she was awake. His throat went tight, worried she had slipped back into unconsciousness. He set his hand upon her shoulder. She stirred while the cat arched its back at him and leapt off.

He was surprised at how relieved he felt when he saw her eyes open.

"To bed with us now," he decided, and he heaved her into his arms, kicking ash over the fire to dampen its flames. He glanced about, commenting, "You've been busy!"

The two women must have unpacked what his brothers had stowed away. He recognised his father's shield on the wall. The tapestry depicting one of their voyages to Shetland had been weaved by his mother. The place was beginning to resemble home.

Rosa looked towards their bed. "I thank you for tending to me."

"You make it sound as though I am a stranger, rather than your husband!" Grimulf replied lightly. "Your health is in my hands, of course I would do all I could to heal you."

"You went without a wedding night."

Yes, the delayed wedding night was fast approaching. He had a surprise for her. Another test. He wondered how she would react to this one.

"I could hardly make you my wife while you lay abed sick with fever."

He settled her upon the down stuffed mattress. She sat there, legs slightly curled towards her chest.

"I am not your wife lest we…" but she could not finish what she wanted to say. She seemed resolved to have this done, yet already she was crumbling.

"Why would anyone else need to know what goes on in our bed?"

"God knows, and judges."

"Are you really using God to command me into your

bed?" he chuckled. Then, as the meagre light caught upon her shoulder, he saw the way she trembled. He rested his hands upon her to hide her fear, but he felt her shake within his grip. "Are you certain? If you are still unwell…"

"I have to do this."

"You do not have to sound as if you are being led to your execution."

"No, I am—I am excited."

She turned and kissed him. Her lips were cold.

Grimulf could not deny her. He carded his fingers through her hair, cupping her head. His kisses were soft but demanding, and soon enough her lips parted and she trembled for another reason.

Women always favoured kisses. Grimulf found some pleasure in trading kisses and bites. It was a comfortable lull while their sweat cooled and they readied themselves for the next round of the hunt.

Sometimes it could soften a woman into accepting further pursuits…but he did not think tonight would be like this. Her hesitant but happy caresses of the muscles of his leg caused a stir of interest. He needed her, aching badly.

Grimulf was stronger than his hunger. He could tame this wolf. He would not frighten his little maiden into bolting.

He loosened her braid, her beautiful black hair spreading out like ravens' wings. He kissed the jut of her shoulder, too sharp from her recent illness. As his tongue wormed into the dip, he thought to himself he would rather have her on his lap, feeding her strawberries and buttermilk until she became hearty again.

"Make yourself comfortable," he growled.

Rosa swallowed, but did as he commanded. She half-lay, half-sat upon the bed, left awkwardly stretched out like a deer slipping on the ice.

"Do you prefer to do this with or without your clothes?" he asked her.

"I should think they would be taken off either way, considering what we are about to do," she responded tartly.

"Good. I find clothes troublesome at rest."

Grimulf pulled off his shirt. Getting the hint, Rosa began fumbling with the brooches at the shoulders of her dress. She tilted to her side.

Grimulf crawled over the bed. He did not waste time. With the knife he kept in his boot, he sliced the brooches free —ignoring her gasp—and peeled her dress from her. He swept his hand along her flank soothingly as he dragged off the shift.

"Come, you're shivering. Get beneath the furs."

He had her settled before he took off his trousers. She watched him, silent and eyes wide, the furs drawn to her chin. He saw fear there and it put a bitter taste in his mouth. He also saw interest brightening them, hungering curiosity as she took him in entirely.

Grimulf threw back the covers and crawled in with her. She shrieked at the cold getting in, squirming from him, but he quickly had her against him. His heat enwrapped them both. She pressed curiously against the hardness behind her. He groaned, thinking he might not be able to rein himself in and she would be devoured.

She felt pliant and at least willing. But he did not want someone who was only willing for some reason he had yet to discover—he wanted passion.

Grimulf wrapped his arm around her and laid his head down. His thumb stroked her stomach, just beneath her navel.

"Do you know of Freyja?" he asked her.

"We prayed to her during the ceremony. Why do you ask this? Is it... Is it another ritual?"

He kissed her ear. "A story tonight, I think."

She would have argued, but his stroking of her side lulled

her. His rumbling voice sounded as soothing as a distant storm that would never get too close.

"She is the daughter of the sea god Njörðr, wife of Óðr. Goddess of love, magic and death."

He told her of the great battles fought in Freyja's name, of the giants who schemed to carry her off to their lands but could never fool her. When warriors fell, she had first pick of them before the rest went to Valhalla.

"Then one day Óðr went missing. Freyja hunted for him, but he could not be found."

"She never found him? Not one sign?"

"The other Gods thought him dead. She remained strong even while she wept, awaiting his return while ruling their lands justly."

Her body slackened in his arms as sleep claimed her. A single sigh escaped, then she was away, off to the next day.

Grimulf smiled, pleased, though it did little to ease his discomfort. Being wounded would be worth winning her over and having her comfortable around him.

"I'll tell you a story every night," he whispered, wondering if it would reach into her dreams, "and I won't stop until you tell me *your* tale."

He too settled for sleep and now his bed did not feel so barren.

CHAPTER 3

"Let me tell you of Melusine," Grimulf murmured low in Rosa's ear.

Rosa moaned in acknowledgement, her senses too focused on the way his hand dragged over her breast. A hint of frustration sharpened her tone, for she knew the touches would not go further.

"She was a beautiful woman found wandering the marshes. A man came upon her and made her his wife. She worshipped him, as he did her, but there was one thing she made him promise. It was a strange request. *My love, you must never watch me bathe. If you do, I must leave.*"

The night sky turned to day, like the blade of a knife catching the light of the fire.

"He obeyed her. And yet, when she banished him to the other room, as he heard the splash of water, the soft lilt of her singing, he ached to know why. Aching as badly as when he desired her. As well as his lust, his curiosity must be sated."

Outside, horses were being saddled. Swords sharpened. Hunting horns swung from the thick, muscular necks of young men eager to prove their worth.

"The man crept to the door of the room his woman

bathed in. Put his eye to the keyhole. All he saw were fragments: water spilling from her hands, the delicate impression of her spine through her flesh, shoulders crawling with strands of her black, slickened hair. He held his breath, but she must have heard the hammering of his heart in his skull, for she turned.

"The door flung open of its own accord, Melusine wailing he had promised her never to look. Her true self had been revealed. Scales blossomed upon her flesh. Her legs entwined to form a serpent's tail and wings burst from her back. Weeping, she flew into the mists, abandoning her husband and the children she had borne him."

Rosa yawned. "I think the moral of this story is for husbands not to delve too deep into their wives' secrets."

"Or perhaps Melusine should have trusted her husband would not care what she hid in the water's reflection."

Grimulf nestled his face against her neck. She squirmed and laughed gently at the tickle of his beard. His fingers gripped either side of her hips and she tensed, thinking it might finally begin.

But, just as it had been these past few nights, he settled for a kiss to her shoulder. He arose and quickly dressed, sliding the knife under their pillow into his boot.

"I must be away. A group of us will be riding out as a hunting party. I'll be home before sundown."

Rosa sat up, pulling the furs higher. Already, she felt the loss of his warmth.

"Who will be going with you?"

"Rudolf. You would not know the others."

She tried to conceal her disappointment when his uncle was not mentioned. There was no hope of a boar accidentally goring the other man.

"Hurry home," was all she could meekly offer.

Rosa had no reason to remain in bed. She climbed out and changed into her overdress and layers of shawls. Grimulf braided her hair when she tilted her head suggestively, enjoying the way his fingers faintly grazed her throat, then he left her to get his weapons.

She trailed into the main room, where Gunhild knelt to start the fire. Morgana lay curled on a sunspot coming from the smokehole, luxuriating in the meagre heat of the day. Grimulf's dog Shuck, who had invited himself into the house when Rosa had been sick, gave her a better greeting. His claws clicked on the stone floor as he nuzzled into her gloved hand. She scratched his ear then went to prepare their breakfast.

Grimulf appeared from the storeroom, a bow and arrow strapped to his back. He did not stop to eat, instead taking bread and cheese for later.

"We'll eat when we've caught something."

She supposed he preferred this. Hunting and the rougher roles in life were what he knew, rather than diplomacy. He could prove to his people his worth as leader if he kept them fed, though would they learn to respect him if they thought the man no better than themselves? Rosa knew she would rather trust a man willing to dirty his hands and feel sweat upon his brow.

She went to him as he headed for the open door. The dog raced out at the scents outside, eager to snare a rabbit.

Rudolf was there with their horses, quick to be off with him. Rosa clung to Grimulf's cloak as she kissed him, as though having to remind him that she was his wife.

Then the pair rode into the distance and all she could do was wait.

———

Gunhild and Rosa were making barley bread. The simple, mindless motion of kneading distracted Rosa from her thoughts, simply enjoying the sensation of her knuckles thrusting into the rough dough, freeing the heady smell of honey and ale.

The old woman had left to get water from the well. Rosa kept on glancing at the door, not wanting to be caught out, but uncertain what she would do if another stood there. Olaf still had not approached since her recovery.

There were shouts outside, followed by screeches of pain. One of the spoons clattered to the ground as Rosa rushed to the door. Her heart thrummed in the base of her throat, thinking it something to do with Grimulf.

She tried peering out. Whatever was happening was concealed by the onslaught of people hurrying to see.

Gunhild joined the crowd, heaving the sloshing bucket along with her. Her face was curious, eager to see what the fuss was about, then she gaped in horror, the wrinkled cheeks screwing up to cry out.

Rosa should have remained inside. Anything could have happened. There might be a fight or someone dying. It would be better to hide, rather than draw the others' attention and ire. She had already done enough to make them dislike their new lady.

Yet, she reasoned, already scraping the dough from her hands, if someone was hurt then it was her duty to help them. She might not be a nun anymore, but she had her skills in healing. It would be a sin not to use them.

Rosa ran into the chilly day. Even with the winds and frost making the air taste sharp, it was unable to mask the bitter, metallic blood she could almost feel upon her tongue. She tried to peer over the outer edges of the crowd, but she was much smaller than them.

"Please... Excuse me..."

No one paid her any notice. Whoever was in the centre now wept, the high-pitched, ragged choking sound letting her know the person was young, rather than a fully-grown man. She glanced around, wondering where Grimulf was. Some of the other men were gone as well, which meant the hunting party had not yet returned.

Rosa tried slipping in amongst the crush of bodies, but she was forced out. Gunhild had somehow managed to get to the front. Rosa wavered, ferrying up her resolve.

If she did this, she would have to see it through. She had no idea what the wounds were or if she could fix them, and if she could not then they might turn on her. Grimulf was not here to protect her.

Rosa surged forward. "Move aside!" she cried. "I am a healer."

Her hands shot out, pressing against bulky sides, and heaved. It was only from surprise that they moved. She took the chance, weaving her way through, any empty space quickly occupied by her. Their wool cloaks and furs dragged over her face. She smelt their smoke and sweat.

Then she reached the centre. One of the young farmhands lay upon the curling grasses, groaning, voice too hoarse to continue screaming. Gunhild knelt by his side, cradling his head, shushing and stroking the sweat from his brow. His left hand gripped his right arm, trying to stem the rush of blood spilling forth. Between the white, shaking fingers were great shards of wood.

Rosa knelt as well. Her hand settled on his throat, feeling how swiftly his heart raced.

"What has happened? Who is he?"

"This is my grandson Björn, mistress," the old woman sobbed. The boy began whimpering and she tried to soothe him. "He's all that I have left of my family. One of the carts fell upon him when a horse spooked. It's near severed his arm."

Rosa quickly examined the rest of him and deemed it was just the arm that was injured, save for a few bruises. She wanted to see the wound more clearly but knew if she were to have him remove his hand then it would gush further. He had bled too much already.

"I need tweezers, needle and thread, herbs to stop the bleeding," Rosa called.

None obeyed her. She glanced at Gunhild and the old woman bared her teeth at them.

"Did you not hear her, you gawpers? Do as she said or I'll blame the lot of you for my boy's death!"

Finally, people were rushing to get what was needed. Rosa pried open one of Björn's eyes. The boy was becoming quieter, a slight haze coating the green eye.

"Forgive me." She removed her wedding ring and slapped him harshly with the back of her hand. He started, crying from his pains. "He needs to stay awake," she explained to Gunhild. "Make sure he does not shut his eyes or else he will be lost."

The boy must have fallen in the pig sty from the crash, for he was smeared in mud and other matter. His pale hair turned into claggy clumps. This would not do. She understood the wound should not be dirtied, for evil spirits might creep in and poison him.

Rosa took Gunhild's bucket and sluiced water over the boy. He gasped and shuddered, clothes sticking to him. Tiny rivulets of dirty water streamed, running across the bare patches of ground where the grasses had curled into sleep.

Another woman brought her tweezers made of bone. She set upon carefully prising out the wooden shards. Most were large chunks she could easily remove, but there were some that had splintered and she had to go further in, the boy hissing, as she cleared the rest of the debris. More water was thrown over him. He shivered, breath steaming as he choked.

"Get him inside."

She made a gesture. Some of the farmers went either side, lifting him. "Gently!" And the ascent was slow and careful.

Gunhild led the way, taking them to a hut near the barley field. Just as one of the men booted the door open, there came the stamp of horses' hooves. The hunters had returned. A boar speared on a spit was carried between two of the riders.

Grimulf rode at the front. He pulled at his reins, guiding the horse.

"What has happened? Has there been an attack?"

"An accident," Rosa answered, and he looked to her with surprise.

"Go inside—"

She interrupted his command, "I will return home when I have fixed this boy." She might defer to him in all other matters, but she was resolute in this.

Knowing he could not win the argument, Grimulf nodded stiffly. He ordered his men to get the boar butchered, then rode to the stables, promising to return. She did not even think of the reprisals he might have planned for her later.

The hut was small with only a bed and chest, where a scythe lay beside a flint, waiting to be sharpened. They set the young man upon the bed and lit a fire in the cooking pit.

Rosa threaded a needle. The dried yarrow and crushed garlic were quickly ground together, mixing honey and water to turn it into paste.

She felt eyes upon her. Faces crowded in the doorway, leaping apart when someone made to shove past. At least they had not piled into the hut.

Such attention did not make her hands shake. It stiffened her resolve. She might as well be at the nunnery, tending to some poor man injured by his farming tools, while the elder sisters loomed behind her, ready to swoop in and take over if she showed the slightest of hesitations. She needed to prove herself.

"Björn," she said softly, soothingly, for that was the voice the men she had tended to always obeyed—even in the throes of agony. "Let go of your arm. I must see it better."

The boy thrashed his head left and right. "No! If I do, it'll pull right off."

She continued, urging him, "If I cannot clean and close the wound completely, devils will crawl into your blood and sicken you from within. Then one of the men out there will have to slice your arm off to save the rest of you. Please, be a good boy."

Shakily, he let go. A red ring surrounded the arm from how tightly he had gripped it.

Now she could tell how deeply the cut went. There did not seem to be any sign of his arm being broken thankfully. He must have turned just in time to avoid the worst.

"Keep cleaning off the blood while I stitch the wound," she told Gunhild, who nodded and took the bowl and cloth.

Her needle went back and forth, forming a tiny wall to contain all that made a man from within. She tugged and the stitches made to meet one another, the wound closing. Only the slight impression of her work could be seen, enough for a hook to slide under and pull them out once they were no longer needed. Rosa smeared the herbal paste over the remains of the wound to aid the healing process.

She did not know what possessed her; it must have been the flutter of her pulse hammering in her ears. She fell upon what always calmed her when she was in a state. Her hands clasped together as she shut her eyes. Only the rush of her breathing betrayed that she was praying.

Gunhild stiffened next to her. Björn whimpered. The poultice must be working now, the cooling paste relieving the itching burn as his wound started to knit together. He sighed in relief.

"Now you can rest," Rosa said. "Do not pick at the wound, do not let it go unclean. Come to me at any time if you think the stitches are not holding."

Rosa stood, though had to pause to steady herself. The adrenaline pumping through her trickled into nothing, leaving her lightheaded. Her hand pressed against the wall.

"There is no need to come in today, Gunhild. Your grandson will be wanting family around him."

"Thank you, my lady."

Rosa ducked her head, flushing. "I'm glad I could be of help."

She made to leave. Those watching her moved, keeping their distance. There were whispers, most sounded relieved while some were astonished.

Had they expected her to faint at the sight of blood? To refuse to help because he was a pagan?

Vikings and Christians might consider one another completely different in nature, but the truth was there was little to tell them apart when it came to it. Hopefully they would see that as well.

She did not look at them, did not offer any smiles, instead striding home. Grimulf waited outside, arms crossed.

"Is the boy all right?"

"Yes, thank goodness." She paused, awaiting his response. "Was I wrong to tend to him?"

"No," he decided. "But it might have turned out differently if you had failed."

"It was worth the risk."

He leaned down and kissed her. He smelt of the woods, smoke and blood not from the wounded but the hunting of beasts. The sweet taste of mead flavoured his lips.

"I must see to my people, but I am grateful for what you have done. They will be as well."

Another kiss, then he was heading for Björn's hut. Rosa stepped inside, smiling slightly as she settled before the fire, waiting for the last strings of her thundering heart to calm with her.

Grimulf would soon return to her side. This was her

home now and she would do all she could to keep it safe and welcoming.

With little else to do, Rosa now had to consider whether she would be in trouble. She had disobeyed Grimulf. Even if it had turned out fine, she had ignored his command. It would be all that mattered to the man.

She wondered how Vikings punished an unruly wife.

Moonlight glowed across the darkening sky like a breath of frost. Water droplets glistened, shimmering on cobwebs and purple flowers growing wild, their petals gleaming, tall, thin bodies swaying in the breeze.

The bedroom curtain lifted then fell. His wife did not turn around.

"Good evening, husband."

Grimulf's footsteps came close, her body shifting as he settled down next to her on the bed. She watched him just out of the corner of her eye. His hand went to his pouch and there came the tinkling scrape of a chain.

Rosa shut her eyes and bared her throat to him. It was like a lamb offering herself to the Gods. Her hands rested atop one another and he saw the way her fingers pressed down, stilling any trembles.

"You are my wife," Grimulf murmured. "According to your Christian laws, I can do whatever I desire." His nail lightly stroked along the pulse of her throat. Her breathing quickened, her heart fluttering beneath his touch. "If I were one of your Christian men, I could beat you, strangle you, force you to slake my thirst even in your weakened state. There would be no retribution."

Grimulf moved to kneel behind her. He pulled aside the loose locks of her dark hair, draping it over her shoulder.

There was a mole on the back of her neck, which he leaned over and kissed.

"A northwoman can inherit, divorce, her fate is hers to wield. You might try to lead me on to your good and holy path, but I'll be dragging you just as hard into the bracken briar you fear."

His tongue crept out to sweep across her shoulder blade and she shuddered, a soft gasp escaping. His teeth sunk into the marble flesh, but not enough to make her bleed.

"I do not strike my women, but that does not mean I will not find some way of punishing you if you disobey me again."

"Of course, my lord."

"And yet, if you had not, one of my men would be dead."

Grimulf removed the necklace. There had been no original plan. He had taken it before burying the rest of the hoard because of its beauty. He had known he would have himself a wife by the end of this year, and this would be his gift to her.

This woman might be his wife, yet she remained a stranger. Nevertheless, he wanted to see her wear this. It was the first thing the emperor had ever gifted him for his service.

He trailed the thin chain of coloured beads around her throat. Rosa started, trying to turn her head to see what this was.

"Be still," he commanded, but would not let her see what he was doing. He had trusted her with a blade to his throat, it was time for her to trust him.

There were pearls strung upon the chain as well, a tiny knot between each one, and in the centre dangled a key. It slithered along her throat as he pulled the clasp to, dancing between the hollow of her breasts. She glanced down.

"What is this?"

"The key to our house," he told her. "You are my wife. The queen of my household. In all matters of the home, I shall bow to you. This is proof to all of your standing."

Her fingers gently caressed the object, understanding the honour he gifted her. Heat burned beneath his collar.

"Is this to be another one of your bedtime stories?" she asked, tone disgruntled.

"Would you rather lie in silence?"

"What I want," she told him, twisting herself until she faced him, "is my husband to hold me."

"Do I not do that already?"

Her cheeks were turning scarlet. She would not relent. Rosa crawled forward, Grimulf falling back, until she crouched over him.

"I am well enough already. I will not break if you kiss me, touch me... make love to me." And the sheer effort of even hinting at that took the rest of the argument from her.

Grimulf smirked up at her. "Are you certain you are ready? I don't think you are. Not until I hear you ask for it properly."

"You!"

"You are not a woman yet, you are still a nun. I don't want you regretting this, for I do not want my wife to sour towards me. So, until you do give me the order..."

Rosa's mouth opened, then pursed. Grimulf turned his ear towards her in interest. Her teeth dug into her lip, unable to even whisper the words after years of being told it was shameful and wanton.

Instead, she thrust herself down, locking their lips together. Grimulf's eyebrows jerked in surprise, but he wrapped his arms around her, fingers tangling in her hair. He wasn't about to push her away if she was going to be this eager.

Rosa rutted against him, grabbing at his trousers, knowing what needed to be done for this to be over with quickly. Her hand slipped beneath, touching what was hidden within. Holding him burned her almost. She felt his response to her and shuddered, not certain whether it was from anticipation or anxiety.

His kisses scattered over the tops of her breasts. She lifted her head, the necklace dangling before his eyes.

"Is this enough of an answer?"

His tongue was curling around her exposed nipple when he looked at her, about to tease her further. Grimulf paused. She did not look at him, instead focusing on something to her right. Eyes clouded, pained almost, but most certainly not happy.

He was cloudy minded himself, but with a fugue of lust. Slowly, he came to himself. She did not truly want him yet.

"Shall I take you quickly?" he growled against her throat. "Rough and with little care?"

"Isn't it how such matters turn out?"

Grimulf shook his head. His fingers circled her wrist and he saw how the tips easily met one another. She was too thin.

"No. Whoever taught you this deserves to have their tongue cut out."

She stiffened at such violence. Grimulf stroked her head, sitting and gently pushing her aside.

"I need to keep fattening you up before I finally taste you. Get under the covers, you're shaking."

Grimulf arose, groaning softly under his breath. He had to leave, before he gave in and ruined all chances he had. She did not want him, not yet. He was not about to force her. A child could easily be begotten, and what then?

Rosa softly called his name, frustrated she was being abandoned. His throat lurched. He dared to look and see her sprawled on the bed.

Grimulf burst out of the room, heading for the storeroom at the back of the house, where the winds crept in and he could cool the fires raging beneath his flesh.

If she was willing to trust him, he had to be certain he was worth such a risk. He could not lose control with her alone with him. He had already lost his sanity before and innocents had perished because of this.

The room had a fire going. He pulled off his shirt, but the chill air could not even give him some relief.

Grimulf went past the bench where his weapons lay, waiting to be cleaned and sharpened. He did this even though there was no call for it—there were no men to kill or hunt now a truce had been brokered between the people here. But it settled his mind, a ritual almost, in the same way a Christian would calm himself with prayers.

He was a man. He was not cursed. He was not some wild beast.

He leaned forward, hands either side on the wall. A mirror of polished metal hung there. He looked at his reflection: a hulking brute who was barely contained, his eyes dilated, shoulders heaving, and a flush that travelled from his neck to beyond the mirror. He saw the hardened bulge of his hunger. The ties strained, the simple knots seeming so complicated in that moment he would happily use a blade to free himself.

There would be no relief waiting for him, unless he took matters into his own hands. It did not seem right, seeing as he had a willing wife.

He tried to recall Rosa's expression when she had felt his interest. Had it been fear widening her eyes or did the flick of her tongue across her lips indicate hunger?

She had offered herself and he had rejected her again. If she did not fall with child soon, his men would suspect his seed was weak. Imagine what they would say over his self-inflicted punishment!

Any other man would have taken her. It was not from lack of attraction or being unable to rise to the occasion. He feared this ache would never ease until release was found.

He wanted her, but he did not want it to be a few heady moments. Something animal, just as it had been during his travels. Those women had been like fire, wild and rash and beautiful, but his desire for them had been borne from lust. Passion soon turned to ash—the same as a moth engulfed by flames.

Rosa was his wife. He could not turn from her if things soured. He did not want to. What he desired, even more than her mouth, was a companion. His mother and father's marriage had been something he yearned for himself. If he was patient, then he might have a mate in Rosa.

What if she is a spy? his paranoia whispered, the voice husky and rough like his uncle. *There would be no happy union then. You will have been made weak by what she has discovered and whispered to her masters. If she is revealed, your men will expect her to be punished. And there is only one punishment. You will have to execute her.*

Grimulf shut his eyes. "Leave me," he said, low in his throat. "You will not taint me further."

The voice became quieter, but it was there, murmuring low in the background like a buzzing midge.

Some of his hunger had abated, but he was in no fit state. His breathing slowed as he tried to calm himself. Even though he tried to turn his mind to thoughts of the smithy and hoeing the fields, another much lovelier vision appeared.

Rosa in their bed. Asleep. Naked save for the necklace, the pearls and bright beads pooling in the hollow of her neck. The key curled over her breast, pale nipple hardened from the cold. Furs cradled her narrow hips, dragged away to reveal her belly button and the thatching concealing her.

She was soft and inviting, gently illuminated by moonlight. Then he realised her eyes were open and her arm rose to beckon to him.

Grimulf groaned, dashing water from a bowl on the side and over his face. None of this was helping. Rosa would be wondering where he was. She might come in search of him.

He'd have to go wading through the river, just as he used to as a young man.

The door opened slowly. Others might mistake it for the winds. Grimulf let out a sigh. He pulled his shirt on, the length of it covering his interest.

"You should not hound me so, Rosa," he teased, patting dry the water clinging to his face. "I'll start to wonder if you really were a nun, but instead an imp."

The footsteps were not that of a woman, hesitant and unsure of her new habitat. It was the cautious step of a stranger.

Grimulf gripped the water bowl but remained where he was. "I know you are frustrated. You must think me mad. Any man would be to deny himself you. And by the Gods, I want you."

The steps came as close as he dared. Grimulf spun around, ducking and dashing the bowl's contents, and the bowl, at the stranger's head.

The intruder must have known what he planned. He stabbed low, the dagger catching Grimulf at an angle. Water sprayed, clay shattering.

Grimulf did not recognise the man who fell back. A net covered his face to conceal his identity. He was without his armour, only wearing thin chainmail.

Grimulf clutched his side, teeth gritted. His sword was behind the assassin.

He didn't need a weapon to subdue this fool. Grimulf lunged, tackling him at the legs.

Rosa put on her cloak the moment she began shivering. Grimulf was not returning.

Her cheeks were flushed with shame. Was this what she

had become, no better than a common slut? She had near begged the man to take her virtue. She was a nun!

But it was her husband's right to bed her. She should not have to demand him to do his duty.

Why did he reject her? It could not be because of disgust. The hard weight pressing against her stomach had been proof he desired her. Men did not stop when it was offered to them, just as a fox preyed upon a rabbit trapped in a snare.

The Viking confused her, she needed to discover more about her husband. He would tell her the reason, even if she had to torture him with the promise of her flesh.

Thinking of him as her husband did not sit right with her. Not yet. They remained strangers. Even though most of her family's marriages had begun in such a way, they had at least celebrated the wedding night and got on with the rest of their lives together. She must find some way of drawing Grimulf close, of having him warm to her, or else he might discard her and she would be abandoned to battle those who pursued her.

The threat of Olaf echoed in her head. If he ever found out she remained a virgin, he would try to carry her off again. She'd rather die than let that happen. Grimulf might be a pagan, but at least he had a better temperament. So far, he had treated her with patience and kindness.

She sighed softly. Surely his reluctance was a boon? He cared for her, rather than roughly forcing her to obey his wants. Perhaps it was her own frustrations which irritated her.

Rosa left the bed, flinching as her bare feet brushed the frigid ground. She put her shoes on, hurrying through the longhouse with her arms wrapped around herself. She at least wanted Grimulf to return to bed, so she could cling to him and leech from him his warmth.

The torches outside had been banked. She recoiled at shapes in the darkness, thinking them Olaf, but they were as insubstantial as her thoughts.

This was not her home. Would she ever become used to

this? Or would she constantly be trailing behind Grimulf, on the same footing as Shuck?

She went to the storeroom, relieved she saw a beam of light beneath. She paused before it, uncertain whether to knock or simply enter. She heard ragged breaths from within and here she was shivering in the dark, as though wavering before the maw of a bear's cave.

"Grimulf," she called, carefully picking her words in case anyone else was listening. "I do want to tell you my story, but I find it hard to form the words. I wish I could shut a door between it and me. I want to focus on the present. Us. Can we not go to bed and see what the dawn brings?"

What she received in response could only be described as a growl. She started, blinking in disbelief. Her fingers curled tightly.

"Is that all I get? I am not asking you to drape yourself in thorns, but to hold your wife and—"

Foul words she had once caught her brothers speaking flashed through her mind. She almost uttered them. Instead, she threw open the door, but did not expect to see this.

Grimulf wrestled with another man on the ground. His shirt had been torn, revealing his broad, scarred chest. The stranger had something strange over his face, concealing his identity. She gaped at the scene. Then she saw the bright gash of blood streaming down Grimulf's side. This was no friendly tussle.

Rosa rushed to where Grimulf's weapons lay, leaping over pottery shards. Gripping the sword—for a wild moment she considered stabbing the man herself but knew she could not stomach it—she slid it across the floor for it to stop near Grimulf's grasp. However, while he was busy with the attacker he could not let go to take the weapon.

Grimulf's shield was also there. She tugged at the strap, gritting her teeth. Her breath whooshed from her as she took on its full weight.

Rosa edged around the grappling men. Grimulf had his knee on the man's throat, but between them their hands were clasped, quivering, around a dagger the attacker was trying to thrust into Grimulf's heart. She had to hurry. This man was going to kill her only protection.

Grimulf's face burned with the heat of exertion, sweat beading on his forehead. A cord of muscle stood out along his throat. Lips wrenched in a snarl, his nostrils flaring.

They rolled together, straight into the firepit. Grimulf's free hand slapped down to steady himself against the man's weight, the back of it catching upon a throbbing mound of peat. He roared in agony. His pain was what pushed Rosa.

The assassin's eyes darted to the side, suddenly catching the swish of her cloak. The dagger was beginning to tilt, towards the man then back to Grimulf's chest. She needed to end this.

Rosa brought the shield down flat on the attacker's head. Grimulf snatched the dagger, throwing it aside. He picked up his sword and held the blade to the dazed man's throat, grip trembling as he fought against the burning in his hand. Rosa went to hide behind her husband, clinging to his back.

"Who is he?" she said in his ear, rising and falling from the force of his breath. "Do you know who sent him?"

"No, but I have my suspicions." His eyes flicked to Rosa. Surely, he did not suspect her? But his attentions were focused again on the stranger, who was starting to come to. "Who sent you?"

The man spat blood at them. Grimulf wrested off the mask to look at him better.

"I do not need to hear your answer. All I need do is send each of your limbs to the chieftains around here and see which one gets the biggest reaction."

"Go ahead, then," the man wheezed. "You are nothing but a beast, unfit to claim your place."

Grimulf swung his sword.

"No!" Rosa cried. "He wants this. He wants to take his answers with him."

Grimulf paused the descent of his blade. "You are right. He wants a warrior's death at the end of a weapon. I'll not give him the glory. Get Thorstein. We'll keep him caged until we find who to return him to."

Rosa nodded, releasing Grimulf. There came a sickening squelching noise and the assassin began gurgling. Grimulf, swearing, scrabbled at the man's mouth, trying to hook his fingers in and pull out what was in there. The man convulsed, then stilled.

"Is he...?"

"Dead. He swallowed his tongue. You don't need to see this."

Grimulf led Rosa out of the room. The boom of his voice summoned a guard, who was sent to check the corpse and carry it off. Grimulf took her to their bedroom, where he leaned heavily against the timber post.

"Surrounded by enemies at every side," he couldn't help but remark.

"But not here," Rosa said, sitting upon the bed. Some of his blood had smeared over her dress.

He smiled wearily. "Not here. No."

She wanted to ask him why someone was out to kill him. It seemed he had a story to tell as well. She had only thought of the past she ran from and had not considered her husband's demons.

His wound needed seeing to. She crooked her finger.

"Tempting me to bed again," he said.

He obeyed her, though. He settled at the commanding push of her hand. The sweat upon his brow started to cool. He watched her with half-lidded eyes.

Just as Grimulf could command the presence of his men with a mere word, Rosa was able to summon Gunhild. The old woman brought what was needed, then left them to their own company.

"What?" he groused, almost like a boy forced to stay put in bed when he would rather be at play. "Am I supposed to be at your complete and utter mercy?"

"Most men with wounds such as these," she said, a little irritated, "would be writhing about in agony and begging for my attention."

He grinned roughly, pulling his lips back just how a dog revealed his teeth.

"I am not one of your feeble English men."

She reached for his bloodstained shirt. Viper-like, his hand shot out. He gripped her wrist, but his touch did not bruise. His fingers gently wrapped around her, acting only as a warning.

"Mind how you go. I'll not take my eyes off you."

"Do you mistrust nuns so much?"

"You're not one now. You're my wife."

"Then you should trust me completely."

She hated to be reminded of her loss. The nunnery had been her sanctuary. Silence and peace to consider God's meaning in their lives. The other sisters had been her family after her brothers had perished. Due to cruel fate, she had exchanged them for this brute instead.

He was paranoid and strange. His faith heathen and wild. He was all these things, yet not inhuman. Grimulf would be her protector from now on.

To be beholden to him did not sit right with her. If he was her warrior, her shield, she would have to be his healer. It was her duty as his wife, besides bearing his sons. She would rather be cleaning his scrapes than considering that prospect. At least, that was what she should think.

Rosa broke free of his hold. She reached again for the shirt.

"Then watch me, husband. Perhaps you'll finally realise I am one of the few people not out to kill you."

His arms fell either side of him. Grimulf watched her with his eyes lazily half-narrowed, head tilted slightly to get a better view.

Rosa peeled off the clothing. There was no need to cut it off, the assassin's blade had sliced it in several places. The shirt had suckered itself to some parts of the wound and she carefully prised it free. Not once did he hiss or squirm as some of her patients had done in the past.

"You have been injured many times before," she considered, as she traced one of the white-hot scars that curved over his chest. "I suppose you've built a tolerance to pain."

"These scars are only another way to tell a story," he told her. "Those ones you're admiring came from a bandit in the East. A dance of the blades I call the way they wield their daggers."

"I do not think there is any glory in pain. I have seen men in the throes of agony. They lose control of their minds, their bodies, miserable and turned into children when death comes for them."

"It is a pitiful end when one has to fight with death's poisoned talons. Better to fall in battle and be given to Valhalla or even the greater honour of Freyja's Fólkvangr."

"There is no glory in dying from an argument or another man's war! Think of who you leave behind. Who will suffer —" She snapped shut her mouth at his look. Her eyes shut briefly. "I am sorry."

She expected fury. It must be a vast insult to disregard the power of Valhalla here.

Grimulf sighed bodily, the low sound rumbling through his entirety. "I suppose it is different for one such as you. You only see the misery of the festering leftovers from the battle. Before we argue any further, will you tend me? I do not fancy bleeding to death and having my strengths measured from my last battle, which would be an argument with my wife."

Grateful, Rosa nodded. She cleaned the blood from him. There was another bowl, full of ice water from the river and mixed with salt, which she placed his burned hand in. Now she got a flinch of surprise.

"It will stop the wound festering," she told him. It would also lessen the harshness of any scars, but she kept this to herself.

The dagger wound gaped. She had hoped it would be shallow enough to knit together on its own, yet she must give it a helping hand.

She felt a squirm of unease as she began stitching him. It horrified her how their bodies could be pricked and cut, and all within them left to spill out. The copper tang of blood burrowed itself in her throat. Her eyes were stinging from the smoke and the stink of burning meat—of burning human flesh she realised with horror.

She steadied herself. Now was not the time to falter. With practised ease, she closed the wound with minute loops. She put her other hand upon the burning hot flesh of his chest to steady him when he tried to move away.

"I am almost done. Be patient."

"Yes, Abbess."

"I do not deserve that title. I was only a mere novice."

"You have the iron will of one."

"I might have had the honour of becoming one, had I been allowed to remain."

His eyebrows furrowed in curiosity. The stare he gave her urged her to speak further. Rosa's teeth bit into the inner part of her lip. She had revealed too much.

"But, of course," she covered weakly, "I must answer my God's commands."

She was nearly done. In the silence, as her needle weaved, she kept on glancing at him. He had watched her the entire time. Not her hands, for they both knew she would not truly wound him further. No, it was her cheek, ruby from her running around in search of him, the lurch of her throat with each swallow, and then finally on her lips. At her noticing him, he met her gaze.

The final stitch was made. She sliced the thread with his knife and sat back on her haunches.

"You have some skill in mending men," he mused. "I did not think a nunnery would come across so many injured."

"Perhaps those men were off hunting for mischief and got what they deserved," she jested lightly.

It was her own gaze preoccupied now. Even though it pulled at his stitches, Grimulf stretched his arms over his head. The muscles in his chest rippled. Gone was the distraction of his blood and all she had to gaze upon was his oak-thick body, a bracken bush of dark red hair coating it, the dip of his navel and then the teasing hint of the outline of his hips vanishing into his trousers.

He said nothing else. Was he enjoying this? She wondered, didn't think it possible, but was he tempting her to stare at him? Her mouth went dry. A curious sensation formed within, like an eel stirring itself from the seabed, disturbing all around it.

His trousers were darker than they were meant to be. She put her hand upon his leg, ignoring the way his lips twisted in an encouraging smile. Her palm came away with blood.

"You've bled everywhere, rather like a stuck pig," she complained. Her fingers hooked in and began pulling at the bands and strap at his waist.

"Quite demanding, aren't you, my lady? Is it not your people's way to lie down and simply take it?"

She smacked his thigh and he laughed. "I need to get the blood out of these or they'll stain and be of no use. This is my house. You'll obey me, or were you lying when you told me I would be queen of your household?"

His hips lifted, allowing her to pull his trousers down in one swift movement. He toed off his boots and they thumped loudly beside the bed.

Rosa had seen men naked before. She had been the elder sister of three brothers and nakedness had mattered little to her patients when they were bleeding to death. She thought it would have no effect on her, and then wouldn't he be shocked —or even amused—at her lack of surprise.

Instead, as the entirety of Grimulf was revealed to her, her blood surged quickly. It went to all manner of places that there was a faint dizziness, an urge to rest her head. It was the fire and smoke and trauma, she told herself, but in truth knew differently.

"Your face looks as though it has been smeared in warpaint," Grimulf commented, and she frowned at his arrogant tone.

And yet while she scowled her eyes roved up and down his form. They had lain together in bed, yet she had never truly *looked*. His legs were thick and covered in scars. The hairs here were finer, singed by blade or flame, and paler from being hidden. She could sit quite comfortably there and compare her thigh to his, and not even two of her legs could amass the same size as his single one.

To be held by him would mean being enwrapped completely. The imaginings of being crushed against such a finely built body caused her to tighten her grip on the bloodied clothing. She had compared him to a bear on their first meeting. He had yet to show her he was truly a man.

Then she took in the hilt of him, surrounded by another briar patch of much darker hair. He was like any other Christian man she had tended to, only larger, but she had been expecting that. The anticipation had not been ready for how she would feel when faced with it, though.

He was her husband. Soon enough, if they did not quarrel and part from one another, she would feel that within her.

She understood well enough the comparisons to a sword, for it looked just the same as a weapon. Would he be as savage in its wielding as he was with his sword upon the battlefield?

It was...different, she noticed. Hardened in interest. She was almost tempted to reach out and touch it ever so gently with the backs of her fingers, as though caressing some wild dog to see if it would bite. *It is only a man's staff,* she thought, *I should not be afraid of one.* Not her husband's, anyway.

"It won't do you any harm," Grimulf told her, as though guessing what was writhing within her mind. "It only wants some attention, and you'll have your pleasure as well."

Grimulf's arm swept around Rosa and lifted her onto his lap. Her rump settled atop him and he let out a groan of pleasure.

Rosa thought this was it, he would throw up her skirts and take her. Then they would be joined together and the possibility of being divorced lessened. She tensed, awaiting the attack.

Instead, Grimulf's mouth settled upon the swell of her breast. The remaining wisps of his shorn beard tickled her and she squirmed, uncertain whether she enjoyed the sensation or not. He seemed to like that.

His hand crept to tangle his fingers in the ties of her brooch, letting them come loose to move on to one of the steadily hardening nipples beginning to show through her pleated shift.

"There, my lovely," he rumbled. "I know enough for you to enjoy this imm—Ah!"

He hunched over, face buried in her breasts, as his hand went to the wound in his side. A fresh stream of blood ran free. Rosa jumped out of his hold, even when he tried to pull her back.

"I'll find you some fresh clothes, then you will have to be still and good so that you will heal."

Rosa hurried off in search of these things. Grimulf let out a heavy sigh of disappointment.

After she had redone his stitches, she put aside the tools and torn clothing. A crest of red concealed the stars for a moment as she dashed the bloodied water outside.

It was difficult to believe a man had perished only moments before. Was this to be a regular occurrence?

Rosa crawled into bed with Grimulf. She ran her nail gently over one of the old scars upon his stomach, white as chalk and slightly raised at the edges. His touch had left her insides feeling uncentered.

Rosa had other matters to deal with. She had to know if there were more enemies out there besides Olaf.

"Why are men out to kill you?"

He took her hand, slotting their fingers together. He brought the covers over them. She settled down, nestling against his uninjured side.

"I was eighteen when I left these lands, and it was not with good cheer. My youth was wild and reckless. I always wanted to fight."

"And you fought the wrong people?"

"No, the right ones. To the east and west are other villages, ruled by their own chieftains. Both men's sons are my age and we often found something to justify a fight. One battle, Thormod slipped from a tower and struck his head. His senses never returned. I very nearly bled to death from a knife wound to my stomach."

Rosa stifled her gasp of horror. It was how their lives were, rough and bloody. It was her life now.

"His father never forgave us, as he now has no heirs. Sven soon came to hate me as well. He had a much-loved younger sister, due to be married to another from Norway. She fell with child a week before the marriage and I was named as her seducer."

And a child as well! Rosa thought as she hesitantly asked, "Did you father the child?"

"I always suspected Thormod was the father, though now we will never know. I thought her still a girl. But that does not mean I have never lain with a woman."

"Oh... of course."

He softened at her stilted voice. "None of them are here, and I know for certain there are no children. It will be you who will bear them. I shall lay with no other while we are wed."

"You speak the truth?"

"I expect you to follow those rules as well," he gently growled.

"To love, honour and obey," she whispered, and he did not quite understand what she meant. "Would they want to kill you for these past grievances?"

"Rudolf was attacked shortly after our return. Those who harmed him spoke of a trap."

"But what could it be?"

He became silent.

Grimulf kissed her forehead. He did not say he thought it her.

"We will have to wait and see. To kill me would mean they could claim my lands. My brother was ruler here. I have only returned, which means my hold upon the people is weakened. There is the hoard as well."

"Treasure?"

He balanced her key over his fingers. "My services as a Varangian Guard earnt me great rewards. I have hidden it away, for winter comes each year and the trade of it will ensure my people are fed even if our stores are empty. This necklace is proof of this treasure." She made to take it off. "No. That is yours. It will never be used for bargaining."

"You do not suppose..." She would not look him in the eye. Her teeth worried at the flesh behind her lip. "Your uncle was quick to arrive. He would know of your return. Might he have been involved?"

"You arrived before him. Somehow, you knew I would be here."

"I was sent here. The vision—"

"God is your master, I know. Olaf is my uncle. I cannot start mistrusting my family."

He was already too isolated. If he had only one person to rely on, even if she was his wife, he knew he would fall into the jaws of his enemy.

"I'm sorry. I won't mention it again." Yet her face remained pale with worry.

"Do not fear. I'll not let any of them near you."

"It is such a beautiful moon tonight," Rosa sighed, turning to look at the smokehole, perhaps wanting to pretend they could sleep in peace.

His heart lay just beneath her ear, the pulse quickening. Grimulf clasped her to him, face buried in her hair. He did not look at the night sky.

"Yes, beautiful," he whispered.

There was more, but he dared not tell her it was himself that could not be trusted. The curse had begun its work, the talons digging in tighter, almost piercing his heart.

He must break it, for all their sakes. He would not allow it to be passed on to any of his children.

Grimulf watched over her most of the night, eyes narrowed slits in pretend sleep. Rosa continued to hold him close. Not once did she slip into the shadows to seek out her masters. She remained by his side.

As dawn arrived, he settled his chin upon Rosa's shoulder. He watched the throb of sunlight glisten through the holes and slits. The rare hint of warmth cradled her face, eyelashes paling in the light, the redness of her lips deepening. Some flesh was beginning to appear in her cheeks.

He leaned over to rouse her with a kiss. A twinge of pain shuddered, his wound resisting him.

To get at him, his enemies would hurt what they thought was the chink in his armour. Even if she might betray him, he had to protect her.

However, if he did keep her locked away, his people would begin to wonder why he did not trust them with his wife. She could not be kept indoors forever. She would need her freedom at some point. It would be better to sever the knot he had formed over this issue immediately, rather than be swayed to wait longer.

"I have reconsidered my order of you remaining indoors," he told her as she stirred. "This is your home now. You are free to go to the beaches, the dunes, but be careful not to stray far."

"Thank you... perhaps I can collect herbs to make into medicine."

She had saved a young man, ensuring he did not lose the use of his fighting hand. The village must welcome her. Now was the best time to let her roam. Those who grew fond of her would become her defender as well. If she remained true to Grimulf, then he would be preparing her for the rest of her life here.

A dull ache in Grimulf's skull, lulling and starting since last night, made itself known again. He would have to leave her soon, if only for a day, though it pained him. He had to make certain she would not be targeted just because she was a Christian.

Rosa did not stray far from the settlement. She had a basket under her arm made of knotted rushes, carrying the feverfew and meadowsweet she had been collecting for common ailments such as headaches or cramps. That morning she had sat with the other women and listened to their pains.

This place would be where she remained for the rest of her years. She must become one of them. They were whispering to one another in their old tongue when they thought her distracted. Rosa couldn't help but feel distant from them. It would take time, she reasoned.

Grimulf had left again, dealing with a dispute between two farmers about some sheep. What surprised her was how long old men could argue; the sky had already turned tawny. Thorstein passed by to light the torches, throwing his fire into the pile of wood in the centre, the red and orange talons cradling the bonfire until completely consumed.

People were beginning to head into their longhouses and huts. Rosa hurried towards her home as well. She quickened her step while the people darkened into shadows and vanished. She thought she'd have more time.

She had seen him in the distance. *Olaf.* When she had first stepped outside, he had been standing on the dunes, fringed by the grasses. She could not see his face, yet she knew he watched her as a heron might a fish, anticipating diving down with its sharp pointed beak and spearing her.

Rosa passed the smokehouse.

A wind cracked hand shot out from the shadows. It clamped over her mouth, catching her scream before it could even form. Another hand gripped her arm and dragged her into the hidden crevice.

She thrashed, kicking out. Her attacker kept himself out of the way. Only when she tired did he move, his foul hot breath dampening the back of her neck. Tears burned her screwed shut eyes.

Revulsion swirled inside of her. She thought she had managed to be rid of this foul creature. The thrall had promised her Grimulf would protect her, but the pair were related. Somehow, she had bound herself even closer to Olaf.

Would he try to defile her here, on his nephew's lands? He might. She could not shout for help.

Olaf's hand did not go groping amongst her skirts. His teeth grazed her ear as he hissed, "I never thought I'd catch up with you. Imagine my surprise when you slowed and entered my nephew's home."

She glared at the wall of the shack. A spider tending to its web idly swung.

"Do you expect me to turn back, tail between my legs?" he continued. "These are my people. I know my nephew. He trusts me. Your prettiness might have swayed him, but you are barely a woman. A nun will not know all the ways to keep a man panting at her heels. He hasn't even bedded you yet, so there's no promise of sons to keep him bound to you."

A flush of shame burned through her at the thought of Grimulf revealing what went on in their bedroom to others. It was not as if she hadn't tried. Was that why he had not taken her, so he could easily discard her without worrying she was pregnant with his heir?

"This is what we will do," Olaf told her, as if they were conspirators. "I will talk with my nephew and make him realise his error. You must then stand at the next feast and announce your wish for a divorce, stating it is because Grimulf has not taken you, that he is not man enough to do his duty. Grimulf will cast you aside to be rid of this annoyance and claim another to prove he is not unmanned. You may go wherever you wish, I will not follow."

She managed to let out a snort of derision. As if she would believe him! This was not entirely about her. She had quickly realised were she to say this, Grimulf would be shamed and lose standing with his people. Was that what Olaf truly wanted?

"It's what I offer you. If not..." Olaf's teeth went lower,

settling upon her throat, not quite a bite but a threat. "I'll tear you asunder. Maybe then what you've cursed me with will be gone."

Rosa could not understand what he was raving about. She could not bear to be locked in his arms any longer. She twisted again, his grip tightening.

She bit down hard at the flabby flesh of his palm stuffed into her mouth. He let out a shout and threw her from him. She staggered forward, then started running. She burst into her house, alone save for the cat.

Olaf did not chase after her. Rosa felt her throat. It was wet with his saliva, yet there was no impression of his teeth. The only proof of what had taken place was the blood staining her mouth and the bite on Olaf's hand.

He could twist anything to what he desired. He might even believe his delusions.

Shaking, she sank down before the fire. Her enemies were everywhere. She did not know who to trust.

CHAPTER 4

The next morning, Grimulf left their bed before Rosa awoke. The side she rolled on to was cold. She dragged the furs over herself but knew she could not nestle down and return to sleep. It was another day of trying to get the villagers to soften towards her.

"He's probably hunting with the rest of the men," Gunhild told her, when she wondered where her husband might be.

With Grimulf vanished, Rosa kept close to the house for fear Olaf might come calling. She was surprised when he did not.

While Gunhild dealt with milking the cows, Rosa knelt amongst the cabbages, checking to see which ones would soon be ready. She had never shied at hard work, often tending the nunnery's herb garden or making bread and cheese. She had loved picking berries as Sister Sweterun always let them savour a few.

"There is God within that simple fruit," the nun had said, while she delicately bit into one. "When the sun comes, they bask in its holy light and turn the pale berries vibrant for us to live upon. That is proof of another's design. Why else would these bushes offer succulence to the birds, to us, if someone had not planned this?"

Rosa patted earth from her hands, using the hem of her shawl to wipe her face. Why did she torture herself with thoughts of home? She could not spend her entire life mourning them, though memories crept after her just as her shadow did. This was her life now. She must find her own joy.

When the hunters did return, the sky draping a dusky red across itself and the birds mere flecks of ash, Thorstein led them. She could not see Grimulf or Rudolf.

The old woman had no answers. Rosa wanted to ask the other villagers but dared not. If they thought she did not trust her husband, they might twist things and lie to Grimulf. It might even make him appear weak.

Gunhild showed her another dish: smoked herrings with pickled cabbage. This time, she did not burn the fish. The two women sat together, talking quietly as they ate. Stars were beginning to appear, the full moon just barely peeking past a cloud.

A third trencher had been set out, but Grimulf did not appear. Rosa's leg jiggled anxiously. In the end, Morgana was given his fish.

When night finally came, Gunhild sat before the fire with her pipe, blowing smoke ribbons overhead. Rosa hovered by the open door, the cat in her arms.

Moonlight draped itself over her face, expression tight and eyes barely blinking as she focused on some unknown point in the distance. Quiet dread slithered in her breast just beneath her heart, flicking at her with its devil tongue and making her fear the worst.

Olaf could have taken her husband somewhere quiet and set his men upon him. The enemies Grimulf had spoken of might have laid a trap.

Or perhaps, and this was most frightening of all, Grimulf

had simply left. Abandoning her in a place she was not welcome.

The cat nudged at her, grumbling softly. Half-asleep, Rosa crawled into bed, pulling the covers over to tuck herself in the shadows. She dreamt of the tent again, Olaf's hunting dogs pacing through it in the form of spitting flames. The sow's blood crept across as an ink pool.

She did not wake at the sound of howls outside nor the frightened squeal of an animal. They wove themselves in her nightmare.

When dawn came she stirred. She had twisted herself in the covers, a slight sheen of sweat marking her from the sudden engulfing heat. Her feet were cold, poking out into the cool air.

Grimulf lay next to her, atop the furs. His arms were wrapped tightly around her. He still wore his clothes, only able to kick off his boots before collapsing.

She cupped his cheek. One of the hands clinging to her was streaked with mud. His nails were splintered, blood congealing beneath. At the side of his mouth was a bruise, slowly darkening, as though something had been tightly pressed against the flesh there.

In her relief she wanted to fling herself down and kiss him. Some sense of unease made her pause.

"What have you done?" she whispered.

His eye cracked open, shutting again as he groaned softly. "You must never ask me that after nights such as this. For your own sake. For mine."

"And yet I still ask."

He forced himself up to stare hard into her eyes. There was something foreign there, dark and cruel.

"Will you give your secrets in exchange?"

Rosa pursed her lips. Knowing he had won, Grimulf shut his eyes and slept. She left their bed and dressed. She needed to see Gunhild. However, outside people surrounded the pig pen. A man struck his foot at the fence, cursing.

One of their pigs lay slaughtered, the great teeth of some beast having cloven it almost in two. None of the dogs could have done this, not even a fox.

"A wolf," an old man decided, mouth puckered in distaste.

"It'd have to be a great big bastard to do that," Rudolf said.

Rosa crept back to the house and sat by the fire, pretending she had seen nothing. By the time Grimulf awoke, the remnants of the pig had been cleaned away.

After what Rosa had done for Björn, she assumed the village would welcome her. That morning, a grateful Gunhild made her porridge sweetened with fruits for her breakfast.

As the days passed, she noticed a stiffness about the other villagers. Before, they had been distant but not unkind. Simply curious. They had seen her as some weak minded, docile creature their chieftain thought sweet enough to bed and get some sons from.

The women smiled tightly at her as she passed them. Rosa turned, bending to peer into the nook the chickens nested in—

"Christian witch."

Rosa did not look around. A confrontation would do her no good. She focused on the sleepily clucking hens, the whispery rush of their ruffled feathers.

When she did look back, the women were gone. Men sat sharpening tools or hunched over vegetable patches eyed her warily. During the accident they had seen how easily she took control and did not like it.

Rosa had expected to at least see Björn again. His

wound would need seeing to and a new poultice applied. Not once did he appear at her door, not even to visit his grandmother.

Instead, she found on the doorstep curious gifts: a flagon of ale, gulls' eggs, even a basket of honey, the comb sticky and gleaming, broken into clumps. When she did manage to catch a glimpse of the boy, he bowed his head to her. It was a quick, nervous jerk, as if afraid.

Rosa asked Gunhild if he was well. The old woman pursed her lips. She batted flour upon the dough she kneaded.

"I'd rather not say, mistress. I don't want you to think my lot ungrateful."

"I would never think poorly of you because of another's actions," Rosa said. "Best tell me why."

"Björn's got it in his head you're a witch and he's superstitious enough to want to avoid you. I know, before you say, that you'd not mean him harm. He's a boy, swayed as easily as sedge in the winds."

Rosa knew she was no witch. It was ridiculous; she was a woman of God!

Now that the village knew her skills in healing, someone who meant her harm had been whispering falsehoods in their ears.

Rosa hoped their dislike would remain as hissed whispers. She could easily ignore them. If she did not react, they might tire of this. Grimulf would never have to know.

Then one of the men began following her. She had been collecting samphire while watching cattle grazing on the marshland. The flat landscape had been tinged gold, the trees still bare.

She quickly returned home, knowing not to be caught before sunset again. Another's shadow followed hers. Sensing something her heart began to pound, the sweat on her throat no longer warm.

The person moved sloppily, drunk. It would not be Olaf, who slithered about with little noise. She hurried her step. An invitation was shouted for her to slow down. Her silence earnt her a curse.

"Fancy you're better than me, Christian whore? You'll be begging to lay at the end of my bed once he's used you up!"

They were close to her home now. The door was opening. Relieved, she thought it was Gunhild. Instead, the person standing there was Grimulf, returned early and wanting to welcome her.

He heard what was shouted. His smile went stiff, then his lips drew back as Shuck's did, eyebrows knitting together. His head bent low, shoulders hunched. He burst out and swiftly charged towards the man.

"What did you say to my wife!" Grimulf boomed. There was malice in his tone, but rather than roar with blind fury the snarl seethed and promised cruelty. "Perhaps you'll learn to quiet that foul tongue of yours if I cut off your prick!"

Rosa darted to get out of Grimulf's way, cringing against the fence. As the stranger tried to stagger off, Grimulf grasped his collar and wrenched him so they were nose to nose, the man's feet dangling.

"What have you to say to disrespecting my wife?"

Their shouting had drawn attention. Women gathered, watching with interest while one had her hand to her mouth. Rudolf stood there, arms crossed, mouth pursed into a thin smile. Here was the excitement he must have been missing since leaving Byzantium.

The drunk scrabbled at the fingers gripping him. Grimulf did not calm. He struck the man hard on the back of the head, flinging him to the ground. The man spat out blood from his bitten cheek, kneeling there, dazed. Grimulf made to strike him again.

Rosa, though she trembled, leapt forward. Dropping her basket, she wrapped herself around Grimulf's arm. Muscles rippled against her breast, her pounding heart impressing itself upon his skin.

"Stop this senseless fighting!" she commanded.

"It is how it is done," Rudolf called, and she scowled at him. "Come, Grimulf, you're not going to let her command your fists as well as your cock?"

This was what she feared. Since Grimulf's return, he had been agitated. No longer did he whisper stories in her ear, instead lying upon their bed stiff and awake. A kiss barely distracted him from whatever plagued his thoughts. She'd dared not trouble him further, hating this sensation of having to tiptoe around a slumbering bear.

Grimulf was not perfect, no matter how gentle or patient. He did have an anger, stirring deep within.

And yet he released the man. Sneering in disgust, he roughly toed the drunk into standing.

"Go to your woman and let her tend you, though I pity what she has to live with."

The man ran, one of the women breaking from the group to join his side. Disgruntled at the lack of sport, people left.

Grimulf shook from the force of his held in fury. A touch on his shoulder. He snapped his head around, teeth bared to snarl.

Rosa froze. She carefully leaned away as a frightened cat might, but something made her stop. She stayed where she was, the hue of unease fading as she looked at him defiantly. She dared him to snap at her again.

Grimulf's tense shoulders began to relax. None of this had been her fault. However, the anger broiled deep, causing him to pant. It would not go unless he found an outlet.

Their bed lay within the house. Gunhild was elsewhere. Tempting as it might be to have him fall into another base instinct instead, neither wanted their first time spent in anger.

Grimulf took her hand. "You've not had much to eat. I'll catch our dinner."

Rosa watched Grimulf pick up a fishing rod, unwinding the line. From a pouch on his belt, he took out a barbed hook and tied it on.

She leaned back, cushioned by the grasses. Gentle winds stirred against her cheeks. Carried on the breeze was the smell of cooking fires from the huts.

While considering, and dreading, her marriage to Grimulf, Rosa had expected a fraught life, constantly uneasy for fear her lie would be found out. Surprisingly, she felt at peace. It was reminiscent of her life at the nunnery. Life unhurried, instead focusing on the simple joy of a task, whether it was sewing, planting herbs or sitting in prayers.

She pulled a face when she saw what else he pulled out. He thrust a wriggling worm upon the hook and flicked his arms, the line spiralling over their heads. There came a minute splash as the hook hit the water.

Then all that could be done was wait, just as with most things: waiting for the pot to bubble, a flower to bloom or for a woman to be won over.

A frost-edged sun looked down upon them. The sky was pale, bright but with little warmth or softness, as if one could tap their knife to it as they did the bowl of water for washing and it would crack and turn to rain. The river had yet to harden with ice, but it was coming.

Rosa pulled her shawl over her head to cover her ears when a sharper wind blew. She need only ask and he would wrap her in his cloak. That was not what she wanted. If she spoke, she knew she would ask to join him. Press her body against his and thieve the heat wafting from him.

If she were to do that, he would certainly wrap his arm

around to cup her breast, thumb comfortably rubbing circles, and lean over for a kiss. She enjoyed his attentions, but knew they were only the first steps to something else. Their awaited wedding night.

Surely it was wanton to beckon a man to bed, even if he was her husband? From the stories the nuns had told her, it was a trial a woman must suffer. To lie back and be the vessel for the man's seed or, if children were already born, to avoid and hope he found his pleasures in a mistress.

She'd felt a spark of her own arousal. Was it sin blossoming? Had it already sprouted now she had wed herself to a pagan?

She knew Grimulf wanted her, rather than being disgusted or having other sorts of attractions. Always, he stopped at the last moment, kissed her cheek and bid her goodnight. At times he would have a pained expression on his face. He had a great deal of self-control.

Might he be waiting for her to feel comfortable around him, considering they had been strangers when they married? It would not be a great surprise if he was being patient for her benefit. Warmth tickled in her chest.

Grimulf was a strange man, unlike any she had met. Nothing at all what she had pictured as she had ridden through the storm. Every day he showed her a different facet.

———

Grimulf could feel Rosa watching him. He did not react, focusing on the gentle lapping of the waters, the minute bob of the hook. He wasn't moving until he caught a fish and fed his wife. She was much too thin. He wouldn't be done with her until her flushed cheeks were their usual roundness.

A taunting voice whispered in his head, telling him he no longer sounded like the warrior he was but a dog fetching something for his mistress. The voice was not his own, instead the singsong tone of his uncle when dealing out his biting teasing. He dismissed it as one might do a fly.

Fishing had calmed him as a boy, when he'd been too wild and foolish to temper his ways. It had been the only thing to keep him in one spot. But he did not want to listen to the waters, the rustling leaves or his own heavy breaths.

Without turning around, he said, "My father often brought me here."

He heard her start, not expecting him to pay her any attention.

"He was the one who taught you?"

"I was reckless then, getting myself into scrapes, climbing dunes with little care how stable the ground was beneath—"

"It sounds no different from now."

"It was, little deer. You'd soon be sick of me if I hadn't grown up. My father certainly was. The beatings never worked, so he had to think of other means. One day he dragged me out of bed, while I was snoring away a hangover, and brought me here. He told me I wasn't moving until I'd caught his breakfast and sat nearabout where you are now."

"Your father beat you?"

"It's the only way sometimes. It was often how I got his attention. Did your father not beat your brothers?"

"Yes, he did."

She became silent. He wondered what she was thinking. His lips thinned as he considered if she might be including herself in her answer. He knew little of her past.

"If we are to have children, will you beat them?" she asked.

It almost sounded like an accusation. Well, he was guilty; he had given her no chance of having children. Yet. She only needed to be patient, then she'd have plenty to quiet any complaints. She would be sick of how many he would beget her with.

He grinned at the thought. A stirring of pride settled,

thinking of her full of life while a second child clung to her hand.

"Well?"

He cleared his throat and tapered down his smile, in case she misread his intention. Not that she could see him, but she might hear it in his voice.

"If one of our boys was causing strife for someone, I'd give him a clip around the ears. Though I'd rather find some other way for him to learn. I know a beating doesn't make a point sink in, but instead turns a boy as stubborn as a mule."

"And any daughters?"

How much had she heard of Vikings? Grimulf knew of some men who would not tolerate a daughter, concocting many ways of ensuring there were only sons... His uncle was such a man. Grimulf was not.

"I find the girls to be more sensible. A stern word and they soon work out what to do."

Satisfied, Rosa let out a soft sigh. "Did you catch the fish for your father?"

"It took all morning, but by noontime I had a bite. The creature was a morsel, no bigger than my palm. But my father dined on it for his dinner. After that I always came here to fish when I needed to calm myself."

There was a pull on the line. Grimulf carefully tested it and there came a tiny answering tug. He grinned, gripping the rod.

"Here's one!"

"Hopefully it'll be bigger this time around. I'm famished."

"As big as two of my hands, then!" he joked, the old excitement returning. He pulled, the fish beginning to grapple. "Best give up now, my scaly one. You're destined for the pot!"

This one was certainly a big one. He jerked the rod and it had yet to arise from the waters. Keeping his grip steady, Grimulf pushed himself until he stood. All his attentions were on the river and the spray of water as something thrashed just beneath the surface.

A tail emerged. Emboldened, Grimulf gripped the line and reeled it in. With a furious yank, he had the fish in the air.

It tumbled down and he caught it in his arms. In that same moment, Rosa's arms wrapped around him from behind. Her chin settled on his shoulder. The fish flapped, river water flicking into their faces. She shrieked, but woven in was her beautiful, joyful laughter. He loved that sound.

"Looks like breakfast is served."

She kissed the bristles on his cheek, hugging him tight. The swell of her breasts pressed into his back.

If he did not have her soon, he'd be coming out here in the dead of night to dip himself into the icy waters and cool the fire in his blood.

———

The calm had not lasted long. Soon enough Grimulf returned to his sullen, secretive mood.

Slowly, her husband was forming an armoury in the storeroom. Some were inherited from his brothers, but there were others with exotic designs. Rosa often found him there before bed, examining the sharpness of each blade.

She would not draw his attention when she found him there. Afraid to discover what he was thinking.

Now she peered at him from the gap in the door. Grimulf turned. He looked at her directly and beckoned. Hesitatingly, she obeyed.

"A fine collection," she offered, while wondering if all these blades had tasted blood.

"Every one of these may turn around and bite, no matter how pretty they are." He selected one of the daggers, feeling the weight of it in his hand. "This will do."

It was a thin blade, hilt ornately decorated with jade shaped into strange reptilian tailed creatures. He freed it from its sheath, holding the weapon out to her.

"Am I to shave your beard again?"

"Another time. I want you to keep this by your side. You're strong enough now. I need to keep you safe, but if there's any time I cannot reach you, I must trust you know how to protect yourself."

Rosa would not take the dagger. To strike a man seemed impossible, even with a blade. To kill one only sickened her.

"I am a nun. I heal, not maim."

"You are a Viking's wife now. There will come a time when you must kill to survive."

A dark voice whispered in her mind, *if you had one of these hidden in your habit, Olaf might not have been able to carry you away.* She accepted it, careful of the blade.

"Then show me how to use this."

His rough, calloused hands scraped over hers as he guided her. How to hold herself so her arms were a barrier to the softer parts of herself. To quickly jab when the enemy drew too near and send them leaping back. Then, finally, how to end the battle for good.

Grimulf held his hand over his neck to protect himself, the other showing the quick, straight jerk of slicing a man's throat. "There is no time for pity," he warned in a low, empty growl. "No one will show mercy. You must be just as ruthless."

"Even to you?" she said, saddened. All throughout he had been rigid, keeping himself distant. This was not the man she was beginning to know. She made the gesture, quick to learn. "Where has my husband gone? He has been replaced with something cold and made of flint."

He started, the dagger catching the burn on his hand. Rosa let go, the weapon clattering between them. She rushed to get bindings while he put his mouth to the wound.

"Stop that," she admonished as she returned.

"Why? It lessens the sting."

"It... Well..." She did not want to say the sight frightened her, for the blood had smeared across his cheek and it made it seem as if he had been hunting. He looked feral. "Let me clean and dress it. You slathering over it isn't going to help."

"It's but a scratch."

However, he sat so she could reach him easily. Rosa settled opposite, focused on his hand. She did not see the guilt upon his face. The bite of the blade had stirred him from his inner turmoil.

"What must I seem to you?" he murmured. "There are things out there you and I would think folktales, but there they are roaming. I should have warned you when you came to me, but I wanted you too much. I thought you had come to cure me."

"Of what?"

Grimulf chuckled, the sound without humour. "Soon I'll tell you. I hope by then it will be a mere shadow I have outrun."

He rested his chin upon her shoulder. Rosa let out a soft sigh, relaxing. She cradled his head, combing through his unruly hair. This was what she had missed.

"Whatever it is," she promised, "I will see it through with you. I was sent here to be your companion, bride, healer... I love you." And she was not surprised when she realised she spoke the truth.

She felt him stiffen beneath her fingers. The breath upon her neck stilled. Then his arms came up, loosely holding her.

"I believe that is the most honest thing you have told me," he said. She flinched, her already wet eyes shining brighter, and made to move. He held on. "I desired you the moment you rode in and demanded me."

But it is not love, Rosa thought sadly. Was it only an emotion belonging to women?

"I need to love you. It happens each morning and night. It first happened when you ran a blade over my cheek, yet each time I dismiss it out of fear for you. When I am free of this, when I am worthy of your sweetness, then I will love you."

He placed a kiss upon her lips as tenderly as an offering. She clutched him, deepening the embrace, afraid she might lose him somehow.

Grimulf had become restless. It was the same as the day he vanished and returned with blood and dirt streaked over his hands. Rosa saw the butchered pig in her mind's eye. Her throat went tight at the possibility her husband was involved.

Perhaps it was something of no import. There might be a simple explanation: a ritual the new chieftain had to go through, and he only kept it from her so as not to disgust her Christian principles.

And yet she remembered the emptiness of his eyes. Whatever he hid from her, she had to find out.

She gazed at the sky while Grimulf paced before the fire, his shadow passing over her. Shuck, who had been following at his heels, had finally lain down. His head flicked side to side, chasing his movements.

Gauze coated the night, tucking away the stars. The moon could barely be seen, a hazy edge encircling the orb. Grimulf pulled on his cloak.

"Husband, won't you come to bed? We can tell stories to each other."

What worried her most was he *wanted* to remain. She saw it in the way he turned to her, fingers hesitating over the silver brooch. Grimulf shook his head.

"I'll return, just be patient."

Rosa watched him step over the threshold. His broad form soon became smaller, like a tree in the distance. She grasped her shawl.

Breezes stirred the grasses, weaving like waterweeds beneath the surface. Rosa followed slowly behind, knowing he might easily spot her. It was only because he was distracted she was able to do this without being noticed.

Another joined her husband. Rudolf. Rosa ducked when he looked in her direction, scowling as he checked the perimeter. Her cheek grazed the ground, a decaying flower tangling in her hair.

When she looked again, they were hurrying from the settlement. She clutched her skirt, quickening. Winds pushed, as though warning her to go back. She would not. Whatever waited for her, she must see the truth.

The men were silent as they traversed. Rudolf attempted roughly striking the other's shoulder in a sign of companionship. It caused no reaction in Grimulf.

They approached a small shack, a smokehouse abandoned to the elements. Rosa stared, curious and horrified, as Rudolf unwrapped shackles, silver gleaming in the moonlight. The pair entered.

She waited.

"I do not agree with this," Rudolf warned, standing in the door of the smokehouse.

Grimulf nailed the shackles to the wall, tugging to see how strong they were. Assured, he clicked them in place around his ankles.

"Did you expect me to tell them during my wedding speech? Give it here."

"You'd be better off going begging to that Christian God

of your wife's," Rudolf groused, yet he held out the leather drinking vessel.

"The healer brought you back from the dead, didn't he?" Grimulf grimaced as he breathed in the surfacing aromas— the marshy bogs had a sweeter fragrance.

"It turned out my wounds weren't as perilous… All in one go is the best way, from what I've had to suffer."

Grimulf choked as he forced the potion down. It burned from his throat to his belt, and he feared the pounding, tilting sensation in his skull meant blood might pour from his ears. Besides the urge to bend over and be sick, there was no other reaction. Rudolf shrugged at his uncertainty.

"Perhaps it'll work when *she* arrives."

The clouds were thick tonight, draping her in shawls of misty stars. The moon lurked somewhere. He held out his hands from behind to be bound.

Rudolf knelt. "They should be warned. More than a pig might go missing."

"This is how I protect them. I'll find a cure soon."

Finally, a gag was placed in his mouth. Grimulf grimaced at the taste of sweat and sawdust. It was best, though. Although the disused smokehouse was a mile from the village, he knew how well a howl carried on the winds.

The moment Grimulf settled on his knees, head bowed in meditation, Rudolf left and shut the door. His eyes appeared in the small slit, watching over just as he had done throughout their journey home.

It shamed Grimulf to be in this state, chained like a wild animal. His father would have raged at him, his mother looking on with pity.

This was his own undoing. He must pay for his crimes. The darkness came and Grimulf hunched over, forehead touching the brittle, discoloured straw, anticipating.

Throbbing in starless black, the moon emerged from her cloudy domain. Although Grimulf could not see this, he knew of her approach by Rudolf's sharp intake of breath. A shiver ran through his body, even as his flesh turned hot and prickly.

Sweat broke out upon his neck and shoulders. Even gagged, noises escaped. The rumble of a growl. His gritted teeth caught on the inside of his cheek, scraping flesh and filling his mouth with a coppery taste. The whispering in his head grew wilder. Every muscle tensed, desperate to lunge and break free, and when escape was not possible fury roared.

The chains went taut, rattling and straining. Grimulf writhed. His heart hammered in his skull. He thought this might be the moment he perished and something new awake. No matter how his mind railed against the change, his flesh succumbed. Time slowed and flashed past, night stretching as endless as the sea.

This was no magical transformation, as in the stories of old. This was a degradation. Man brought down to the base urges of a wild animal.

Shadows danced within his eyes. The last vestiges of himself were leaving. As he tried to hold on, Grimulf turned to thoughts of his brothers, his comrades, then finally to Rosa.

The drum of his heartbeat pounded furiously, but it had found a rhythm. His fever cooled.

Her eyes would be wide with shock if she saw him in this state. The hollowness in his chest sharpened into ice shards. In his mind's eye, she did not run. She crouched by him and offered her hand, a small, sad smile on her face. Moonlight fell upon her and she glowed, turning the light into something ethereal and beautiful. She cupped his face... and then he was no more.

Rosa watched Rudolf emerge, but Grimulf did not. The other man crouched on the balls of his feet, lighting his pipe. Smoke spiralled around him.

Not long passed before the noises started. She clutched herself at the first low groans. She might pretend they were the winds, but she could not ignore the human quality to them. It must be Grimulf who made such awful despairing sounds.

Sea mists had rolled in. Gulls flew overhead, mere smudges of ash in the unclear skies. It was as if the village was not beyond the slope, instead the three of them somewhere distant and alone. With nowhere to escape.

Grimulf began to gag and cough, as though choking on something sharp. Rudolf twisted, the smoke pattering quickly from his pipe.

Snarling, then a great weight threw itself at the door. It was as though a wild dog thrashed within, desperate to kill everyone beyond its cage. Rosa covered her ears. She shook, eyes stinging.

Her mind frantically clutched at any explanation it could muster, yet none made sense. This was what Grimulf meant to warn her of. Were all the men in his family cruel monsters?

He was right to believe she would be terrified. She had not outrun the wolves, only flung herself into the maws of another pack.

Rosa did not return to the cocoon of her bed and pretend this was another nightmare. She remained. She would sit through this. Her fingers went taut as she pulled her shawl over her head, until only her wide, wet eyes could be seen.

The violent pounding upon the door stopped. Rudolf arose, stamping the stiffness from his leg. He peered in from some slit in the door. Tapping the spent ash from his pipe, he left. Rosa eyed him with growing incomprehension. Where was he off to?

As monstrous as Grimulf had sounded, she could not

abandon her husband. He might have suffered a fit or swallowed his tongue. She shuddered, remembering the horrid noises that had come from the assassin.

Rosa crept over. Going on tiptoe, she peered inside.

"Grimulf!" she whispered, horrified.

Her husband lay upon straw and ash, his hands bound. He had bitten through the leather strap muzzling him. Shards of wood lay shattered, from where he had torn his chains from the wall.

Blood coated his mouth from the exertion of his thrashing. He lay hunched in on himself, panting raggedly. His head shifted and she almost fell back in fear he would notice her and grow wild again, but it was only a twitch in his sleep. He must have struck himself in his frenzy and fallen unconscious.

It was awful. No better than a wild animal, bound and waiting for the hunter to finish it off. This man could not be her husband, yet here he was.

If he was awake, would he even recognise her? She pushed her fingers through the gap, but that was all she managed. She did not have the key. Even seeing him bloodied and fearsome, what she yearned to do was hold him, stroke him into calmness.

"You still look a man," she said.

There were no scales or fangs, as Grimulf had described blooming or thrusting from the shape-changers in his stories. Not even a change in his form. He bore the features of her husband and that was what stoked her empathy.

"If there is a way to save you, then I must. You are my husband now. I will not lose what is mine."

Rosa watched over him. Only when she heard the scraping footsteps of Rudolf returning did she slip back to her hiding place.

It was still dark when Grimulf regained his senses. Rudolf was releasing him from his chains.

"It went faster this time," his friend said, shuddering. "I was not certain what it was you became, not any beast I could name."

Grimulf snuck into his house with the shadows, a shard of dawn gracing the top of his head as he ducked inside. He set to scrubbing blood and dirt from his face and hands. The cat watched, her green eyes glinting, sharing in the secret.

Exhaustion made his movements clumsy. He held his breath as he approached his bed. Rosa's shape was visible beneath the furs. At the sight of her peaceful and slumbering, some of his pain fled. Carefully, he crawled in, laying his head with a weary sigh.

She rolled over, settling into his chest. He wrapped her in his arms delicately, almost afraid to touch her, yet he greedily took the opportunity. This might be the last time he held her. Come the next full moon, he could be lost completely.

He hungered for sleep but could not quite grasp it. Instead, he watched as day needled its way into the night sky, purples and reds with capes of bright light. Rosa stirred. She kissed his tender cheek, as though knowing he had been hurt there.

"Where were you?" she asked, drowsy.

"Wandering about in your dreams," he answered cryptically, and she frowned at him.

"I'd rather you kept to our bed or else I'll be forced to follow you into the mists."

"There are places you should not tread."

His time was slipping from him as quickly as the sands. Any day he might be completely consumed.

If he wanted to live a normal life, to continue his lineage... If he wanted Rosa to embrace the man he truly was, rather than be savaged by the beast he was becoming, he must purge this wolf.

When Grimulf left to deal with the petty squabbles amongst his people and hear their concerns, he kept an eye on the animal pens. There were no signs of torn feathers or blood spots; the livestock had survived the night. He must not have broken free of his cage.

Tiredness dulled his frustration. He had hoped he would be celebrating. That the potion worked and he had been cured, remaining in bed with his woman and finally giving her all he had promised.

Instead, it was a brittle sort of day, as insubstantial as mist. He was tense, anticipating something.

Rosa remained by his side. She barely spoke, but her presence was of comfort. He might be able to forget the night he had left behind and step into the day as the man he was.

The potion had been the last of his supplies. He must go in search for another cure. Once his people were ready to survive the next winter, then he would travel. Further inland there was talk of women who could change their forms into birds. They might have some way of helping him control this sickness.

He would have to tell Rosa. He didn't dare leave her longer than a few days. Would she risk going with him? Wherever he rode, the moon followed.

Men were heading for the marshes to dig peat for their fires. Grimulf took up his own shovel.

Birds were settled atop a tree trunk or something of that shape. At the men's approach they took flight, tawny wings flapping, obscuring everything. Then all was revealed.

Small streams of water lapped at a pair of boots haphazardly stretched out. Reeds lay broken and curled around the man's chest, soaking up blood seeping from his throat. His eyes were wide in horror, mouth twisted to screech —expression ashen and frozen.

The fangs of a beast had torn his throat. Many smaller bites peppered his legs, as though he had run and a pack had clawed and dragged him. Sounds of disquiet went through the crowd, trying not to alert the women, but they sensed and approached.

"How?" one labourer muttered.

"I heard something," another said. "I thought it a foul nightmare, but it must have been true. Accursed howling sounds!"

"My lord," one woman demanded, "what shall we do? Will you hunt the beast?"

Grimulf was very still, gaze locked upon the man's features. He knew who he was: the man who had insulted his wife. Grimulf had threatened to maim him.

And some great beast had hunted him down.

His grip around the shovel slackened. His breathing paused, then came out in rapid bursts.

Had he done this? No memory of the night remained. Rudolf had said nothing of him escaping, but this corpse could only mean…

Grimulf looked desperately for some clue this was not his doing. The drunk's hurried tracks and thrashing concealed any sign upon the ground.

"A party will go out. We will find what has killed this man." His voice boomed, yet inside horror writhed.

There would be nothing out there, for the monster must be here, roaming amongst them. They were all in danger. No matter his precautions, a man had died. He had another's blood upon his hands and he was further damned.

There was only one solution. The one he should have done before. He should have never returned, should have never married. Now he had ties to bind him and they must all be cruelly severed.

He sent them away, the men to prepare, the women to bar themselves in their homes. The old ones carried off Ivar's body to give him a proper burial. No matter his sins in life, he had fought hard with death and deserved the proper honours.

Head bowed, Grimulf strode home. He did not notice Rosa chasing after, his thoughts mired in what he must do. Rudolf waited for him outside.

"I heard."

"Did you leave my side at all last night?" Grimulf demanded.

His friend crossed his arms, shoulders hunched. A grimace of frustration marred his cheek.

"I had to. I thought I heard someone approach."

Grimulf had been left alone. He could have easily slipped out in his frenzy. Bravely though Ivar had fought, all men fell to the teeth of the wolf.

"You know what I ask of you?"

They went inside, the cat skittering from their feet. Grimulf took his sword but not his shield.

"Is there no other way? Surely you have not exhausted all the healers hereabouts."

"I cannot keep this up. I cannot lie to myself! Who will fall next? You? An innocent child? My wife?"

"Grimulf," Rosa called, trailing as a shadow did, wavering and confused.

"It must be done. You will protect her?" Grimulf demanded. "Should anyone seek vengeance..."

Rudolf bowed his head. "I'll protect the woman."

"Listen to me! Do not ignore me!"

Now Grimulf turned to her. Dark bruises ringed his eyes. He seemed smaller somehow, a creature condemned for the axe. Rosa flinched, far more frightened than when she had faced his anger.

Rather than kiss her, he clasped her hands. He pressed their foreheads together.

"Forgive me. You wedded a beast, not a man."

He wiped her tears, then the two men left. They walked in the opposite direction of the steadily forming hunting party, to the smokehouse where Grimulf kept his secrets.

And where those secrets would bleed out and perish.

Rosa glanced over her shoulder as the village became engulfed in morning mists. The ground was damp, slightly spongy. She panted heavily while the men pushed forward, much faster and used to this uneven terrain.

She had only wiped the sleep from her eyes, now suddenly she was running after her husband. It was a morning of madness. She thought she might be in one of her fever dreams.

None of this made sense. A man was dead and for some reason Grimulf blamed himself. She recognised the corpse, knew Grimulf might be suspected had a sword slain him, but he had been mauled by an animal.

An animal Grimulf believed himself to be.

Rosa hurried. Their figures were fading in the marsh-smoke. Rudolf gripped his spear.

"Come at me, then," he shouted. "I'll dispatch you straight to Valhalla."

Good God, Rosa realised, throat lurching, *they mean to fight to the death.*

Grimulf thrust out with his sword, roaring. Rudolf dodged, blocking with the staff of his spear and pushing him back.

Grimulf meant to die as reparation. Rudolf would give him the fight needed to put him on the path to Valhalla.

They weren't going to go easy on the other. The Gods were watching.

Rosa knew Grimulf could not have killed Ivar. She had watched that entire night, even when Rudolf left his side.

Neither would listen to her. They thought they knew best.

"Are you willing to abandon me?" she cried, lunging between them. Her protector planned to throw his life away, what did danger matter? "Stop this! The others will soon notice."

"Move, Rosa. It must be done. You'll be free to take another worthier of you." Grimulf crouched, his blade furiously quivering in his hands.

Rudolf scoffed. "Stand aside, woman. You know not what you interrupt."

"It is a waste of an honest soul. Whatever you fear you have done, I know you have not. I watched you."

"What?"

"I followed you and Rudolf. When he left, I peered in and saw you in your..." Unable to describe the sight of him, she finished uselessly with, "Your state. You are not that man's killer."

His sword slowly tilted towards the ground. Rudolf loosened his grip on his spear.

"Please," she continued, "tell me what plagues you. We will find a way of fixing this."

"But first," Rudolf interrupted, "the men will be ready to ride out now."

Grimulf went with the hunting party to search for the mysterious beast. Mothers whispered stories to their children of a hulking shadow that turned into a ferocious dog with flames for eyes, warning them to run home when daylight began to fade.

A bonfire flared, hungry for the remains of Ivar. Those who knew the man surrounded the flames, mere shadowy outlines. The shape in the centre was soon consumed, his soul sent to the Gods for judgement.

Even though the man had abused her, Rosa prayed for him. She knelt at the side of her bed, rigid against her shivers and aches.

Part of her prayer hoped a beast might be found. Some feral, inhuman creature whose head could be carried through the village. Because then there would be no doubt at all over Grimulf's involvement.

Her husband returned as the sky put on its cloak of night. Shadows crawled over his face. She went to him, helping remove his armour.

"Nothing," Grimulf breathed out wearily. "I knew it would be the case, for it is not out there but here."

Her hand passed over his chest, fingers curling in his chainmail. "You are innocent, Grimulf. I saw you. No matter what you say, I know you are only a man. My man."

She turned to put away the chainmail. His arms crept around her, tightly caging her against him. The armour fell from her fingers as water did, ringing as it hit the ground.

"How are you not afraid of me? Do you not understand?"

"I do not know everything, but I know enough." She shifted to look back at him and he put a large steadying hand upon her stomach. "Even if I was frightened, I would not leave."

"Do you tie yourself to this brute because of another's orders?"

She flinched. "You still mistrust me?"

"I'd be a fool not to. You have little trust in me. I saw you after I lost control of myself. You were afraid."

She faced forward, staring into the fire. All he saw was long waves of her hair curling around the delicate column of her throat.

"I cannot stand men with little control over themselves. It is… It is weak. A woman is near broken to ensure she never descends into hysteria. Surely a man must be able to be just as strong?"

"Our blades are sharp, but our minds not so much."

Grimulf lifted her in his arms. She made a sound of surprise. He did not carry her to bed to drift off with another story. Instead, he set her on a stool and knelt. He leaned over, arm resting on her knees. She tangled her fingers in his hair.

"I should have told you all that I am before we were joined," he said.

"There was no time. I was the one hurrying you."

"You did not know. How could you? I have been gone for so long not even my own people know. Even they would fear me."

"*Why?*"

"I was once a berserker. No, not once, it will never leave me. I *am* a berserker."

She knew nothing of what the word meant. She looked upon him blankly, as if it was something simple as being a common warrior.

"I know you are not a farmer, but you are not a raider either."

"It is something deeper than that. A berserker is a warrior turned mad. His weapon is a part of him as his hand is. There is no sense or reason, only the fury of his blade and the thirst for blood. Seven years I spent in the East, as a Varangian Guard for the emperor."

"And what caused you to leave?"

Grimulf breathed in deeply. His fingers curled, not quite forming a fist. The memory of his time exploring was like a shadow creeping closer. His room flickered from him the same as fluttering candlelight.

What returned was the shadowland recesses of a temple, a fire before him. His face wet and glistening with warpaint, bare chest daubed red to mimic blood, thin trails of chainmail curled over his biceps. Legs crossed, hands gripping his thighs, the muscles in his arms clenching and unclenching, an eel tattoo rippling.

The flames sparked with a blue light. Otherworldly. Inhuman.

He knew he was not truly there. He knew he had escaped. And yet he smelt the crisp, burning smell of herbs he had thrown in. It settled in his throat along with the slithery sensation on his tongue of the fungi and bog-myrtle he had consumed. Heat burned behind his eyes. Head tilting, he heaved out a roar and bit deep into the metal of his shield.

Grimulf was no more. Another man stirred beneath his scarred flesh. No, not a man, a beast paced in his blood, snarling, desperate for the hunt, the cornering of prey and the triumphant snap of teeth.

Fingers stroked his knuckles, turned stark by the jut of his bones. Grimulf blinked and he was home again, bowed before his queen. Rosa sat there, concerned but patient. He swallowed the bitter taste of his memories.

"I was ordered to destroy a band of rebels that had been robbing the emperor's merchants. My men and I cleaved through. They were no match… I should have known then. When we burnt the bodies, I discovered they were not bandits but priests who had angered my master by spreading their faith. I cannot stand to be misled—" He saw her hand stiffen atop his, but let it be. "I challenged the emperor and bested him. I would have finished him as retribution, but his daughter threw herself before me and begged for his life."

He settled his chin upon her lap. The black of his eyes flicked up.

"I do not think your God means well for me, considering what I did. Now you know what you have tied yourself to. A man easily led, no smarter than a beast."

Grimulf pulled away to let her escape, not wanting to see her struggle and weep. A pang in his gut jabbed him at the thought she might run. Rosa gripped his unruly red hair to keep him before her. She drew so close he could see each dark strand of her eyelashes.

"You did not know," she reasoned. He made to shake his head, but she held him in place. "*I was sent here.* There must be a reason for all the cruel misfortunes in our lives or else there would be no point in existing. Those priests brought you home and my vision came just as you returned. Your regret will be your counsel. I will do all I can to make you a better man."

"More than the memory of what I did came with me over the seas. One of the priests lived, though only long enough to curse me with his last breath."

"God's wrath?" she whispered, glancing at the ceiling as though she expected the roof to rip apart and a storm to invite itself into their home.

"He invoked the dead to come for me, to twist me into a beast only vaguely resembling man. Its snout is long and teeth sharp, and always it awakens and howls on the full moon. I cannot lie with you, for fear I may lose control and harm you. Any children sired might have this curse passed on. Can you not understand why I keep my distance? You do not deserve a wolf-coat as a husband."

"Have you ever truly changed on the full moon?"

"My men chain me and keep watch, as you saw." He remembered the rough scrape of sand against his back, how the moon seemed an orb of burning holy water about to burst. "When I slept, I woke another man. I tore at my bonds, cursed them in a savage tongue, howled even, then fell about in convulsions."

"But no claws or teeth? It could have been sickness or..."

"Madness. I should have warned you before our wedding."

"It does not matter. I will free you of this curse."

"You might be able to heal the wounded, Rosa, but you cannot go against the Gods."

"It was my God who cursed you. He sent me for a reason." She took one of his hands, placing it over her stomach. "No child of ours will be cursed. Any that form within me shall have God's blessing."

"You do not know me. You were forced into this."

"I am your wife now. Everything will be shared between us."

She tugged, but he was too heavy for her. Grimulf followed her direction and pushed himself up, their noses brushing as he hovered. She would be the one to make the first move. Rosa's tongue ran over her reddened lips. His stare honed in. He tensed, more creature now, yet he was not certain if he was the fox ready to pounce or a hare turned rigid, straining to hear the predator.

Then she kissed him. This was not what he had been searching for, yet it was exactly what he needed. He had held back too long. Never mind her secrets, she was soft and willing and that was all that mattered. Her teeth gently bit into his lip as though rebuking him for tantalising her so much.

He surged forward. Her gasp of delighted surprise gave him entrance to her mouth, entwining with her shy, curious tongue.

Grimulf effortlessly lifted her. Her skirt rucked over her thighs as her legs coiled around his waist, barely able to get her ankles to hook together due to the width of him. He stepped backwards, too distracted by her kisses and soft sighs in between. He lifted the curtain and threw them both down once his legs hit the bed.

He rolled over, pressing her into the mattress, hands either side of her head. Her hair fanned out, spilling over his fingers. He felt every dip and curve of her slowly recovering body and she must feel his thickening desire desperate for attention. He made to rise, to not crush her, yet one small hand clutched the ties of his shirt. She pressed herself along the length of him.

"Keep that up and I'll not be able to draw this out," he warned.

"Good. You've been dithering for far too long."

He shook his head. He liked her eagerness, but he knew she truly was untouched. He was tempted to be quick, but gentle, he would not hurt her, and see just how she would handle a rough and tumble.

No matter how arousing her breathless cries would be, the night had barely swept across the land. He planned to give her no chance for sleep.

Grimulf did not expect his shirt to come apart at the throat. She'd been busy while he was distracted. He sat up to remove the clothing and she grumbled at the loss of warmth. She busied herself just as quickly with his trousers. Her hand settled over him, about to but not quite giving him some relief.

Rosa's other hand trailed appreciatively over the hardened expanse of Grimulf's chest, every raised ridge of his scars knitting itself in the tapestry of her memory. All she needed to do was shut her eyes and she could weave the life's work that was his flesh.

Her flushed face turned scarlet, mouth suddenly dry. She was remembering all the times she had seen him naked. The surprising size of him. Her thoughts turned to whether he would even fit.

She had wanted this, yet was it not the man's pleasure that mattered? Women weren't meant to enjoy this. She would have to grit her teeth and endure, for there was only one way for a man to trust a woman. To bind him to her.

She found it difficult to believe there was no pleasure. There must be something luring women to men besides protection, titles, riches and a handsome face. The curious stirring sensation in the pit of her stomach promised more.

Perhaps there was a reason why the church railed against a wanton woman. They could be keeping a melting pot of pleasure out of reach, fearful of what women would be transformed into.

He dragged her skirt up, thick fingers carding over her legs. She willingly lifted her arms for her dress and shift to be tossed aside. The moment she was laid bare, his rasping breaths travelled down her lurching throat, tongue flicking out to mark the places where her skin was freckled.

There was the thumping of clothes being thrown, the crash of boots hitting the side. When he drew her to him again, the heat flaring from him near scalded her. The heaviness of him dragged against her stomach and the doubts returned. It jutted as mightily as any weapon and she thought —*it is being wielded against me.*

Sensing her unease, Grimulf kissed her forehead. "I'll do nothing to harm you. Both of us will enjoy this."

Rosa nodded jerkily, spreading her legs to allow him admittance. Rather than diving into her, he continued his caresses. Every kiss, whether it was her navel or the inner flesh of her elbow, was ticklish from the bristles of his beard. His thumb circled her breast, nail lightly scraping the delicate flesh.

Even while she burned she shivered, biting into her cheek to stop the embarrassing noises she wanted to let out. Grimulf gazed at her with eyes dark with mirth, as if he knew the sound of her pleasure already. He suckled at the tiny rivers of veins cupping her breast and she arched as he traced the curve of her spine, resting at the base to support her. She braced herself.

Now? she wondered and tilted her hips. An ember burned there, needing something. Needing him.

She must have spoken, for he smirked.

"Impatient vixen."

He kissed her and she thought even with his teasing he would finally claim her. There came a pressure against that part of her she knew so little of. She held her breath.

Something thinner and gentler grazed her within. Confused, she saw his finger had taken the place of his member. It was a curious mix of sensations, a part of her wanting to cleave, another to embrace him tighter. More were placed within, crooking and expanding her, until she trembled. She followed the rhythm of his thrusts, hips canting, her entire body moving while only his hand worked her. She was under his control.

Suddenly he left her and she was empty and begging, tears pricking at her eyes. "Don't just leave me this close to—" She did not even know what she had been running towards.

"I thought this was what you wanted?"

And his manhood was pressing into her and she thought she might cry out with passion and pain. It was too much. She truly would be cloven.

Grimulf took her weight in his arms. Shushing a fallen tear, he kissed her cheek and rubbed her back. Slowly, she relaxed. Tentatively, she shifted and almost jumped at the groan that earned her. He settled her upon the pillows.

"All right now?"

She managed a smile. "I think so."

He kissed her fingers. Then he started rocking into her, her whimpers dissolving into moans. She clung to his dampened back, felt the muscles moving beneath his flesh. Rosa knew he could break her, but instead he was as gentle as summer. He was slow, nudging her over the edge she had been teetering on before.

He drew the skin of her neck into his mouth. His thrusts became erratic. A ball knotted in her stomach, sensing, anticipating.

Grimulf bit her just as his orgasm exploded. A cry of

pleasure left her. Then she stirred, cradled in Grimulf's arm. She was lax, all her earlier tension flooded away.

She felt her neck, wondering if there was blood. Grimulf had not broken the skin, instead leaving a mauve mark the size of a ring. Between them was a small streak of blood: the spilling of her maidenhead. Such small amount, considering the magnitude of its loss.

Could it truly be considered a loss? She had freely given it and thoroughly enjoyed the taking.

Moonlight came through the smokehole, the flaking orb bright as it sank closer to the horizon. It cradled Grimulf's shoulder and hip, the rest of him drenched in shadows. Her eyes focusing in the darkness, she gently traced his features: the strong jawline, plump lips, the thick arches of his eyebrows furrowed slightly even in sleep.

Covertly, she raised the blanket. His manhood slept as well, not quite as threatening as before. It was still a weapon, only now she thought of herself as the sheath, keeping it bound and safe from becoming dulled.

She was stroking the hairs surrounding his navel and another tattoo, this one of a swirling sea snake, when there sounded a breathy sigh of laughter. One of Grimulf's dark eyes opened.

"I thought you'd want some rest before renewing any further pleasures."

Rosa felt a slight ache within, almost like a warning left behind by her virginity. She shifted, considering. "Might we do this again in the morning?" It was no worse than her monthly courses and they never gave her fun in exchange.

He chuckled. "As you command."

Her head rested on his chest, hair spilling over his scarred breast, concealing his past pains. They lay there, comfortable and silent, but not quite able to slide into sleep.

"God sent me to you," she whispered. "He had his reasons. I will trust in his judgement, just as I trust you."

"Will you be the water to put out my fire?"

"No, for that would kill you. I like your passion. I would rather have a husband happy to argue rather than one who ignored me and did not care."

Grimulf pulled her close, until her steadily quietening heartbeat rested atop his. "Rest now," he murmured, combing the damp hair from her face.

CHAPTER 5

R osa lay curled in bed, wishing to cling to the night before. Grimulf leaned over to kiss her shoulder. She mumbled something, snuggling deeper. There was no hope of shifting her.

Chuckling softly, Grimulf arose, tucking the covers around her. As she dozed, she half-listened to the splash of water as he washed.

She needed the rest; they'd been up with the moon. Her body was a mere anchor, her inner self floating slightly above.

She had never felt so satisfied before. This bed was where she wanted to remain forever. Here, with her husband. What she wanted even more was for him to return. Her hand extended, beckoning him as a lazy cat might tempt the mouse to come closer.

"How can I say no?" And he was back in bed, pulling her close and entwining their legs.

After everything, her suffering, her fear, she had found not sorrow but joy. *Let this never end*, she thought.

Most would know their hearts beforehand or end up hating one another through being forced together. Grimulf's patience meant they had slowly come to accept their desires.

Rather than tumble into lust and watch the flames degrade into ash, it burned even brighter.

They could not yet settle into their places, living as they wanted to. A demon lurked in the shadows for them both. Rosa might pretend Olaf was not out there, lurking about as a friendly uncle offering his wisdom, but his gaze always followed, unnoticed by anyone else. He still had her on his mind.

Her fingers trailed over the length of her husband's spine, pressing him closer and closer until he got the hint and slid inside of her. It was a slow coupling, not quite chasing off her thoughts but none of them seemed to overwhelm her as they usually did.

Her lips settled against his chest, almost tasting the strong pulse thrumming there. Grimulf gripped her, fingers pressing in, nails gently scraping, but there was nothing abnormal—no claws. As he licked her ear, his lips drew away from human teeth.

And yet her husband thought himself a wolf in man's flesh. She could not hear any growls buried deep within him or some beast crashing against his bones, desperate to be freed.

The night before last flashed over her eyes, of Grimulf crouched and chained. Her arms went around his shoulders, clutching him tight, as though she might be able to crawl inside and chase it out as one would a stray, hungry dog.

Rosa started with her herbs. She picked camomile and lemon balm to ease anxiety and calm rage. There must be a physical explanation for what she could only describe as fits, if she did not want to consider a supernatural cause.

There had been a young woman living near the nunnery who suffered from sudden fits while attending church. The elder nuns had given her such things to calm whatever bedevilled her.

As Rosa ground the herbs, her grip tightened around the pestle. She tried not to remember, but the girl had soon been tried as a witch by the local priest. The poor creature had been forced to carry silver from the fire to prove she was innocent, hands blistering and weeping.

Grimulf trustingly drank whatever she gave him. Around his neck he carried a pouch of lavender. They would not be able to tell if any of this worked until the next full moon, awaiting the bone-white orb's return with a held breath of anticipation and fear.

Sacrifices were made. Not blood and high-pitched animal cries, but silver and grain. She had him bury coins. Grimulf only performed these rituals in the dead of night, with the fire banked and only the dark, glistening eyes of the roosting seagulls to watch. In the daylight Rosa saw him kneel at Thor's tree before the start of his work, as if asking for forgiveness.

What Grimulf most craved was her caresses. No longer did he hold back. After one taste, he found it impossible to ignore her touches, the lilt of her voice asking for a deeper kiss. Any chance they had was spent tangled in the bedcovers.

It was the same as worshipping. The way he clung to her hips as he thrust within, becoming lost, might as well be him clasping his hands together. If he immersed himself in goodness, the curse might slither free and pass on to a more deserving man.

Always, in the last moment, he pulled from her, afraid of her falling with child.

It only took the once, though…

Rosa was careful where she wandered when gathering her herbs. Since Olaf's arrival, he and his men had been subtly digging their claws into the earth. Two months had almost passed. Their tents were slowly erected, consuming the landscape.

Stray dogs roamed, snapping and fighting with those who slept in the mead hall. Some of the people in the village were reunited with family, others clashed when a father caught one of Olaf's men sneaking from his daughter's bed.

Reparations were made, his uncle quickly taking control of the situation and smoothing things over before Grimulf had the chance to. Villagers were going to Olaf to air their grievances rather than approach her husband.

Strangers had begun to appear. It did nothing to ease Grimulf's paranoia.

Rosa walked past one of the longhouses housing Olaf's men. The door burst open. A woman was thrown out, sprawling on her hands and knees. Rosa rushed over and knelt by her side.

Olaf stood there. He only wore a kirtle, the hem of it swaying over his pale, knobbly knees, the hairs on his wrinkled legs sparse tufts. He looked like an old man caught attempting to do something crude. Laughable rather than sinister. For the first time since he had abducted her, Rosa was not afraid. She sneered at the state of him.

Olaf swore at her and slammed shut the door. Rosa turned to the woman, who was only slightly older than herself. Her hair was long and slightly curled, black as burnt wood. The eyes were wide and pale. Squint just a bit, and they could be mistaken for one another.

Rosa scowled in disgust. She knew what Olaf was up to. Must the man always plague her? Such a vile creature.

"Did he hurt you?" she asked the woman. "My husband is chieftain here. We can go to him."

"No, it is all right." The woman did not brush her off but took her hand. "I'm used to worse."

It was then Rosa realised the woman was not from the area, though she was still struggling to recall everyone's faces. She must be a prostitute brought here by Olaf's men or had even followed them of her own volition to earn her bread.

"It does not excuse what he did. Do you have somewhere to stay? What is your name?"

"I'm sure I'll find someone willing to share their bed... and I'd prefer not to give my name. It is better that way. I pass just as quietly as a ghost."

The woman began walking and somehow Rosa found herself following. She watched as the stranger readjusted her dragged on dress, scraped back her hair and straightened, regal as any queen. It was amazing how easily the woman shed off what had happened, as though it had been an entirely different person. Rosa wished she had this skill, as it felt as if every speck of her past had burrowed beneath her flesh.

"Why was he so violent to you?" Though Olaf being a brute to other women was no surprise.

"Some can only find pleasure in violence. They're broken, you see." The woman's bruised lips stretched into a cruel smile. "But this time I angered him. I laughed. I couldn't help it."

"At what?"

"He's like a strutting cock, bragging how hard he'll swive me and how long, that I'll be begging for more. Only he couldn't rise to the threat!"

Rosa's eyebrows crinkled. The woman laughed at her confusion.

"Don't you understand? I would think you'd have learnt by now, seeing as you're married. His cock, woman. It didn't even stir and I laughed at all his boasting and it angered him." She paused by a door, knocking. While the person dragged themselves out of bed, lazily stumbling to the door, she whispered, "Now, be off with you, else he'll think you're included in the fee."

Rosa hurriedly moved on just as the door opened. The prostitute leaned against the doorway, hip cocked and with a saucy grin. A few words were exchanged, then she was allowed inside.

Olaf would be more spiteful considering his predicament. Now his hatred and fear made sense.

Olaf believed Rosa had unmanned him through the power of her God. *Good*, she thought. At least he could not try to force himself upon another woman.

Her joy did not last long. What would Olaf be willing to do to her, if he thought he might get his virility back?

The revelation caused Rosa's heart to hammer in her ears. No matter her reassurances to herself, it would not settle. He thought she had cursed him and like all men he believed the only way to free himself was to destroy her.

She needed comfort from someone higher. Rosa rushed home, lavender falling from her basket as she entered. She heard no other noises save her own heavy breathing. She was alone.

Rosa had not given up her prayers, even amongst heathens. She was hoping for some sort of sign, proof she had done the right thing.

So far, she had attempted to pray before Grimulf returned or while he slept. Uncertain how he might react. He might forbid her from doing this. And what would her response be then? This was all she had left of her old life.

Rosa fell to her knees. Clasping her hands together, her wet eyes screwed shut. She felt the tremor of her pulse in her throat. Her thoughts roared in her head alongside her blood.

"Dear God, grant me this…"

He was the one she could whisper her fears to. She did not dare speak them aloud in case another might be listening.

Olaf dogged her shadow. Grimulf knew she kept something from him.

"Amen." She let out a great sigh, opening her eyes.

"I wonder what plagues you to need to speak with Him?"

Rosa started. Grimulf sat on the bench behind her, arms folded. He had snuck in without her even realising. He clutched the fallen bundle of lavender. The sweet calming scent crawled free as he crushed it between his fingers.

Flustered and a little irritated, she stumbled up, blood rushing to her head. Grimulf was quick to steady her, pushing her atop the bed. He settled next to her, leaning on his side so he might peer into her face.

"It was only a prayer," she said, avoiding his gaze. How long had he been there?

"You are not in church anymore. It is not your God in the sky."

She tried to turn from him, but he held her hip to stop her from escaping.

"He comes with me. You cannot banish him with a single command."

"But I can." He stroked the corner of her mouth. "I forbid you from praying. I'll not have my sleep deprived by your muttering."

She stiffened. "No! You cannot take this from me."

"I am your husband. You must obey me."

Rosa flung his arm from her. She rolled out of bed, got on her knees and slapped her hands together.

"What are you doing?"

"Praying." She watched him with one eye open, as though daring him to silence her.

"Get back in bed, Rosa."

"No. If I'm to obey your whims, I want something of my own. You might not understand praying, but I do."

He leaned over the edge of the bed, holding out his hand.

"There. You have it back. I never planned to take it from you. Now will you get in."

She let him pull her into bed, grumbling, "Then why did you say it?"

"I was curious to see if you would disobey me."

"Oh." And she had. What would he make of that?

"I am glad. I would prefer it if my woman kept true to herself and rebelled in bed, rather than on the battlefield when I need to keep you safe. But you are distracting me again. What distressed you?"

She had wondered if Grimulf would consider praying to her God to be rid of his curse. She had not tried suggesting it yet but knew it might be their last hope.

"Why don't you try praying?" she asked, not wishing to answer his question.

He shifted, uncomfortable. "I doubt he'd wish to speak with me."

"You might be surprised."

Grimulf, cursing the cold while Rosa remained bundled in furs, climbed out of bed. He knelt before her, sloppily clasping his hands and resting his chin upon them.

"It begins like this…" And she went through with him the prayer. His voice rumbled along with hers. Then he shut his eyes.

He did not rise for a good while. Silence lapped amongst them. At some point, Rosa began to doze. She started awake at the dip of the bed. Grimulf lay there, face tight and gaze focused on the ceiling.

"Did…Did you hear something?"

"I do not know. Perhaps," he told her.

"Was it an answer?" She was tense, almost jealous. Since her arrival here, there had been no sign or response to her own prayers.

"The wolf remains," he told her, and she shut her eyes. "However, another problem was made known to me."

"What?"

He turned and held her close. He clung to her as if someone might snatch her away.

"My brother Ragnar truly was murdered."

"How come you to think this? You were not there."

"Some of the old men have been speaking with me," he told her, and she wondered if he had not mentioned it before because interspersed with it were condemnations about her. "From how they described it, I believe he was poisoned. Even my father and brother died too easily in the shipwreck, when they were both experienced seamen. Perhaps all of us were cursed... or someone from this world had a hand in it."

Grimulf would not go any further. He rolled on his side, not even attempting to try and sleep but staring at the shadows. All Rosa could do was hold him from behind, praying he would not be torn from her.

Olaf only came near when Rosa was with Grimulf. His eyes were small, pinched tight. She stared at him, not breaking eye contact. Grimulf's arm around her waist was a steady reassurance. The wind whipped about them as they stood upon the dunes.

"What is it you carry in your pouch, nephew? I've been curious for some time," Olaf inquired.

"A few herbs. I have had trouble breathing."

"A good clear sea wind ought to fix you right," he replied. "I am glad it is only that."

"What else would you believe it to be?"

"Some might think you'll start wearing the Nailed God's crucifix, if it was asked of you."

Olaf's eyes flicked over to Rosa again. She barely managed not to reach for her throat. Her own crucifix had been snatched from her when he carried her off. It must have been lost to the sands by now, yet his hand seemed to creep towards his waist. Her throat lurched, eyebrows furrowing slightly. The crucifix had belonged to her mother and was greatly missed.

"My Gods are in the sky and seas," Grimulf answered him a little tersely, and Rosa wondered how many times Olaf had approached her husband, trying to undermine her influence.

"Good. My men caught a stranger attempting to ingratiate himself in our camp. I believe him to be a spy for the Lady of the Mercians."

Aethelflaed, the Lady of the Mercians, ruled the lands that were free from Viking control. Since her husband's death, she had been ruthless in her attacks upon settlements such as theirs. Her men would most likely be just as harsh if they caught a Viking lad, yet Rosa felt cold.

Grimulf's arm tensed and, covertly, she rubbed her thumb soothingly over the inside of his wrist. She remained silent.

"What have you done with him?" Grimulf asked.

"We interrogated him, but nothing could make him speak. We took away his tongue as he seemed to have no use for it."

Her head began to swim at what played out in her mind. The flesh beneath the collar of her cloak turned clammy.

"You had no right to do this on my lands without consulting me," Grimulf snapped. "Don't think I haven't noticed how *comfortable* you've made yourself."

"What would you have done differently? I apologise for being overbearing. I still seem to think of you as a boy, rather than the man you are now. Your brothers would often let me perform the bloodier aspects of what was required. They relied on me."

"You've been meandering too long. You'll start to take root."

Rosa smiled sweetly at Olaf. *Yes, go and scurry into a hole, rat*, she thought, yet none of this showed on her face.

"Soon I'll be gone. Don't be quick to chase off what's left of your family. I'll stay long enough to see the sacrifice made."

Now Rosa spoke, unable to help herself, "What sacrifice?"

It was Grimulf who answered. "The man will be staked upon the sands. Left until the hightide comes in." He would not look into her horrified eyes.

"But that is…!"

She pressed her lips tightly together. She had hoped Grimulf would understand the futility of such a sacrifice. Blood did not water the fields. He continued to cling to the pagan ways.

"It might even sort our fish problem," Olaf said, ignoring her outburst. "Though no doubt the seas would prefer a more worthwhile meal to savour."

Rosa was led home by Grimulf. She couldn't help looking back at her uncle-in-law. He grinned at her. She knew he had been thinking of her as the best sacrifice for the sea.

She should keep quiet and pray for the poor soul. To do anything else would put her in great jeopardy. Yet this man was one of her people. He had been the only one she had heard of in a long time. If she could sneak off and free him, it would feel like a great triumph against these Vikings.

Valerian stirred into a warm drink would soon lull a person into sound sleep. While her husband lay in bed, Rosa crept out of the house in that fragile, cloudy moment before sundown.

A fire had been left snapping and spurting on the sands, yet the Vikings had abandoned their sacrifice to the waves. Rosa walked along the beach, getting closer to the dark shape spread open like a starfish.

Not quite light, not quite night, the sky had a grey hue that meant she could see without a torch but pulsing behind it was darkness waiting to fall. Opposing waves formed small arches, then crashed. Birds hunted for shells and crabs to crack open and pierce with their small, sharp beaks.

Rosa caught up her skirt to stop the wet sands slowing her. Stakes pinned the man's hands and feet, yet in these shifting sands the spikes were starting to topple. The young man did not move, only the ropes trailing around his arms shifted at the nudge of another wave. One particularly tall wave thrust over his body, his face, then slowly dredged back, dragging him ever so slightly. It seemed almost as if it was a hand trying to pull him further in.

She knelt, but she already knew she was too late. The Saxon spy had bled out from his wounds. Hand shaking, she shut his eyes. Under her breath she muttered a soft prayer to guide his soul to somewhere better.

There was movement in the corner of her eye. She tensed as a dark shape emerged from the waters. It was sleek, without fur or feathers. There was something almost human about how it bobbed, yet she could not see any sort of face.

The winds were seething around her, buffeting at her hair and cloak. Could this be one of the Gods the Vikings thought consumed their sacrifices? Perhaps it would come for her instead.

The creature did not surge forward. It sunk into the waves and no matter where she looked it did not emerge.

The birds scattered, shrieking towards the dunes. Olaf must have known she would be drawn towards the boy. He had appeared once he saw her shuffle down the gap leading from the village to the beach.

Rosa's hand went to her boot. "Stay away," she warned.

He laughed. Rather than frighten her, it only made her angry.

"It was foolish to come out here," he called. "I told you what would happen if you did not do as I demanded."

He was striding over. Deep imprints of his boots followed

him. A wave pushed forward, completely covering the corpse and soaking through her shoes.

"Grimulf does not want you here," she said as powerfully as she could, alone with the grey sky splitting into night. "He is my husband."

"And you are in his ear? Quite a crafty creature, aren't you, I hadn't even realised. You've got a keen sense of survival, just as I have. Now you've made it impossible to leave my nephew out of this and it's your fault."

She grimaced at the thought of them sharing anything at all. What he said last made her stiffen in attention, though.

"What are you planning?" Her heart throbbed in her throat. A thought occurred to her, what Grimulf had spoken of after he had prayed. "Were you troubling Grimulf's brother when he perished?"

It was a mere flash, quickly swallowed by the darkness that descended. His eyes had widened, then there was a surge of emotions, sorrow, regret, but in the centres an evil glee.

He was only a smudge of shadow now. His breath panted from him as he lunged for her, the sands scraping.

Rosa lashed out with the dagger she pulled from her boot. She did not think of where to aim, only tried for somewhere she thought would cause him great pain. He did not even realise she was armed. There was a shout of pain, the hot rush of blood hitting her hand. He sagged heavily against her, arm locking around her neck. She thrashed, twisting them around and forcing him backwards, until his heel knocked against the corpse on the ground and he fell.

She stood there, heaving, not knowing what to do next. Her dagger was raised, thinking she could end him with one thrust.

It hung there a moment, but she could not finish the movement. Instead, she crouched, feeling through the pouches on his belt. She found her crucifix tangled around a bone from an earlier meal.

Rosa stumbled in the dark and only just managed to find the path home. She crept into bed and held herself, shivering, afraid she would jostle Grimulf into wakefulness and he would smell the sea salt in her hair.

What upset her most was Grimulf started to suspect her again. The next morning, he sat at breakfast and ran his tongue over his teeth, as though chasing some strange taste, while eying the shadows beneath her eyes.

Feeling guilty and wanting to reassure Grimulf she was still loyal to him, Rosa set to cooking a special meal.

She had heard plenty about the dish called haggr. She was not certain what it meant, only that wives served it to their men on important occasions. After the week Grimulf had, she wanted to cheer him up. She also wanted to try this, curious about what her husband would have eaten in his youth.

Gunhild eagerly helped. The old woman led her to the river, bag jostling with the ingredients.

"This'll do nicely," she told her warmly, pleased Grimulf's new wife showed willing, considering she was a Christian. "Grimulf won't be back until tomorrow evening, and it'll be finished just in time."

"It takes that long?"

"It needs a thorough cleaning, little one."

They knelt by the water. The bag was opened.

"We've no deer to hand, but a cow should do well enough."

Inside, Rosa blanched. She had thought it would be well butchered meat. She could make out quite clearly the stomach, heart and lungs of the beast. The loudest thought inside her head was the innards of an animal were not so different from a person's. They could be butchering a man for all she knew.

She would do this. Just as her husband had provided for her, she would for him. Steadying her nerve, she swallowed the spit that suddenly welled in her too dry mouth and righted herself.

"What do we do first?"

They cleaned the cow's stomach in the river and carried it inside, where they scalded it entirely. Then came the fiddly task of turning it inside out.

Rosa had begun to feel lightheaded again, but all they had to do now was leave it in a bowl of salted water. A night passed.

When they arose, the rest of the organs needed to be prepared. Seeing how pale Rosa had become, Gunhild cheerily offered to do the heart and lungs, and for her to clean the kidneys and liver. At least it was familiar to the nun. She remembered serving a dish of kidneys to a visiting lord they were hoping to pry donations from.

And yet it was too much. At the first bright burst of blood over her fingers, Rosa ran outside, heaving as she vomited. Once she swilled out her mouth, she came back. She resumed washing the meat, biting into her cheek to force down another surge of nausea.

It was certainly something she had never encountered before. She was not certain if she could stand putting this in her mouth once it was finished. Yet she had not expected such a violent reaction.

As the meat boiled in the pot, they mixed chopped onions, oatmeal, minced trimmings, seasoning, and poured it all in. They spooned the haggr inside the stomach, sewed it up and pricked it with a knife.

It took three hours to cook. Rosa spent the rest of that time tidying, sometimes pausing to look out of the door at the horizon. Her heart pounded, the excitable flutter within her she had coined as her arousal turning into a frustrating ache—she wanted Grimulf home. She anticipated his return and sating his hunger, both in his stomach and elsewhere.

Then, just as the sun started to set, the horses could be seen pounding across the flat landscape. Rosa waited outside, hands clasped together just beneath her breast. There was his horse. She saw his silhouette atop, strong and tall. He was safe. A great heaviness like a waterlogged shawl fell from her shoulders.

Grimulf rode straight to the house and dismounted. His boots squelched in the mud at the force of his descent. He rushed over, sweeping her in his arms and pressing a rough kiss to her lips.

"By the Gods, I'd rather listen to you than have to spend another day hearing Knud boast about his make-believe conquests."

"I have missed you as well."

Grimulf kicked off his road weary boots and stepped inside. The fire was already going and he sat beside it, chasing off the chill of the sea.

"I've cooked something for you," she told him, voice slightly hesitant but light with hope.

"Oh, aye?"

Rosa pulled from the pot the haggr, slitting the stomach open and spooning upon their trenchers the contents within. She poured them ale.

"Gunhild showed me how to make this."

"She's done a fine job in teaching you, and you in learning. It looks just how my mother used to make it."

"Mighty praise indeed!"

They sat to eat. Grimulf, ravenous with only bread and cheese to rely on, dived in. She listened to his appreciative noises for a moment before turning to her own food.

She reached for her spoon, but instead took a sip of her weak ale instead. Her stomach lurched. She had been unable to properly eat all day and she knew she must be starving.

She put some on her spoon, only covering the tip. Her mouth opened, settling it upon her tongue. Chewing, she found she did not mind the taste at all, yet her throat closed tight as if in rebellion. She forced herself to swallow.

And then promptly found herself running out to spit what was in her mouth and stomach, which turned out to be only bile. Hacking, she barely registered Grimulf's hand rubbing her back.

"It is an acquired taste, Rosa."

She nodded, unable to speak. Not many would likely enjoy haggr, considering what was needed to be done to make it, but she did not think it entirely the case. There was another cause…and it might be for a happy reason, if she was correct.

The next morning, Rosa had to quickly untangle herself from Grimulf's arms to be sick again. It was all the proof she needed.

She was with child.

CHAPTER 6

Rosa might not be with child, yet deep within there was a certain contentment she had never felt before. She knew. The knowledge was tucked inside like a beloved secret.

She wanted to tell Grimulf but was uncertain how he would react. He would believe any child of his might become stricken with the curse as well. There were herbs that could blow away the dream of a child as easily as dandelion heads. Her throat went tight, fearful he might demand she found those herbs.

While the child was as fragile as a seed and in need of protection, Rosa held her tongue. When she could no longer hide the child, then she would tell him. Hopefully the joy of her pregnancy would be enough to stop him realising she had been whispering falsehoods in his ear.

The kitten Morgana quickly grew as the bitter winter months softened into damp spring. Rosa found herself watching with a soft smile, considering the child within her was growing at much the same rate.

Alongside this time the moon spun from a farmer's sickle to a droplet, like an eye slowly and painfully blinking.

Grimulf slipped off to the smokehouse whenever the full moon was due. When he returned, the darkness remained beneath his eyes, a muscle in his cheek taut from his gritted teeth. Rather than desolation, the hope in his eyes refused to fade, growing brighter. He believed in Rosa.

No pigs were slaughtered or men hunted down. Grimulf stayed in his shackles, the howls quietening.

But the true monster, the one that had killed Ivar, had yet to be found.

Olaf had not been washed away with the corpse of the Saxon boy. After Rosa fought him, while dawn flickered its eyes, the old man limped his way past the dunes, disgustedly dashing sand and blood from his clothes. She could not see his face but sensed the fury darkening every craggy incline and pockmarked wrinkle.

Rosa remained close by Grimulf's side, keeping him in bed longer, her arm linked with his as they walked. She wondered if Olaf would dare name her as his attacker. He did not, she was relieved to find out. She reasoned he could not stand the humiliation of being thrown to the ground by a mere woman.

Rosa kept her crucifix hidden, as she would have no way of explaining how she came to reclaim it. Whenever she was alone, she clutched it tightly. Her own talisman against the curses and pagan songs surrounding her.

One night as Grimulf slept she hesitantly pressed the crucifix to his cheek. It might burn him, reacting to some evil lurking within. Instead, it gently sunk into his flesh. She removed the crucifix and soon enough the slight impression vanished.

Even though he had promised, Olaf did not leave the settlement. He sent word to Grimulf he was sickening. Olaf blamed his wounds on the Saxon boy, who had struggled while being staked.

Any mention of him leaving was met with gripes. Was he to oust the last remaining person who shared his blood, cruel, uncaring man! A healer was called for, and he easily closed the wound, but Olaf still complained of pains.

"Perhaps," Olaf suggested to his nephew, "your wife could cure me of my ills."

Rosa was grateful Grimulf did not order her to tend to his uncle. However, she did agree to when he asked if she would be willing.

"I know he is gruff and overbearing, and thinks he knows best, but he is the last of my kin. One of the few I trust." He leaned in, kissing the spot below her ear and enjoying how she shivered and arched. "Besides you."

The sooner Olaf was cured, then he would have no more excuses. Whatever he had planned, he could do little if Gunhild was by her side.

Olaf and his men had set up their own camp further down the dunes. Rudolf escorted Rosa and the old woman there. Thankfully, a blood feud between two brothers needed overseeing, meaning Grimulf could not attend. Now she did not need to worry about Olaf letting anything slip, either in the throes of sickness or on purpose.

Rosa felt eyes upon her. Olaf's men watched her progress curiously. None recognised her. They were unable to compare her striding through, strong and tall as the chieftain's wife, with the hunched, shivering creature who had been dragged by her hair.

Her steps slowed as she took in the tent. It was the same one she had been imprisoned in all those months ago. Her hand passed over her stomach reassuringly. She should not be afraid; no longer was she Olaf's captive.

Rudolf lifted the tent flap, the two women ducking within. He remained outside.

Very little light eroded the hazy darkness. The air was heady and nauseating, thick with smells of sharp, bitter medicines and acrid old blood. Olaf lay on his bed, the furs lifted to reveal the deep gouge she had left in his side. He tugged at his kirtle, barely able to conceal himself, and it left him in a pathetic, vulnerable position.

It was a dark red gash, closed neatly. The flesh surrounding it was reddened, most likely aching and itching. Although she was a healer, she felt some pleasure in seeing his discomfort.

"What ails you?" she asked brusquely. Gunhild said nothing, perhaps in deference, but her lined face was stiff and she would not look at him.

"Come see for yourself."

Rosa's eyebrows quirked. "A mere woman? Surely you fear I'll make a mistake and kill you." And her teeth were slightly bared as she said this.

Rosa examined Olaf. The covers were lifted further, the reveal of his pale, sagging flesh making her grimace. Little could be done about the wound, only wait for it to heal. There were other signs of malady, which Rosa knew she had not dealt.

The flesh thinned in places, the veins small, pinched things rearing over his knuckles. His eyes had yellowed. Each wheezing puff of breath was rancid, but that could have been usual. The fingernails were turning brittle, beginning to peel.

His stomach bore the worst of it: distended while the rest of him wasted, the flesh there a vivid purple as though bruised. She pressed down, rougher than she would any other. He hissed and writhed, and she remained pressing for a few seconds longer before releasing him.

Rosa could not understand what affected him. She found herself murmuring, "It is almost as if you have been poisoned."

Olaf heard her. The wrinkled, slightly sunken Adam's apple jerked.

"What did you say?"

"No, it is nothing."

Her boot nudged against something half-peeking out from his discarded armour, causing it to rattle harshly. The flash of white caught her attention. She recognised the hue of bone.

She crouched while he spluttered for her to leave it be. Gunhild pulled off a cloak of sable.

It was the oddest, most disquieting skull Rosa had ever seen. She thought it belonged to a dog, but it was leaner, the back rearing upwards. There were a great many teeth crammed in. She flinched as she dragged it out and the jaw seemed to open and snap.

"A trophy from my travels," Olaf said, voice turning into a low hiss.

She pried open the jaw and saw gore and blood packed between the vicious teeth. Dried now, though, and the colour of earth.

"What creature does it come from?"

"A mere seal. They leave their pups upon the beaches hereabouts. Lazy, fat things that barely move."

"Then it must have been a worthless diversion to hunt one of them."

She remembered the night she saw the strange creature emerging from the sea. She could just imagine the oily, smooth flesh over this skull, peeling its lips away to reveal fearsome teeth.

There was something else. Rosa struggled to understand what it could be. It was the teeth, she knew it had to be them, but she could not be certain if it was because of how gruesome and monstrous the creature looked with its inner self laid bare.

"Leave now!" Olaf commanded, before she could say anything further.

The tent flap shifted, Rudolf peering in. Olaf waved his hand in a dismissive gesture.

"I tire of her poking and prodding. She can do nothing for me. Return her to my nephew. She's of more use to his needs."

Flushing furiously, Rosa left with Gunhild before she could be ushered out. Soon after she returned home, Olaf demanded to see Grimulf. Before he departed, Rosa asked him to look for the skull.

"It is a curious oddity," she told him innocently, wondering if he saw it he might be able to name this strange tugging sensation within her. "I've never seen a seal before."

Grimulf breathed thinly through his mouth as he entered the tent. It reminded him too keenly of his nights locked in the smokehouse, surrounded by the scent of his sweat and fear.

"How are you faring, Uncle?"

The threat of sickness still made his hackles rise. His eyes darted about, rather than settling on Olaf. He saw no sign of the skull Rosa had spoken of.

The cruellest threat to a warrior was the fangs of disease. It offered no honour in the tearing of a blade, instead nipping and spreading its poison, eroding man into a frail, pitiful creature. No matter a man's riches, strength or connections, a simple sickness could sweep him off.

Grimulf forced himself to look in his uncle's glazed eyes. "You will be well?"

"I'm not yet done with life." Olaf's ashen cheeks flushed a violent hue, veins pulsing. "Your wife seems to think I am being poisoned!"

"What?"

"She said she was mistaken, but I feel the taint of it in my bones. If we've had spies, who's to say we haven't had poisoners as well? Your return to these lands would have alerted that Mercian whore. She will want to strike us at our weakest moment and put a puppet in your place."

"You think our troubles come from an outside threat?"

"It would be better if it was, rather than distant kin. We should teach this Queen to fear us. They once ran from our raiders. *My* raiders. But now we have settled and we farm and fish, and they think us weak. Ride to the centre of Mercia and strike her down."

"And then she will bring her armies upon us."

"You shy from bloodshed?" Olaf wheezed. "My brother would be ashamed."

"You are older than your ambitions. I have already left one war."

"Before your return, a priestess of Freyja came to me. She spoke of a new age of the Viking, with the Mercian woman another body upon the battlefield. I thought it mere idle fantasy at the time, but then you arrived and I could see in your eyes the need to fight."

Grimulf flinched. Whatever he had seen had most likely been a wolf pacing, desperate to break free.

"Prophecies?" he snapped. "I'm not about to lay the safety of the village on a woman's delusion!"

Olaf's lips thinned, but he did not speak. Grimulf heard the response clear enough: he had married a woman based on her vision. He roughly shook his head.

"I seem to have fallen into a web of intrigue," he remarked bitterly. "All because of Ragnar's death."

"Such a sad occurrence… I did all I could." Olaf's hand passed over his eyes. All the grief and sorrow showed stark in his weathered face.

"I know you did. My brothers might have favoured Father, but I know how much you cared for us all."

156

"As I had no sons of my own, I thought it only right to watch over you all."

All the irritations Grimulf had felt at his uncle's overbearing attitude began to fade. He realised perhaps the old Viking was lonely, unable to find companionship amongst his band of men as he had done when younger. He did not have the luck of encountering a woman such as Rosa to settle with.

Grimulf had been rebelling against him, newly arrived, wanting to make his own mark, when he should have been listening to his counsel. His uncle had never led him astray. He had been his tutor in sword and bow when his father found him too unruly to deal with.

He gave his uncle a moment to recover. The old man's eyes hardened.

"Why do you sound suspicious? Do you think a hand other than fate ended his life?"

"I fear it is so. The way Ragnar perished reminded me of a poison the saboteurs at the emperor's court would often use."

Olaf's nose scrunched up. "Then you should be on your guard. I doubt they would try something so apparent again, but I am certain the Mercians will target you. They might already be ready to close in."

Grimulf clenched his fist, knowing it would be when he was at his most vulnerable he would be caught. He tensed, awaiting condemnation of his wife, ready to defend her. He must. He was so devoted to her he could not believe she was the enemy, not when she kissed his wounds and he heard the love straining in her voice as he moved within her.

Olaf shakily clutched his shoulder. "Fear not, nephew. You are the last of my blood. I will keep watch over you, old and frail as I am…if you will let me."

Unfortunately for Rosa, Olaf did not leave. Time was wasted as he "recovered". Even when he was hale enough to leave his bed, she was not given the blessed sight of his retreating back vanishing in the horizon. Something had unsettled Grimulf, now he wished for his uncle to remain.

Each evening Grimulf would creep away to discuss battle strategies with Olaf. She only knew of his return when he crawled into her arms, rousing her with soft kisses to her throat and his weight pressing down on her insistently.

She was afraid.

All Rosa wanted was Grimulf. That night the storms screeched outside, winds rattling the house's foundations and scraping against the closed smokeholes. There were shadows sloping past along the sands, like men stretched into twisted shapes.

If she had her husband here, then at least she would not be alone. He would bundle her into his arms and whisper his stories. She could sleep and dream of magic and far off lands rather than the nightmares roaming her waking world.

He was out there, though, conversing with his uncle. Olaf might easily tell him of what had happened at the nunnery, twisting it so Rosa was the enemy. Then what might Grimulf do if he knew she was already wed, and to his uncle of all men? Now Rosa did not wish for Grimulf's return, for fear he would bring his sword...

Tears fell from one eye, gravity dragging it over her face to rest upon the pillow. She should have told the truth when Grimulf sat before her, head tilted trustingly while she shaved his beard. He would have had to have listened.

A weight settled itself upon the bed. It was too slight to be Grimulf. Rosa stilled.

"Who's there?" the words came out as a rasping whisper. She received no answer. Slowly, her hand crept under the pillow, where Grimulf kept one of his daggers.

Instead of being grasped suddenly, a warm lump settled

against her back, exactly where she ached and shivered. There was a strange rumbling noise. Rosa released the dagger.

"Morgana."

Rosa sat up, petting the cat, while overhead lightning flashed. She would not be cowed into submission. She had almost died to get here and become Grimulf's wife.

Olaf might be in her husband's ear, but she was in his bed. Grimulf had chosen her. Come tomorrow, she would tell him. She must.

She could only pray he would believe her.

"Husband, there is something I must tell you."

Grimulf sat, fussing the dogs gathered at his feet who had slunk in at the scent of food. Whatever scraps remained of his earlier meal vanished in their slathering maws. The cat lounged upon one of the benches, eyes gleaming from the firelight, tail flicking lazily about the floating embers, somehow avoiding being singed.

On the table was his sword and shield. They gleamed, damp from the polish he had rubbed on. Rosa's own little dagger was there, newly sharpened by him.

One side of Grimulf's face was ablaze in light, the red of his beard bright as garnet. Creeping over the other half were shadows, only the tiny pale eclipse of his eye shining through. He paused, mid-way scratching one of Shuck's ears. The hound grumbled low in his throat.

Rosa had never called him husband in a good way before. Grimulf straightened.

"Aye, what is it, wife?"

This simple exchange had distanced them, as though they were strangers only just meeting one another.

Rosa's hands were clasped behind her to conceal her fidgeting, though he knew anyway. She focused on the fire instead. Her eyebrows drew together, teeth worrying her lower lip.

"We have been together for four months now."

"Not regretting it now, are you?"

"Be quiet for once!" She gasped in alarm at what she had done. "I only meant... Always you are joking. I will not be able to do this if you keep interrupting."

"It is because your face is so stern," he answered, amused by her harshness. "I'd rather see you laughing. I'll hold my tongue, so there'll be no need to punish me."

As much as he tried to avoid the seriousness of this, there was something wrong. He wished he could carry her off to bed and let her forget that way. He had done it plenty of times recently.

Grimulf forced himself to be quiet, bowing his head for her to continue. To think, when they were first wed, he would have done all he could to worm the truth from her. Now he wished to stopper his ears when it finally came.

"There was no vision that made me leave the nunnery."

Rosa glanced at Grimulf, hesitant, wanting some sort of reaction. He did not give it to her.

"I never set out to lie to you," she continued. "I did not know who you were until..." Her thumb went to her mouth, teeth grinding on her nail.

Grimulf took her hand, rubbing his thumb in the centre of her palm. He made no move to pull her into his arms. There was nowhere she could run to. She had to confront this.

"Vikings raided my home and burnt it down. The man who led them had come to us before, as a pilgrim, and deceived us. I must have caught his eye because he carried me off to his camp."

His grip on her did not tighten. He stared at her, face still. His fingers weaved with hers.

"He did not... violate me. I thought he would. I knew he wanted to. Yet all he did was lock me away. I thought he might ransom me to my father, but it was not that. He dressed me as a pagan bride, slit the throat of a sow... and married me. I was in his tent when the dogs went wild. He could not get near and he stormed off. One of his thralls helped me escape. She told me to come here, to throw myself upon your mercy, because this Viking was afraid of you."

Too lost in her memories, she did not notice Grimulf releasing her hand, but the calming sensation of his stroking was missed.

"I did not know who you were. I could not believe you would offer a stranger, a Christian, your help. That is why I made out a higher power had sent me, because I thought you would be less likely to argue with Him."

Rosa shut her eyes and let out a breath. There was some relief having spoken of this. Keeping it hidden had made it grow and pulse in the base of her throat, choking her as she tried to keep silent.

This was not yet over. There was Grimulf to deal with. She opened her eyes again. Her mouth went dry. She could not tell at all what he was thinking. Now she wished for him to interrupt and joke with her.

Grimulf set his chin upon the back of his hand. His eyebrows were furrowed.

"Who was this man?" he asked.

"He... He never said his name."

"No. You would have heard during that time. During the wedding, his name would have been spoken."

"Does it matter? I am here now. I got away!"

"Got away? It seems you tied yourself to one Viking, then collected up another. You are married to another man. You did not divorce him."

"I was not willing. It doesn't count. *I married you.*"

"Freyja blessed your wedding to him! You were so quick to catch me, you did not follow proper custom. I thought a little rashness would not be bad, but this is... Our union is cursed. Why would you simply not ask for my help? Why demand marriage?"

"I thought you would not give it," she argued desperately. "If you married me, then he might have no claim." Her face was growing hot. Her slim fingers curled into a fist.

"But he does have a claim, and a much stronger one than mine."

"No!"

"It would be the same in your own precious church. I have heard of nuns deciding to marry, but only one man. Not being greedy and claiming two."

"I did not consent. I—"

"I have had no reports of a nunnery being sacked. My uncle would have told me of such an event. Someone might have stolen you, but you still hide things from me. Did your husband send you as a spy? Once you have found all you wanted, tasted all my weaknesses, will he come and claim you and take these lands from me?"

"I am not lying to you!"

Her trembling fist swung out. Grimulf raised his hand. He could have easily caught it, but instead she struck his arm ring. There was a dull metallic thump.

"Then tell me who this man is."

"I cannot!"

The hounds had scattered. Morgana watched them with mild interest.

Grimulf shoved back his stool, arising. Rosa did not shrink or cower as he loomed over her. Tears streamed down her reddened cheeks. She stared at him, desperate to argue, to force him to believe.

"You are not my wife. What do you expect from me? This

is what your lies have sown. You should have told me from the start. It could have been done right."

He strode past her. The door banged open, then shut.

Rosa sank down. Her face buried into her hands.

She had thought he would believe her. He promised he would. Instead, he had proven her doubts real.

What now? He was right. She was not his wife. If they had not been pagan weddings, she would be tried as an adulteress in church. She knew the punishments for such crimes.

If what Grimulf said was true, Olaf could claim her. Vomit burned her throat, but she forced it down. She could not remain here and weep.

There was the child. Grimulf's son or daughter. Surely that meant his claim was stronger? She knew, furiously, what he would say next. How was he to know the child was his, even though he had bled her? It might not even matter. She had wedded Olaf first, all children might come under his ownership.

She shuddered in horror, even while the fire warmed her back. She would die rather than let that madman near her or her child.

If Grimulf was not willing to protect her, if she was no longer welcome in his home, then she would have to protect herself. She should have done this from the start.

Rosa arose, dizziness assailing her. She clung to the bench, leaning forward. Morgana sniffed curiously at her wet cheek. She stroked the cat to calm herself.

"I'm sorry, I'll have to leave you behind. I'm sure one of the other women will take you in, ferocious little beast."

Another sob came out. This moment of joy had been too short. She had prayed it would last forever.

Rosa went about the house, first finding a bag, then collecting her warmest clothes and food. She must be gone before Grimulf returned. She did not want anyone following.

If Olaf did come after her, she would not run. She had nothing left now, only survival and her dagger.

She soon left the house. She had planned to leave her necklace and key behind, as a sign Grimulf had lost her, but had thought better. The chain the key was on would give her enough coin for bread once she found a market.

If Grimulf thought she was ruthless, she would prove him right.

Rosa briskly walked across the sands. Her shawl was not enough, her hands kept on moving up and down her arms, ruching the lace-like material. The flesh was pale and prickled with bumps. Winds kept on playing with her hair, dragging it over her damp eyes.

There was no one on the beaches, not even the familiar heaving backs of the fishermen hard at work. Slight shelves had appeared in the sands, impregnated with stones. The surging waves crashed against them, flicking seafoam.

Grimulf's voice in her mind had faded, replaced by the seething of the winds. Her eyes squeezed tight. She would not weep. It would only take the rest of her already flagging energy.

She could either turn right, towards the ruins of her nunnery, where she might find some of the other nuns. Or even left, which was unknown but at least took her from here. She wished she'd had the sense to take the horse with her.

The day had barely begun, yet already a golden dusk hued the clouds with a single strand of pinkish sunset. Waves had a brittle crystalline edged curve as they rose and fell, running along the stretch like a thread pulling off a spool. Froth spilled, sluggishly she stepped back and still got the toes of her shoes wet.

How dare he, she thought as she stood there, wavering on

her decision. The way to the right was clear and bright, where the sun must be hiding. She saw the dunes, fringed with grasses and bracken bushes clinging on, the sands running endlessly.

On the other side the mists had drawn in. She knew it was another stretch of beach and rocky cliffs, but all of it was cocooned in spider's silk. Rosa went into the unknown. Her figure soon vanished in the mists.

She wanted to weep, her throat knotted tight, chest burning, but the tears could not be conjured. Her face turned rigid, teeth gritted. A great anger bubbled inside. If she made to sob, she knew she would instead turn towards the sea and scream in anger.

Grimulf had spent most of their marriage promising her nothing could make him turn from her. She had dared to hope!

And now look where she was: alone and walking the beaches, carrying the child of a man who thought her another spy. He had sided with his uncle. Thank God she had not revealed the Viking to be Olaf or he might have shown her how deep his loyalty to his family was.

What had she expected? He had no Christian values. Not that she believed a Christian man would be any different. She had hoped for more from Grimulf. She had begun to...

Whatever it was, it must be crushed beneath her heel. Thinking on that would not help her or the child.

A lone seagull stomped across the waterlogged sands, its webbed feet sinking in. Waves came in, catching the bird and dragging it to sea. It allowed itself to be carried off and now calmly bobbed, as though suspended.

Rosa had not got far, yet the mists she had stormed through pulled a curtain behind her. It was as if she was in another place entirely.

She watched the journey of the bird. Though the waves kept on rolling, the seagull remained in the same place. Her breathing slowed. The exhaustion she had been resisting unfurled.

She finally sat. As she stretched out her legs the wet sands clung to the skin of her calves. The heel of her boot dragged through, parting sand and pebbles.

The seagull continued bobbing along. It seemed easy, when she knew its feet must be moving frantically to keep itself afloat. The bird was tiny compared to the waves, but it kept fighting.

Rosa must be the same. Her soul might be lost, but her child's soul remained in question. She would raise this child to be good and honest and Christian. It might be half-Dane, but it was half of her as well.

"I will be all you need, my darling," she murmured. "Your father might have cast us aside, but I will love you so much you will never miss the love he owes you."

Even if it meant her heart would break each time she looked at her child and saw Grimulf in their eyes.

Grimulf's anger was like an ember, quick to spit and flare, but just as fast to cool. He had walked a short distance into the settlement, where the campfire roared, but had stopped, feeling a fool. Like some witless brat who had stormed out while his mother shouted after him.

It hadn't been his mother, though, had it? He'd left his wife while she wept and shook with rage, all the while begging him to understand.

His own fists were clenched. All he wanted to do was pinch her tongue between his fingers and steal the name she kept curled within.

What else was he meant to do? Strike her? The thought sickened him. Remaining meant he would have to accept what she said. Everything centred on who he could trust. After the assassin's attack, his life was always at risk.

Rosa's face flashed over his vision. The reddened, shining eyes wide and earnest. Hands clutching her stomach to swallow down her ball of rage. During his years as a soldier, he had learnt to read men's faces. Women, not so much.

She had clouded his senses. He wanted to believe her but did not know if he should. She reminded him too much of a deer peering at a hunter, uncertain what the glint of the arrowhead was. However, if he was wrong, he might be the prey instead.

Grimulf stared straight into the fires. Some of the women sat there, gossiping as they weaved. They were mere shadows, heads bowed. Light danced over his face, oranges and reds to make him seem aflame. There was only silence in his mind, gone was the fury, but there were no solutions offered for his predicament.

He had to make his own choices. Grimulf ran his knuckles along the edge of his beard. Even if she was lying, there was the possibility she spoke the truth. She needed his protection and he had abandoned her in the house with a traitor on the loose.

Cursing, Grimulf hurried home. He thrust open the door. "Rosa, I—"

She was not there. He searched for her, but the only hints of existence were the disordered bedsheets from the night before, the cat asleep upon one of the askew pillows.

Her clothes were gone, as was some of the smoked fish and bread. At least she had left of her own volition, rather than being taken.

Grimulf had not seen her in the village. She would have gone in the opposite direction, not wanting to be seen by anyone. None of his horses or the white stallion had been taken.

So, she was on foot. Grimulf knelt outside his door. The

earth was damp from recent rainfall and he soon found a fresh half-print: she had been running. Soon enough he followed the marks to the beach.

Grimulf saddled one of his horses and set off in search of her. She might have a head start, but he never lost his prey.

He needed little skill to track her. She made no attempt to conceal her movements, most of it pacing, then the decision to go left. Her furious footprints wounded the wet sands, tiny pools forming in them.

It would not do to have her easy to find by his enemies, Grimulf thought, already planning on teaching her how to hide any sign of herself. He had to capture her first and bring her back, even if she fought him.

Grimulf found her a mile down the beach. Her bag had been flung to the ground. She jerkily tore out a piece of driftwood sticking out of the sand, adding it to the steadily growing pile. He knew she had seen him, yet she made no gesture of acknowledgement.

"What are you doing?" he called, as another piece of wood was harshly thrown over her shoulder.

"I am making a bonfire, my lord. Unless you think I am attempting to signal my masters?"

"And how will you light this fire?"

"With my flint." She snatched at her bag, peering into it. Her shoulders stiffened, then slowly fell. "I must have forgot."

"You were so enraged it is a wonder you took what you did." He leaned against the horse's neck to peer down at her. "Why would you need a fire when we've got a perfectly fine one at home?"

"Because it is not my home," her voice wobbled. "You made your thoughts quite clear. I will not stay where I am not wanted."

"You foolish—" Recrimination would get him nothing. He tempered his tone. "We only argued. I'd have spent the night drinking and you weeping, then I'd come back and all would be forgotten. I didn't expect you to run off!"

"Forgotten? We were not arguing for the fun of it."

"Not all arguing has to end in misery...it sometimes lights fire in the belly."

She made a sound of disgust.

"I have held this inside me for too long. An argument would not have settled anything. A choice had to be made." She paused. "What made you return? I would have had more time if you had gone drinking."

"Come with me and I will tell you."

"No, I've decided now I'm going to look after myself."

But she was looking at her meagre pile of wood, some parts glistening with seawater. She made no sound, only came over to the horse's side and clutched his mane. She faced the white shoulder, face red.

Grimulf did not drag her onto the horse. Sighing heavily, he dismounted and knelt before the woodpile. He always kept his flint with him. Soon enough he had a fire going. The horse settled upon the sands while Grimulf sat beside him, shielded by the winds.

He held out his hand, beckoning her. "It is time we talked."

Grimulf pulled her so she sat before him. He made no remark on how easily she folded. Even women had pride.

"Who is the man who has done this?" Grimulf softly demanded. "I want to trust you, but if you will not reveal who he is..."

"It is with good reason, I swear. It is I who cannot trust you. I might have given his name, in time, but now I know I must hold my tongue. You proved me right in being cautious."

And now he would have to gain her trust all over again. No amount of shouting would loosen her tongue.

"Is it not enough that I am your wife?" she reasoned. "I have given so much of myself to you...and more."

Even though they were married, had shared kisses, traded their lust with love, it was as if they were strangers. Their marriage had been built upon a cracked, uncertain foundation. Any threat and it crumbled and they must begin anew. Yet they had not given up. Every time it happened, they crawled back up again.

Her hand went to her stomach. Grimulf was not a complete fool. He remembered how sick she had been recently.

"You are with child?"

He almost asked if it was his. He held his tongue, but she must have seen the uncertainty in his eyes. Instead of fury, there was only weariness in her voice.

"I bled when we first joined. I came to you untouched. Do not even try to deny this child."

"I would not."

"It is my choice to be here, Grimulf. I have lost everything. My home. My family. My faith. What I promised still stands. I am a stranger here. My loyalty lies with you. Whatever path you take, I shall follow." She shut her eyes, pained. "I only ask for that same loyalty. We must keep one another alive. I do not even ask for love if you find yourself unable to give it."

Grimulf cupped her cheek, turning her head to kiss her brow. "You have my love. Not quite my trust, but I'll give you my heart. Forget this for now. Tomorrow will be a new day."

They lay there, watching the grey skies unravel into total darkness. Too tired to do anything else, their hands roamed aimlessly, mapping one another to memory rather than hunting for completion.

CHAPTER 7

The child was here now. Nothing could be done to ferry it off, not any method Grimulf would consider. When Rosa looked up with hopeful eyes, he caressed the growing swell of her belly softly as if cradling eggs.

The trials of carrying a child bore heavy on her, cheeks glazed with an ashen, nauseous hue. It had been the same with his mother when she had carried him, according to his brothers. Instead of weakening, Rosa stood taller. There was a glow about her, eyes flicking heavenwards as her hands pressed together in thanks.

While out hunting Grimulf found wild mint, setting a great bushel at her feet. The smile she gave made him look away, heat stirring in his chest. Somehow shy, even when they had traded kisses and touches. This was tenderness that lay outside the bed, which he was unfamiliar with.

No matter how many times she reassured Grimulf, he was reluctant to continue pursuing their pleasures. It was common sense to refrain, yet Rosa told him she felt an ache within when he was not close.

She did not complain about his gentleness when he did hold her. His fingers ghosted around her hardened nipples, tongue running words across the thrumming pulse in her throat. Their coupling akin to adding wood to the fire to keep it burning, rather than thrusting at the dying embers to spark anew.

No other knew about the child, kept hidden like one of his treasures. When her stomach became too noticeable, she wore long shawls knotted around herself.

"There, a kick," she whispered in his ear one evening before the fire.

Their fingers entwined. She placed his warm, heavy hand over the spot. He felt the strange sensation of something thrashing within.

"Such energy." Pride and joy made his voice almost breathless. He grinned. "A son, from the strength of him."

Later in bed, he watched Rosa sleep. She lay upon her back, mindful of her stomach, yet her head turned, her hand reaching for him, fingers curled.

He feared for them both. Yes, the child was strong, but where did that strength come from? Did it kick with a small human foot or scratch with a wolf's paw?

His trips to the smokehouse were shorter than they used to be. He returned to himself much sooner after his fits. Even Rudolf admitted he was improving, though warned him not to be complacent.

"You're enjoying yourself with your pretty wife, but you'll get restless again. It might be best if we returned to where it all began. You know I'll always watch over you."

Grimulf could not leave Rosa now. He had his wife and child, he must be their sword and shield. There was a peace about him he had never felt before. Perhaps the beast was pleased at proof of its virility.

The wet dew of spring dried into uncomfortable, muggy summer. It was with relief that the cooler nights of autumn came, leaves fading, veins white and stark as those upon a dying man.

Fields flourished, but the fishing nets were empty and cattle sickened. Pickled cabbage would not see them through the oncoming winter.

Grimulf vanished one evening, though not to the smokehouse. He returned with some of his strange jewels from the East and sent a man to go trading for hides and cured meats. Grimulf had Rosa visit houses, giving enough to see the village through.

Even the lands hereabouts seemed to be crumbling. Some boys playing upon the dunes had the very earth beneath them come apart, the marram grasses tumbling. Grimulf and the men had to dig them out or else they would have suffocated.

These were ill omens. Olaf had no explanation for them, save suggesting the lands were urging them to face the Lady of the Mercians.

The village's worries eased with the approach of Yule. Rosa watched the preparations gleefully.

"Wait until it is the day of the holly and ivy," Grimulf told her, amused. "Depending on which one crosses the threshold first, the man or woman rules the household the following year."

"I thought I would always rule here," Rosa teased, wrapped in Grimulf's cloak as they walked around the village.

Frost crunched beneath their shoes. There was the promise of snow, though the sea salt-tinged rains might dash it into sleet. Her lips were reddened from the cold. He kissed her to warm them up.

She might miss the festivities this year, for the child was due soon. Labour ferried a woman off just as the hightides did a man.

Another feast was held in the hall. This time Rosa saw it from within, rather than an interloper bursting in. She sat at the high table, slightly lower than Grimulf's raised throne. She had to keep stretching her arm to touch him, yet he interlocked their fingers whenever she needed reassuring.

Dogs dashed between tables, chased by flushed children. Travelling musicians were invited, the sound of lyres muffled by rough laughter and a woman trying to sing. Fires lurched within hearths and lapped at cooking pots, tickling the bellies of pigs upon spits. Smoke clotted the room, thickly spiced with bursts of ground mustard and cumin Grimulf's men had brought from their travels.

Nausea went through her in minute waves. Rosa felt Olaf's narrowed, predatory eyes upon her. All the joy of that night left her, cheeks paling. Her smile became smaller and smaller until only a thin line remained. She grasped her cup and drank quickly, thick mouthfuls gushing down her throat.

"Careful now," Grimulf bent low to murmur in her ear. "You are not used to the strength of this mead."

She managed a smile for him, and it was a challenging one. "I'll have you know the monks always let us sample their wines."

"No wonder you miss the nunnery, if all you did was make merry!"

"The mead hall is just the same as home," she joked. "Only your men are not as rowdy as the older nuns could be." Her heart twisted at the memory, knowing it was mere ash now.

"You forget, my sweet one."

"Forget what?"

"This is now your home. You must put aside all yearning for your life before."

She turned again for her cup but saw Olaf out of the corner of her eye. As if disgustingly bewitched, she looked at him fully.

Olaf had a chicken leg to his large, mottled lips, teeth dragging across the white flesh and suckling at it until the meat came free to disappear into his mouth. He grinned. It felt as if he bit into her.

The music had become too loud, stabbing into her ears. The heat of the fires felt like a ring tight around her neck. Rosa wiped her hands to try to rid herself of the grease on her fingers, only managing to smear it further.

If only she could leave! She had enough sense not to run. It would do her no good for people to believe Grimulf had tied himself to a frail creature unable to handle the rigours of the mead hall.

She would have to steel herself, be strong and keep steady until it was time for bed, then she could give in. Losing herself to Grimulf's caresses would ease her. This was her main discomfort: having him close but being unable to crawl into his arms and let herself relax.

Tonight, she keenly felt her child slowly knitting into life, as if it was also tense from nerves. To distract herself she picked at what remained on her trencher.

A nudging at her knee reminded her to drop scraps into Shuck's awaiting mouth, the dog's lips smacking together as he snatched the offering. Morgana lurked, high where the dogs could not bother her. The cat stiffened, then leapt with ferocious speed. When she clambered back, something huge and dark hung from her mouth.

Men sat at the tables below guzzling their mead. Snatches of their jokes reached her, creating a strange mishmash of anecdotes. Never mind Olaf. He was only one man. She was amongst friends and her husband. He could not get to her here.

Feeling slightly better, she reached for her drink. Another's hand came out, passing it to her.

"Careful now, lest you have another fainting fit and spill it everywhere," Olaf said belligerently, kindly smile sharply twisting his lined face.

Rosa put the cup to her lips but did not drink. He might

have done anything to it while she had been ignoring him. So much for making herself feel calmer. She would have to keep an eye on him.

Her hand drifted, going under the table to give her stomach a reassuring rub. She was joyous she was pregnant, but she could not keep her child tucked away forever. Rosa feared the labour, knowing what could go wrong. Even if she and the child survived, she would be involving them in this unsteady existence. What if Olaf harmed her child to get at her?

If he dared try to, it would not be Grimulf he need fear. She would make him suffer.

Fingers interwove with hers, squeezing gently. It did not come from Olaf's side, which was a relief.

Grimulf faced forward, watching his men to ensure none became too intoxicated. His hand had snuck over to hold hers. He turned her palm over, slipping her something small before letting go.

She waited until Olaf was distracted with grabbing a serving maid before examining what she had been given. Her eyebrows jerked in surprise, then knitted in confusion.

Grimulf's gift was a small piece of bone. It was brittle and bleached from age. There were symbols carved into the side: runes. Rosa had no clue what they meant.

Her nail dug into the indentations. Looking upon them, a beloved sensation thrummed. She smiled. Beauty could be found in what others thought disquieting and heathen.

The doors opened. A horse strode into the mead hall, the stallion black as dried blood. No storm heralded this arrival. The rider sat straight and regal, dark hair flowing behind and merging with her cloak. The reins were held aloft in her clenched, upturned hand.

Everyone heard one woman remark in disgust, "Not another bloody woman after our men." The horse's hooves echoed against the stone floor.

Rosa's heart hammered, because she hoped the rider might be one of the other sisters, who had survived and come to take her home. Yet where was her home now? Surely it had become something else.

When the woman's face shifted into focus, she did not recognise her. Tattoos pricked her cheeks. Rosa grimaced. She had thought Grimulf's markings painful, how strong must a person be to withstand them on their face? Her lips were red as blood, eyes hooded. It was as if wherever she stepped she belonged. She reminded Rosa of Morgana.

"Freyja has called me to your doorstep, Grimulf, son of Heimer," the woman declared, voice ringing in the hall.

She released the reins, crooking her hand to one of the guards who stood rigidly to the side. He approached and she swung her leg over to drop into his arms. He delicately caught her as one might a bird, afraid of the scratch of talons. Her arm curled around his neck, nails combing through his hair, then she was on the ground with her back to him, an instant dismissal.

Rosa looked to Grimulf. A muscle stood taut in his rigid jawline. She feared the little shards of peace she had been hoarding were about to tumble from her grasp.

She knew who Freyja was, but not this woman's relation to her. She said the Goddess had sent her, just as Rosa had lied and told them God had urged her on this path. Did that mean she was a priestess?

Grimulf gently nudged Rosa's hip, pushing a newly filled cup to her. Getting the hint, she took the drink and went around the table, offering it to the new arrival. She was the hostess and must be the one to welcome her.

The woman took the drink with a stiff jerk of her hand. The kohl around her eyes smeared at the corners, eyes watery from the pinch of the winds. It was the only sign of her humanity. The cup was drained in one go.

Grimulf stepped out of his chair. He indicated for the stranger to take his place.

"It is an honour to be visited by a prophetess. Please rest, eat, drink—"

"I am not here to celebrate. I come with a warning. A vision burns behind my eyes. All I ask for is the proper offerings and it will be told."

Rosa watched as the woman ascended the small steps, drifting around the table to sit in Rosa's seat. She stared ahead, a queen.

Grimulf called commands. Men went outside, there was the squeal of a creature in pain. When they returned it was with their arms streaked bright with blood, hands cupped around the... the... A knot formed in Rosa's stomach. They carried a pig's heart to the table and set it upon Rosa's trencher.

Rosa turned aside. She could not watch the woman eat it raw. Her sense of being tilted. Olaf eyed what the stranger was doing, brow furrowed with concern.

This must have something to do with him, Rosa reasoned wildly. Was it common Viking practice? Would Grimulf believe her if she suggested it was a ploy by his uncle?

A knife scraped the trencher. Rosa turned back. The only sign of what had happened was the petal like stain at the corner of the woman's mouth.

The stranger tipped her head, shutting her eyes. Mouth opening, mist steamed from her lips while all around her fires crackled and cast their orange hands upon the walls. When her eyes opened, the pupils were gone. Veins pulsed in the whites.

"I come with a warning, Grimulf. You have chosen the wrong path, turned your back on the Gods and Goddesses, and we are angered."

Her voice changed from a soft, lisping hiss to rasping fury dredged from the depths, shattering upon her ribs. Rosa embraced her stomach. She waited for the winds, lightning and thunder to burst in and carry her off. The drumbeat of her heart throbbed in her ears.

"The seas will not be calm and steady, they will rage and devour the lands you rule, until all that remains is the ruins of your people's homes. Gone will be your lands and your name. Your approaching child will sicken and take with it your wife."

People were rising now. Their voices roared all about. But Rosa realised with horror it was not to abuse the prophetess—they agreed with her.

Rosa trembled. Her nails dug into her arms, tiny pinpricks of pain the only true thing she felt in that moment. How had the woman known she was pregnant?

Grimulf, teeth gritted in a snarl, grasped the woman and dragged her from the chair. They knocked into the table, cups falling and splashing wine and mead. Trenchers tumbled with a leaden crash, scattering bones. Rosa made to follow, but could not quite manage, instead half-crouched, back pressed against the wall and mouth gaping.

"Divorce your Christian bride and renounce her God," the prophetess continued wildly. "That is the only way you can ensure your survival—and hers. Death awaits if she does not return to her own land. She will perish in a blood-soaked bed, with a child that will never draw breath!"

As the woman ranted, Rosa stared at her with wide, glassy eyes. Lips dry and slightly parted, feeling against them the flutter of her quickening breaths.

She knew her. It could not be, yet it was—Adelina. The thrall who had saved her from Olaf's tent. Now she stood with her hair turned black, markings painted to her face, and without her child. Afraid, Rosa put her hand over her stomach.

She tried to meet Adelina's eye, but the woman would not look at her.

It was another trick devised by Olaf. Would the man never stop? As she looked around at the men eagerly listening, their drinking horns half-raised, she knew it was working. Adelina told them what they wanted to hear.

Rosa choked. This was the consequence of holding her tongue. If she had been brave and admitted all to Grimulf, Olaf might have been banished. They could have searched for Adelina and she would be free rather than damning her.

What had happened to her desire to find her fellow novices? She had been too occupied with spinning lies to keep herself safe and loved, not wanting to break the unsteady peace she had salvaged.

Now it had led to this.

Grimulf dragged Adelina. Men tried to stop him, but he batted them away. He threw the woman out.

"I deny your prophecy!" Grimulf roared up, as though speaking to Freyja herself.

Olaf had arisen from his seat. Others did the same.

"She is a false prophetess," Grimulf called as he strode through the hall. Men moved closer, some coming from behind. "Sent to weave lies and divide us. My wife is a good, honest woman. I may not be my much-loved brothers, but I will be just as they were."

"And you might have been. Once," Olaf said.

Rosa clutched the bone shard tightly, the ragged edge biting into her palm. She was shaking from the sudden blast of cold. The long table and crowd were between her and Grimulf. Her heart started to pound. She needed to be next to him.

Olaf still spoke, though, and the men were closing in.

"I had hoped you would return a great man, just like your father. However, tonight I have proof you are nothing like Ragnar or Harald."

"You expect me to stand by and let my wife be abused?"

"The marriage is not valid," Olaf boomed. Rosa gripped

the table, the sea of faces before her blurring. "This witch has enchanted my nephew, turning him against us for her own evil plans for the Mercians."

"You speak as a Christian priest would," Grimulf snapped. "Ranting and raving. Hold your tongue."

"Nay, nephew. I must save you. I know of her foul deeds because I too was afflicted. Some months ago, I came upon her and she bewitched and wed me! Only the presence of one of Freyja's women helped me break free. Before, I was transfixed, caged inside my flesh, while she threatened to curse my seed and turn me from man to beast."

The bone clattered from Rosa's hand, her palm coated in her blood. Her heart had stopped beating, constricted in the base of her throat. The world around her was twisting and turning.

"I fear it is too far gone with my nephew," Olaf continued. "Think of your mauled livestock, the wild howling at night. Ivar had his throat torn out by him when he roamed as a wolf!"

"That is a lie!" Rosa shouted. "I watched him that night and he did not change." Desperately, she looked to Rudolf. "Rudolf knows. He was there. He saw."

Rudolf stood. He had something in his hands.

Olaf took it from him. Grimulf stiffened. His uncle held out for the crowd to see the chains Grimulf used to bind himself.

"These are the chains I shackled Grimulf with. I thought them strong enough," Rudolf said. "I was wrong. He tore through them and vanished, then poor Ivar was found the next day."

"No," Grimulf choked out.

They had grown up together, battled side by side. When

Grimulf had been haunted by the eyes of the first man he had killed, it had been Rudolf who offered his comfort and wisdom.

All this time his ally... his brother had been whispering his weaknesses into his enemy's ear. How long had he been lying to him? Rather than distant enemies or rivals, it had been his own blood conspiring against him. Rudolf might as well have thrust his spear in his chest; it cut him just as deeply.

A wolf had slaughtered animals. A man who had spoken against him had been attacked. All signs Grimulf could not be trusted. Grimulf knew the only blood he tasted on his tongue had been his own.

They would not believe him. Not when Rudolf stood with his uncle.

"My lord," one woman called, "where do you go on the night of the full moon?"

Grimulf's eyes were glazed. Teeth bared. He knew. The monster Rosa had been running from turned out to be his kin, now the betrayal was complete.

His uncle had known of the curse all this time, having Rudolf describe to Grimulf all sorts of gruesome transformations when truly he had lain unconscious. Lurking in the shadows, tormenting Rosa with his presence. Was that why she had kept silent about who her abductor was, because Olaf had threatened her?

Grimulf snarled, lunging for Olaf. Men leapt, holding their chieftain down. Olaf looked on in disgust.

"No better than a wild animal. I fear he is beyond saving. We must try, though. Bind him. I will take over his duties. The first thing I shall do is break this witch to see if there is a way of ridding this curse."

"Run, Rosa!" Grimulf roared.

It was too late. People fell against them like waves, dragging the couple further apart. Rosa knew she had to get away from Olaf. He would slit her throat given the chance.

She staggered through. Hands gripped at her clothes, her hair. One caught the key hanging from her necklace, tearing it from her. Grimulf's gift tumbled, lost amongst the straw.

Rosa fell to her knees, her cloak falling open, the shawls coming undone. Grimulf struck one man in the face with his elbow, knocking down another when his fist was free. Weapons were drawn. A blade pressed warningly to his stomach, another to his back.

Those from Grimulf's fellowship stood half-risen, surprise etched upon their faces, while those who had sided with Rudolf stopped them from aiding their master. And yet they charged, fighting off the guards with only their fists. Villagers surged against one another, fighting and arguing.

Someone dragged her by her hair. Rosa's teeth sank into their wrist. There was a high-pitched cry and she was struck about the face. All that mattered was keeping her stomach protected. To protect her child with her very bones.

Wide hands caught her, gently holding on even while she kicked out. He hefted Rosa above the heads of the men and women, out of reach of their grasping hands.

"I have the witch," Thorstein boomed. It was he who stood between her and the crowd. "But even I would not kill a witch quite clearly laden with child. Not when part of it is Dane."

Good, honest Thorstein made them pause. They eyed her stomach and began whispering.

"You heard the priestess. It is a cursed child," Olaf countered.

"Then we'll see when the child is born whether it has teeth and claws."

Rosa could see Grimulf pinned down by ten men.

Uselessly, she reached out as if she might touch him, even though they were on other sides of the hall.

"I say," Thorstein continued, "we have a trial. They will have another night as lord and lady, barred within their home. Then come tomorrow we find out what sort of creatures they are."

He had done all he could. They had one more night to live.

Gunhild did not appear when the door of the longhouse was forced open. Thorstein carried Rosa inside, Grimulf dragged along by the villagers.

"The old woman will be their jailer," Thorstein decided.

"I hardly think their own servant should be given the task," Olaf began, but was interrupted by Björn.

"Are you saying you do not trust my grandmother?"

"Gunhild was Heimer's servant for forty years and nursed all his children. She will want to ensure Grimulf is returned to how he was," Thorstein explained, the calm, rich timbre of his voice lulling everyone into obedience.

Olaf gritted his teeth, would have liked to argue, but he bowed his head. "The old woman will be our witness during the trial."

Rosa was thrown upon the bed where Morgana lay curled. The cat yowled, leaping and hissing. As Thorstein bound Rosa to the bedframe, the cat scratched him, leaving a ragged stripe along the length of his arm. He grimaced, though made no move to swat the cat away. It had once been his, but now it had other loyalties.

"I've always trusted the instincts of animals rather than men," he whispered in Rosa's ear as he bound the other wrist. "Do not fret. We'll find some way out of this for you."

"But what of Grimulf?"

"Does his flesh truly change?"

"He says it does," she answered truthfully. "I have never seen it."

"And are you a witch?"

"I am a nun!" She screwed shut her eyes, calmed herself or else the other men might come in. "My duty is to heal, not harm. Any talk of magic has come from your people."

"That's the trouble. You're not one of us. A thrall that is different is no matter, for it is soon beaten into submission, but there are many who are jealous of you."

There came a cry from the other side of the house, the banging crash of a chest being knocked over. "Thorstein!" Olaf roared. "Stop petting about the woman and hold down this beast. We need a place to put him."

"The lord shall go where he belongs—at the back with the other beasts!" someone called, followed by laughter and jeers.

"Wait," Rosa said, panicked. She had to warn Thorstein. "Olaf cannot be trusted. He has been lying to you all. Ragnar's death is down to him."

Then Thorstein was gone. The old man had not made her binds too tight, yet they were impossible to slip out of. She angled herself so she could eye Morgana, who remained arched and spitting.

"Can't you use your claws on these?" she whispered, the cat edging closer, though only to nuzzle her head and settle again. It would only be when her fish was not forthcoming would she begin to complain.

An ache spread through Rosa's back, frustrated she could do nothing while elsewhere Grimulf was treated no better than a wild dog. Outside, a battle raged. Grimulf's men might prevail and rescue their friend. However, there were too few and the people they fought would be fathers, brothers, perhaps even sons.

When silence descended, Rosa shut her eyes. More people dead or locked up, awaiting trial just like them.

What would such a trial entail? She knew how Christians dealt with witches: the fiery teeth of the bonfire or thrust into the frigid womb of the waters. And such trials were considered *civilised*. She trembled at what the Vikings had planned. Olaf would be sure to choose the cruellest method as payment for humiliating him.

She knew he hated her, but how could he turn on his family? He was worse than a viper. She prayed Olaf's involvement in Ragnar's death was not true. If he could easily rid himself of one nephew, then he would think nothing of disposing of Grimulf.

Why? Mad he might be, but he did have something to gain. As the last surviving member of the family, he would inherit the lands and riches. If Grimulf died, there would only be two obstacles.

Rosa and her child. Viking wives could inherit. Not even a daughter would be safe if she gave birth to a girl.

The door opened. Rosa tried to sit to see who came for her. She braced her feet upon the bed. Morgana tensed.

Olaf must have come for his revenge. It would be a quick, quiet death, before she had the chance to reveal his lies.

It was not the Viking. Gunhild crept inside, hand cupped over her lamp to hide its glow. Another also entered, concealed by a cloak.

"Please don't believe them," Rosa begged as the old woman approached. "Olaf lies. I am no witch. Grimulf is not a wolf-coat. He is only plagued by nightmares."

"Shush. I believe you." Gunhild set the lamp down, turning to the stranger. "Off with that. Hurry." To Rosa she said while the person disrobed, "Of course I wouldn't think ill of you. You saved my grandson. Men such as Olaf fear women like us, the ones willing to say no. I know what he is like. I knew it since he was a boy. He was always jealous of his brother."

The cloak dropped to pool on the floor, revealing the prostitute Rosa had helped. She started unlacing her dress.

"You're helping?"

"Thorstein offered me coin for this," the woman told her.

"What will happen if you are discovered?"

"I know how to vanish. All us women are witches. I'll turn into a crow and fly away!"

Rosa did not believe the bravery in the woman's words, but this was her only chance at survival. "What of Grimulf?"

"Thorstein plans to free him once you are safe," Gunhild explained. "He'll have to fight his way through, but he'll find you. Those loyal to your husband will prepare a ship at Gernemuth for your escape."

Gunhild cut her bonds and Rosa rolled out of the bed. Set upon the bench was a basket full of provisions from their stores and her dagger. She hugged the old woman, then the prostitute.

"Will you tell me your name now?"

"Nay, I'm Rosamund Thorne now. I like the thought of having such a grand name."

"If you get away from this, go to Wessex. I haven't seen my family in so long I'm certain my father would mistake you for his daughter."

The other Rosa smiled in the darkness. "I might just do that."

They changed into each other's clothes, Rosa pulling up the hood of the cloak. She grasped the basket, Gunhild taking her other side.

"You must walk from here to the beaches. A horse will be too noticeable."

They left the house. A warrior stood guard outside. Rosa's heart floundered in her chest, a tremor in her hands from their brazenness. She did not dare speak.

"The prisoner has been fed," Gunhild told him as she and Rosa walked past. "I'm taking my daughter home."

The man grunted. For a second, his eyes flicked over them. Rosa turned aside her face, but he must have seen.

"Safe journey, maid," was all he said.

Rosa let out a breath of relief. It made the pain in her

breast lessen to know there were some who did not despise her, who were loyal to her husband. What would become of them once she escaped?

She had her child to think of. She could do nothing for them.

Gunhild walked with her some of the way. As the torches became mere firefly flickers, she gave her one last reassuring embrace.

"Come with us," Rosa whispered.

The old woman shook her head. "My family are here."

Rosa could not waste their sacrifice on her terror. She had to keep going. Rosa charged on ahead, getting further from the light, darkness her only companion. She could weep as she walked, though. Hot, wet trails tracked down her cheeks. Her face burned. Sobs merged with the noises of the night, owls hooting as they settled in their nests.

She had lost another home. Would she ever find a place to settle? This was not the life her family had planned for her. God had truly abandoned her.

She hid beneath a sand shelf, crouched tight. Her hands clasped together. She did not know who she prayed to, only that she needed Grimulf to come find her.

Grimulf started from where he crouched amongst the pigs. Someone had rapped against the back wall. He put his ear to the spot, where a small gap was.

Thorstein whispered, "She is gone. Be ready for your own departure."

"My men?"

"They are ready."

"And you?"

Silence. Then Thorstein answered, "I stand or fall here."

"I will see you in Valhalla someday."

Grimulf's hands curled into fists, body hunched in readiness. It reminded him too much of an animal cornered.

Olaf might be right, he was cursed, but none of this was Rosa's fault. He would use all at his disposal—his sword, strength, *teeth*—to keep her and the child alive. His enemies would soon learn not to threaten a wolf's pack.

The rain-like hiss of flames grew nearer. Swords crashed. He shut his eyes, drew in a breath. He saw the flames of the invocation fire when he had called for the berserker within.

Why not kill those who had betrayed him? He hungered to see terror on his friend's face. Rudolf should know not to anger him. He would have Olaf's head on a pike. Then Rosa could return, safe to give birth to their child. They would reign over the corpses of their enemies.

The human side of him knew this must never be. Life could not go on with him slaughtering everyone who stood in his way. He understood this now, just as his brothers had already known.

The guard stationed at the byre unsheathed his weapon, shouting a warning. The crunch of breaking bones came, then a hammer ploughed through the door. Grimulf leapt free from his prison. One of his men thrust his sword into his hands.

"Go now," Grimulf commanded. What mattered was their survival. A new life could be found overseas.

They split up, the man diving into the flames. There were houses on fire, the shadowy outline of corpses. He had never wanted the destruction of his youth to follow him here. These were meant to be his people.

Beyond the veil, did his brothers look on with shame?

Grimulf hurried through the village, not stopping to fight. He did not want to slaughter farmers who only knew how to wield a scythe. His eyes roved for another. If Olaf came to him in that moment, he would rid the snake of its head. The traitor's luck held.

Flames roared. A horse stormed through, the white stallion Rosa had arrived on. Grimulf snatched the reins and heaved himself atop, riding towards the dark blue horizon of the sea. His steady grip and the soothing rhythm of his voice swayed the beast into obeying.

A burst of pain struck his side. Grimulf slammed his hand down, expecting flames to put out. He knocked against the arrow jutting there, sending the head in deeper. He grunted, clutched the arrow and in one fluid motion tore it free, tossing it to the grasses. Blood poured, splashing his leg and the horse's side, staining the beautiful white flesh.

Grimulf looked over his shoulder, sweat streaming into his eyes. The village blurred. A figure stood on the roof of the hall, bow half raised. A mocking gesture of farewell was made. The fox bidding the hare to run.

***

The seas had bitten deep into the sands. Great shelves were carved along the coast. Discoloured, wet lumps of seaweed coated the humped backs. Waves swept over.

There was an overturned crab where Rosa crouched. She thought it dead, dashed on the stones. All the lands around here had lost their vitality. Then she saw the faint twitch of its legs. It was pretending to be dead in the hopes she would ignore it.

Rosa curled in on herself. Her face buried into her knees.

There was nowhere she could run to. If she climbed out, Olaf's men might see her; the land was endless and flat. Her fists shook, nails sinking into the flesh of her palms.

Horses pounded past. Sand juddered free from the shelf, coating her hair. None stopped. The hoofbeats became quieter. Panting, Rosa hesitatingly peered over the edge. The beach was empty, only a vague flicker of shadows in the distance.

The cold carded its fingers through her hair, flipping the loose strands. Rosa righted the crab. When nothing else disturbed it, it scuttled home.

She struggled to her feet, cradling her stomach as she teetered. The stretch of beach seemed as endless as eternity.

"We can do this," she whispered, determined. "We planned to walk this far before."

Something stampeded down the dunes from the village. A white horse. Rosa made to crouch down, but it was too late. The person cried her name. Relief flooded her.

"Grimulf!" she sobbed, scrambling over the shelf. He flung himself from the horse to meet her, heaving her into his arms and carrying her over.

"There is no time. Quickly, let us be away."

Rosa clung to his waist once Grimulf climbed atop. Her leg brushed against the wet slick of the horse's side.

"He's wounded?"

"No, he isn't."

Rosa blindly groped at Grimulf. He sucked in a breath as she caught the arrow wound.

"There's too much blood." Rosa pulled at her skirt to tear off a strip. "I have to stop the bleeding—"

"No time," he pushed out. "Later."

The waves were tilting and spilling into the sky like an hourglass. He kicked off and the horse bolted across the sands. Rosa's hand pressed over the wound, stemming the waste of his precious life's blood.

His eyes streamed from the winds, whipping hair flaying his cheeks. Rosa hid her face, clinging to him desperately. She might have reason to.

"Olaf," Grimulf shouted over the snarl of the elements. She started, looking back. They had yet to be chased. "All this time and it was him."

She could pretend not to hear him, she was struggling to, but this conversation would be waiting for her. Better to have this over with. Then they could see where their loyalties lie.

"It was he who sacked the nunnery. He came to us as a pilgrim. I was welcoming, as we are with all our visitors. He... I only knew what he wanted when he kidnapped me. Everything I spoke of was the truth."

"If I'd known, I'd have severed his head from his neck."

"Then none of this would have happened." This was her fault. If she had warned him, Olaf would have been chased out before he could turn everyone against them. "I did not know if I would be believed."

His hand came over hers, squeezing. Their fingers were drenched in his blood.

"I would have listened, but I might not have wanted to believe. He is my uncle. *How could he?*" He snarled something in his mother tongue. "I'll stop him, Rosa, I swear. We'll get you home. Our child will be safe."

She kissed him between his shoulder blades. "I believe you."

The hunting dogs caught their scent a half mile from the village, as they left the beach for firmer ground. They hadn't dared stop to bind Grimulf's wound. Rosa's fingers were scarlet. Hopelessly she clung tighter, as though she could stopper his life and keep it for herself.

The stallion was like a streak of lightning passing through the night, the dogs rainwater slithering down the hill. Water arced around them as the horse's hooves glanced over the river. Grimulf urged him onwards, voice rough even as he tried to soothe. Once they were over, they would have a better chance of survival.

The horse surged through, water lapping at his chest. Fangs sunk into Rosa's cloak. She screeched as a dog tore her from her seat. Grimulf lunged, catching her in his arms before she hit the river. He took the brunt, stones jabbing into his side, icy waters engulfing him.

He reared to the surface, holding Rosa aloft while she curled over her stomach. The dog thrashed, clawing itself back onto the riverbank. The rest of the hunting pack paced, barking, snapping at the air.

Grimulf strode through, a bloom of red trailing in the water. He grasped the horse's reins, pushing Rosa onto the saddle. Arrows shot past, just slightly higher than their heads.

Grimulf heaved himself behind her. Panting heavily, he slumped forward, unable to remain steady and to cover her in case more arrows flew down. Rosa cried out, holding on. The horse darted across, hooves slopping through the muddy bank as he forced himself free.

The hunters rode after them. Water sprayed in the air.

Rosa clung to the horse's neck, angling him towards woodland. Branches scraped her cheeks, leaves wet and damp, catching in her hair. Grimulf's heat enveloped her, but she could not be certain if he breathed.

They burst out of the dense overgrowth, riding over dunes and down until they were hidden. For the moment. The lands about here were almost flat, it meant their enemies would always know which direction they took. But she had to stop Grimulf's bleeding.

Grimulf clasped her, voice unsteady, as he pointed to a slightly raised mound.

"There. A barrow."

He was leaning away. His side, suckered to her hand, slowly peeled free.

"Grimulf!" She clutched him to keep him upright.

He was too heavy, dragging them both off. He cushioned her fall. She cradled his head, feeling for his pulse. They could go no further. They must hide themselves as mice did and wait for the cats to pass them by.

Rosa led the horse along the path. "Thank you. You've helped me so many times."

She kissed the creature's nose. She could only hope he would be found by kindly travellers.

She struck the horse's flank with the flat of her hand. Shrieking, he reared, bolting along the beach. The white mane became a tiny flicker in the distance, swallowed up by darkness.

Heaving Grimulf's arm over her shoulder, she dragged them into the fringed maw of the barrow.

———

Rosa peered from their hiding place, terrified she would see the hunting party charging for them. The boom of the horn came.

Terror paled her face. She went still, as a hare might when it knew its scent had been caught. She remembered those dogs well. When she had been trapped in that monster's tent, they had circled her, nudging and herding a trembling lamb. This time, they were on the hunt. Not even the promise of a morsel would make them disobey their master's orders.

Shudders wracked through Rosa. She was soaking wet. There would be no chance of running, not with every squelching step of her boots an effort. Part of her hoped their fall in the river had weakened their scent, but she wasn't about to risk their lives on hope.

The desperation to run thrummed. She looked down at the man in her arms, her husband, and knew she could never abandon him. Olaf would frighten her no more. Tonight, she must make a stand and protect what she loved. Just as Grimulf kept her safe, it was her turn to be their shield.

The moon was a bright, broken shard in the cloudless night sky. None of the stars were there. Trees buffeted this

194

way and that, and she could almost picture the talon-like fingers of the winds twisting them as a cruel child might.

Shadows crawled over, the water drenching her becoming colder, heavier. All she desired was the warmth of a fire, but she must hold out.

She scrabbled in her basket and found smoked herrings, red and glistening. Checking they were potent enough, Rosa sniffed them. Brine dampened the tip of her nose and oak wood whooshed into her lungs. She spluttered, the normally comforting scent overwhelming. Hopefully it would overpower the wolfhounds as well.

Now she had to be daring. Rosa emerged from the barrow, hunched in her sodden cloak. Wet grasses slithered over her bare ankles as she hurried to where they had fallen earlier. Where their footprints were, she scuffed earth and smeared the herrings. The fishes' crushed bodies and askew scales sent out another burst of strong scent.

Constantly, she checked over her shoulder, fearful she might be caught in the last minute. She went to where the path slid down the small hill, leading to the beaches. There were rocks, which she crushed most of the herrings beneath. Then she threw the final fish into the dark depths, lost amongst the undergrowth.

Lights flickered between the trees. Rosa ran to the barrow. There she hid, crouched before Grimulf.

The dogs arrived first. They swarmed the fields, heads bent, noses dragging over the ground. Their fur so black they were like liquid darkness spilling past. Their eyes glowed yellows and oranges, catching the firelights of the torches the hunters carried.

Rosa could not look, for she feared the impression of her shaking gaze might be felt by those she watched. Instead, she turned, burying herself into Grimulf's arms. His heat burned into her, but there was no response. Unconsciousness claimed him.

She heard scraping footsteps and claws, the heavy panting of dogs, and she imagined bright red tongues lolling. A rough, short growl. Then the dogs were bounding, barking wildly, not to the barrow but down the path she had smeared in the scent of red herrings. The hunters chased after them, crying out foul encouragements, excited at the thought of catching the hated Grimulf and his beautiful Christian wife.

She nuzzled into Grimulf's chest, for comfort and in another desperate attempt to hear his heartbeat. What if everything she had done was for naught? Her husband might have perished and she would be alone again. Bitter tears stung her eyes. She could not bear such a life any longer.

It might have been minutes or even longer, time had lost all meaning. A thud vibrated against her ear. Her own heart quickened as she registered the slow, weakened pulse. Grimulf was still on this mortal plane. God, either his or hers, had not stolen him from her. Yet.

The night would be long. She herself teetered between faintness and wakefulness. They would have to recover themselves until morning.

Rosa glanced around her. She rubbed her arms, rounded belly going taut.

Barrows were sacred places. It was where the people who were not Viking but a far older race were laid to rest with their magic and artefacts. To save her family, she had risked the wrath of spirits.

"It is only pagan nonsense," she tried telling herself, voice hollow as wispy candle smoke. "God is by my side. He will protect us."

Many of her prayers went unanswered since Olaf stole her. It had been her own wit and lies, and the protection of Grimulf, that had ensured her survival. In this land, something wilder commanded this domain rather than her God. It was better to be cautious.

Rosa clasped her hands. "We mean no harm," she

whispered, the words thrumming in her throat. "Let us remain until sunrise, then we will depart. Please, keep us hidden from our enemies."

There must be a sacrifice, she reasoned. The epics Grimulf had told her while they lay entangled in bed had always featured an offering.

Deeper in the barrow there was a fluttery, hissing sound. The wind she thought at first, sneaking in with them. It roared outside. However, no breezes slithered over her shoulders. Only the whispers. There were words she recognised, muttered in the darkness, but she would not acknowledge them.

Rosa removed her knife. She took her hair, which dripped water at the ends. After slicing it, she braided the cut locks and left the braid upon a shelf-like alcove. A spider slowly approached, then began weaving its home around the offering.

Now she must tend to herself. Shivering, she heaved off her dress. There was a mound of broken twigs dragged in by past creatures, which she hesitated over before giving in and striking a flame with her flints. She left her clothes nearby the meagre fire. Steam arose.

Shadows curled around her nakedness. Sweat peppered Grimulf's face, yet he shivered. She put her hand to his cheek, knowing with dread a fever had begun to set in. Her brothers, brave and strong and undefeatable in battle, had been taken easily as a child might by such a fever. She would not let it ferry off her husband as well.

Rosa stripped him of his chainmail and trousers, they too were set before the fire. His cloak was only wet on the outside. She cocooned them beneath it, resting her head under Grimulf's chin. She rose slightly at the movement of his breathing, then slowly came back down. Her cheek settled upon the fluttering pulse in his throat.

She felt a faint stir as their bodies pressed together, her

flesh remembering the other times they had held one another in this way. If only they were in bed, soft and happy, without the threat of dogs biting at their heels. Exhaustion dampered her desire. She cupped her stomach, thumb rubbing where she thought the child slept.

She needed to rest but could not. Every noise, whether it was the whistle like shriek of an owl or the boom of crashing waves, had her starting awake just before she succumbed. She could not believe her plan worked, she kept on expecting the hunters to return and rip them from their hiding place.

Rosa kissed Grimulf, patting away the sweat on his brow. "Let me see your eyes," she whispered, then settled. Her fingers curled in the hair of his chest.

Softly, she recounted the story of David and Goliath. It was a tale her wet nurse had often told her, which she had loved as a child. Her eyes were half-shut, words drowsy. Perhaps she could pretend they were home and this time it was her turn to tell the adventures she knew.

CHAPTER 8

Grimulf stirred. He shifted, registering the soft weight of a woman atop him. Interest stirred at the drag of her heavy breasts against his chest. There was an answering thrust, clumsy from sleepiness.

Then his body fully regained its senses, all its aches and pains. By the Gods, he felt as if he had been dragged behind a herd of horses. He grimaced, scraping a hand over his clammy forehead.

Instead of disgust, lips pecked his face, settling on his mouth to suckle it open and get hold of his tongue. In between came the breathy exclamation of, "Grimulf!" A rocking motion began between them, his member fully alert to her attentions.

Grimulf cupped her buttocks, squeezing the roundness of them. "Rosa," he groaned. He broke their kiss to lick a stripe up her throat. "Where are we, sweetling?"

This was no room, but somewhere close and dark with a heady, earthy smell. They might be caught in the mouth of a giant. Rosa did not answer. He did not ask again, too busy angling himself so in the next thrust he entered her. He wanted to roll them, smother her entirely in his bulk as she loved, but he was mindful of the child and lack of room.

His body burned hot even while he shivered. Her heat distracted him. He concentrated on her body, her gasps of pleasure and the way her muscles tightened as he stroked her.

Soon enough, they lay limp and sated. His fingers carded through her hair and paused.

"Your hair..."

She yawned, nestling closer. Her answer was half-hearted, as though she had done something quite normal.

"It was an offering for the spirits to leave us be."

Now he realised where they were. The barrow. Shards of daylight crawled in. The fire had completely gone out.

Grimulf wanted to see what waited out there. Rosa dug her fingers into his bicep.

Eyes still shut, she said, "We lost them in the night. Let me rest, my love. I have been on guard all this time."

"Very well." His nail traced the shell of her ear and she shuddered from the ticklish sensation. "Offering yourself up to spirits? What would your God say to that?"

"He'd think me sensible. Willing to adapt."

"Best be careful or it won't be you making me a Christian, but me turning you into a pagan."

She smiled faintly. He kissed her forehead, soothed by the sound of her gentle breathing.

They must conserve their energy. Olaf would think he had chased them out like a pair of rats. Let him believe that. His uncle would pay for his betrayal.

As soon as the sun emerged, it was quickly embraced by the dull metallic sheen of the sky. Misty clouds seemed pinched, as if about to unravel.

They emerged from the barrow. Quickly they dressed. Rosa let out a soft grunt of exhaustion without meaning to. Grimulf took her arm.

"Slowly," he told her, "but we cannot pause. My men will

not set sail until I arrive or they have word I am dead. We can make a new home in Denmark, Rosa."

History was repeating itself: his father settled in East Anglia after the Jarl he served, who had lusted for Grimulf's mother, attempted to kill them. He had never been to his father's homeland, preferring to go to the unknown, thinking he had no need to see the mighty fjords or rainbow dragons in the skies, as they already ran in his veins.

Now, his blood called him home. That place was no longer here. Perhaps it had never been. A hollowness settled in his chest, finally understanding what Rosa must have suffered. He held her tighter.

Homes could crumble or be stolen. It might be better to place such a concept at the feet of another for, so long as the woman stayed true, home would always be at her side.

They knew the day would be short, but it surprised them how quickly dusky red spilled across the sky. Like a stray ember, it blew out and night descended.

They had walked miles, yet the landscape barely changed. Only the sun moved, racing ahead. The proof of their progress were the tremors running through Rosa's legs, the lurch in Grimulf's cheek from his gritted teeth, and the dirt clinging to their boots.

Rosa could do little with Grimulf's wound, cramped and coated in the darkness of the barrow. She had bound his side with cleaner strips of her skirt, tightly jerking at the bandages to close the wound. As she eyed it, she saw the bright gash of blood had dried, no longer warningly shimmering with wet. A flush coated his face, fever creeping in his bones.

He seemed driven, she thought, able to transcend the wants of his body. Just as he must have done as a berserker. She only hoped it did not stir his wolf's hunger for violence.

Clouds parted their fingers. Shining through were shards of pale, beautiful moonlight. Rosa tilted her head, relieved some light kept the path clear before them. The faint rain shower had begun to lessen, leaving a heaviness which kissed damp imprints upon their cheeks.

Then more clouds pulled away. It was not a sickle or half-moon, not even the near closed eye of a waxing crescent. Misty halos ringed the faint orb. The full moon was coming.

Grimulf stared in horror. They had been running for so long they had lost track of the moon cycle.

"Rosa, bind me, quickly!"

"We cannot stop," she argued, while he removed his belt and thrust it towards her. "Olaf still chases us."

"I can at least slow them down."

He held out his hands, going on his knees and gazing at her imploringly. It frightened her, seeing him afraid. Afraid for her. Gently she bound his wrists together.

"Harder," he begged through gritted teeth. She wanted to disobey but pulled the belt tight until the flesh beneath reddened.

He lay there on the ground, on his side, and watched her. Sweat marred his forehead, cool winds tugging the collar of his cloak. His pupils bulged, wild and distorted. Animal.

"Run," the word did not come as strongly, the faintest of wheezes. He mouthed the word at her. "Run, Rosa."

Rosa's skirt blew in the winds, hair clinging to her face from the rain tangled there. Olaf would stop to claim Grimulf. She could escape and vanish in the night, then none of these men would be able to find her.

The child twisted within. She would never abandon Grimulf. It would be akin to tearing a shard of bone out, leaving behind the gaping wound to bleed and fester.

Her eyes were wet as she stared at him, helpless, and it had been her who had put him in this state. He faced the blackened grasses. Grimulf's lips twisted, dry cracks splitting anew, blood droplets shimmering over his mouth. His teeth gritted, shadows making them appear sharper, larger, as though pulling free of the gums to elongate and curve.

She knew this could not be true. She had felt his lips upon her flesh, his gentle, scraping caressing bites to claim her. Not once had he broken the skin. His teeth had been the same as hers.

Grimulf clawed at his bonds, gnawing at them. Snarls issued from his lips, brutal and nothing like the man she knew and loved. She wavered over him as one would over a rabid animal, knowing it was trapped yet afraid it might break free. The moon pulsed above her shoulder. When he looked up he squinted, as if unable to withstand its faint glow.

There had once been an exorcism in the nunnery. A woman, who had been running from her husband, had fallen about with fits, saying she was cursed because she had allowed her child to perish. One of the older sisters had prayed with her. Then the next morning she was cured.

Rosa did not know if there was a true incantation that brought God to scoop out evil within a person. Everyone had been barred from entering the room, but Rosa had crouched by the door, wanting to see if a miracle would occur.

Prayer beads had clicked in a slow, rhythmic beat. What the two women whispered between them had been reassurance. The elder sister had told the young woman none of it had been her fault, there was no curse, and God's love would not allow her to be stricken.

Rosa knelt, the moon hovering over her head. She held out her hand, shaking slightly.

"Grimulf."

His eye focused upon her, the white cracked with red veins. Hair matted over his forehead and cheeks, yet it was only his hair, no fur sprouted free.

"You were a wild creature when the priest spoke those words. You fought, drank, intoxicated yourself into a frenzy."

She wondered what exactly he had imbibed as a berserker and whether it continued to affect him. "The curse worked, did it not? You are no longer a monster, you do not fight for the hunger of it. You came home to become a man again and I found you just when I needed a good, honest man to keep me safe."

She lifted her hands, as though cupping the moon. The gentle glow spread across her fingers. Her hands clasped together. She bowed her head.

"God will forgive you. He has seen how hard you fought and been betrayed for your goodness. He would not leave you to suffer when this child and I need you to be strong."

The prayer was a simple one. Grimulf watched avidly.

Rosa's fingers carded through his hair, stroking it from his face. She brushed his cheeks, put a cool, soothing hand to his forehead. Once or twice, he made to avoid her touch, but then gave up and slumped.

"This moonlight can no longer poison you. With each stroke, your affliction will be taken."

The enlarged pupils receded, small and watery. His all too human eyes gazed at her, weary but familiar.

She could not bear to see him bound any longer. As he had convulsed, she feared he would break or dislocate something. She knew he had done so in the past, while sailing here and under Rudolf's treacherous care. She tore at the bindings until the knots came undone.

"You should not—I am still—"

"You will not harm me," she said softly.

"You are a foolish woman," he muttered.

"I am an honest and a brave one."

"Aye, and a loving one."

Rosa sat with him, her cloak wrapped around them both to keep warm. Slowly, he dragged himself onto his hands and knees. He needed rest, but they knew they should not have stopped for even this.

They must be close to Grimulf's ship. Their progress was halted, though. Any sounds that weren't the scraping croaks of fen-nightingales or the rushing sweep of waves meant ducking into the undergrowth. Sometimes Rosa caught sight of large shapes draped over the sands, resembling bloated corpses.

"Seals," Grimulf murmured in her ear. They gave these creatures a wide berth even though they simply lay there, lazily flapping their fins.

Rosa cradled her stomach, body swaying from the weight. Grimulf seemed to hear strange noises and make them hide whenever her exhaustion became too much. She did not want to be the one slowing them down.

There was a pain Rosa dared not voice. Too afraid admitting it would make what she feared come true. It was not a sharp ache but a scrabbling sensation, an urge to exhale even though she felt pinched and stiff.

Then Rosa saw in the sky the jutting point of a church tower. It might have been a shadow passing over her eyes, but she excitedly grasped at Grimulf.

"I know this place." Relief made her voice high. Her pointing hand trembled, buffeted by the winds tugging at her hair and cloak. "We're safe. We're finally safe."

"You are, my dear, and for that I am glad."

She was already running ahead, finding a break in the dunes. Grimulf heaved her until they were able to clamber onto land, sand scuffing from their shoes.

The church stones were made of local flint, glistening wet from rain. The thatch roof was discoloured, birds huddled beneath marsh reeds to keep out of the cold. Ivy had been left to crawl and burrow into the tower, as if it was a chain keeping it anchored there. An archway stood over the door, draping shadows over where they must enter.

No lights were on. It was as though the church slept,

turning its back on the terrible things that happened at night.

When Rosa looked upon it, all she saw was home. Grimulf thought it another trap.

"Those men betrayed you," she said. "You cannot think of them as family anymore."

"I am not welcome here. I am a pagan."

"You will... You will convert. That is why we are here. To pray and find somewhere to bed down. You are my husband."

And that was the issue. Rosa had married a pagan. She might believe she had him on the road to Christianity, but the men inside would think differently. They would welcome them at first, then they would notice in the candlelight Grimulf's tattoos, the sword at his belt and his blood-red hair. They would know him for what he was.

His people ransacked churches. In Grimulf's memory, he had the blood of priests buried beneath his fingernails.

They would think he had stolen Rosa and would try to take her from him. Or else they would castigate her and then she would be exiled when Grimulf could offer her no home or safety, only a hare's death.

Rosa clung to him. She saw past what made them different. Surely, these priests would welcome converts. The rain drummed harder against the sands.

"Let's go inside, then," Grimulf relented, "before you're completely soaked."

The door's iron handle was stiff. Rosa tugged at it. Grimulf had to lean over and twist it himself. The door groaned as they dragged it open.

Leaves blown in crunched under their feet, papery and like ash. Grimulf stood in the doorway, faint traces of moonlight entering as Rosa ventured further in. Her nose crinkled, sniffing the air, hunting for the faintest traces of proof there was some sort of life here.

"Is it abandoned?" Grimulf wondered.

"It can't be. I was here before the nunnery burned. There

were men here..." She trailed off, horrified.

What if Olaf had ransacked this place as well? But the thatch remained. She passed a table and saw a golden goblet. No thieves had come.

At the centre, before the stained-glass window, was the altar and its cross, the intricate detailing lost to the shadows. It had been an age since she had seen an altar. All she had was the fires and the tree the Danes prayed to. She went to it as one would an unknown animal. She did not kneel, instead standing there as if waiting for it to snap at her.

Once, she had thought these holy symbols beautiful and sacred. As she looked at this one, the golden gleam seemed dulled. It was a mere trinket. It was no more or no less important than what the Vikings used in their prayers.

There was no horror at this thought, only a tiny tremor in her breast. Rosa truly had left behind the woman she once was. She had changed and was uncertain whether it had been for the better. She was certainly stronger now.

"I came back," she whispered, but knew there was no welcome here.

She had done what was needed to survive, if that meant she was damned then so be it. Her child and husband were her life now.

"Come in, Grimulf, no bolt of lightning will strike you down." A wry smile. "From God or Thor's Hammer."

Footsteps came towards her. His warm, heavy hand reassuringly pressed upon her shoulder. She leaned into it.

"You must have missed the peace of this place a great deal."

Somehow, he understood when she had never voiced these thoughts before. "And yet I find it is not as much as I feared I would."

The doors leading to the antechamber opened. A priest appeared, Edward Briar, who she had met when she last visited here. He clutched a candle rigidly, the light flickering over his narrowed eyes. Another priest, one she was not familiar with, peered in from around the doorway.

Briar glanced from Rosa's heavy stomach to the sword at Grimulf's side. "We do not have much here. There is very little to steal."

"We are not thieves!" Rosa exclaimed. "Do you not recognise me?" She thought he might have done, there was a light in his eye. "Rosamund Thorne," she answered for him. "I was a n... I came here some time ago. You once told me you welcomed all under your roof who needed shelter. My husband and I need your help."

"He is a northman. A marauder. A plunderer."

"I am not a Viking," Grimulf said quietly, but from the way Briar flinched the soft rumble might as well have been a boom. "I am an explorer."

"Is that not the same?"

Lightning flashed over the rudimentary stained glass. Rainwater sliding down made it appear as if tears wept.

"I am a Christian woman," Rosa explained. "My husband is Danish, but he wishes to convert. Others that are his kin were against this and they have chased us over these dunes. All we need is somewhere to rest for one night."

Pleas were on her tongue as well, but they shrivelled into an intake of breath at the sneer twisting the priest's face.

"A husband does not convert. It is the wife who takes on the man's faith, even if it is heathen."

"That does not have to be the case—"

"Who says you are husband and wife?" Briar interrupted. "He is no Christian yet. A church would not wed you. So, it must have been a pagan mating. Certainly not one ordained by God. Especially if you are already wed to a higher cause."

He had recognised her! Rosa gritted her teeth. "We are asking for sanctuary. Is that not enough?"

"We do not accept heathen whores who have lain with beasts and carry their diseased seed!"

Grimulf snarled, moving protectively before Rosa, fingers curled around the handle of his sword. The priests flinched, but Grimulf did not unsheathe his weapon. Candlelight illuminated the grim satisfaction on Briar's face.

"Just as I suspected. Nothing can convert a pagan to the true way. It is only a mask of our faith that might be set upon their faces, easily dashed aside. You will have to slaughter us for our bread and water, but we will become martyrs even while your kind burns in the flames."

"I am an honourable man," Grimulf breathed. "All I want is for my wife and child to be safe. I would go out there, if it meant you would take her in, but I see from your words you would not be the type of man I would trust with a woman. I pity you, for you are worthless if you cannot do what your own God commands."

He went to the door, Rosa following. "You disgust me," was all she managed. She wanted to open her mouth and let her anger spill out and drown them. This was what she feared: rejection if she ever returned.

She thought her heart might break, her soul blackening as the doors shut behind them. All her life she had only known the kindness and pure light of the nunnery. The moment she had strayed, she was given not understanding and redemption but condemnation.

More than rain fell over her upturned face. Grimulf's breathing was ragged, head bowed. His hair twisted together, becoming waterlogged, the colour of his beard almost black.

"What will become of you if I am dead?"

Rosa leaned against his arm. She stroked the tattoo on his wrist, of the eel entwined with seaweed.

"I won't let you leave me alone. We'll get through this."

There would be little time for sleep when that was all their aching bodies wanted. They must find shelter. Rosa did not want to falter and be weak. She could keep going, just as she had always done.

Then Grimulf carefully heaved her into his arms, mindful of their child.

"But—"

"Rest. I've carried heavier loads than you."

She tucked her face into his neck, knowing he was right. There would be plenty more miles for her to walk later.

"Just for a short time. Promise to wake me."

"Oh, I promise."

"You have your fingers crossed, don't you?"

"Must I answer?"

Finally, they were laughing, near broken and half-exhausted, but at least there was laughter.

Rain continued to fall. Rosa's face twitched from the flurry of their many kisses, even as she floated in hazy darkness, gently rocked back and forth. Icy cold trails ran down her cheeks, tiny pools settling on her lips.

Grimulf unclipped the brooch keeping his cloak together and lifted it over their heads, able to hold her with one hand tucked beneath her. She made a soft sigh of relief but did not fully stir. The moon was high above them, full with the waters. The ground had turned claggy, his boots slurping free only to sink again.

Some time had passed since they had been ousted from the church. Rosa had promised there was another place of worship, there might be hope of sanctuary there. Grimulf doubted this to be true, yet there was no other course of action. He walked, knowing it was hopeless.

He had disobeyed her. She would be furious to know he kept her asleep. Yet the weight of her mattered little. At least he could keep her close and safe and warm. It might be the last time he would be able to. Greedily, he clung to this moment.

Once they reached another church, he would not enter. Her safety was paramount, even if it meant breaking all ties. She would weep, deny it bitterly, but they both knew she had a better chance of being taken in if they thought her a widow rather than a Viking bride. They would never see Denmark together.

He thought he saw the flicker of lights in the distance, perhaps the candles of a church in prayer, but did not speed up. He did not want to jostle and rouse her nor shorten his time with her.

If she remained asleep, he would set her upon the ground and go. Then she would be forced to enter the church alone. No matter her promises to follow him, she had their child to consider.

And then? All that he cared for would be out of reach. He would have nothing left. Olaf, his traitorous uncle, could not be allowed to get away with what he had done. His village might be behind his uncle, yet Grimulf would get the older man. He could not risk Rosa or the child, for allowing Olaf to continue breathing meant they would still be under threat.

Grimulf paused, peering at his wife's slack face. Her eyelashes fanned out across her cheek, a strand of damp hair curled around her slender throat. She seemed as gentle as a doe, yet he had seen her wielding shield and blade, withstood sights a warrior would baulk at. She was more than what she appeared, just as the moon hid her mysteries within her ethereal halo.

It had been curiosity and loneliness that had made him tie himself to this woman. He thought they could at least tolerate one another, perhaps grow to love once they were grey and scarred. Never had he expected such a powerful adoration. It made him both weak and strong. It was more addicting than any of the fires he had worshipped.

There were many ways it could have ended, he was

thankful for what they had shared. She would have his child. There would always be that to bind them together.

Grimulf knelt, unbuckling his cloak completely to lay it on the ground and protect her from the drenched grasses. He stilled. Held his breath.

Under the pound of the rains, he heard the stamp of horses' hooves. Too many to be travellers in search of shelter.

"Goodbye, my love."

Grimulf crushed his lips to hers. She woke, surprised, then pressed close. He unsheathed his sword.

"They have found us," he told her raggedly. He could not look in her eyes, did not want to see the sorrow there. "Go. Run to the church."

"No, I—"

"Do not argue with me, woman. Obey my last command. Go!" he barked at her, and she flinched. He slapped his sword upon the ground, water droplets scattering.

Grimulf turned to where the horses approached while Rosa raced on ahead. He could not see them in this darkness. Good. That meant he could surprise them. He remained where he was, the sword grasped in his hand.

The rasp of burning fire flickered in his mind. His breathing quickened. A knotting sensation crawled over his flesh, every muscle becoming taut. There was no need to be gentle and good anymore, his only reason was gone.

Olaf would learn to fear him again.

Rosa had not run far. She crouched amongst bracken bushes, concealed by the talons of stricken twigs and shadows. It was a foolish thing to do, yet she could not leave him.

She huddled there, shivering, perplexed as to why Grimulf remained kneeling. He should run as well. There was a chance they could keep running together.

No matter how painfully his name lodged itself in her throat, it was trapped within. Her breath misted as thinly as a snake. *Get up*, she urged him. *Fight for us.*

The horses drew near enough for her to see the flash of their hooves as their pursuers' lanterns splashed light across the ground. One rider broke from the others, approaching Grimulf. His hand was to his mace, but he had not drawn it.

The silhouette of a rope flicked in the murky darkness. Were they going to capture him? Rosa squinted her eyes but did not think she saw Olaf. Perhaps these men wanted to drag Grimulf back so Olaf could watch his execution in person.

Rosa clutched one of the bracken arms of her hiding place. It was she who noticed the roll of Grimulf's shoulders, the subtlest of movements.

His sword thrust upwards with ease and stabbed through the man's head from his chin. She was distant enough for them to be mere figures in the darkness, yet close enough to smell the scent of blood and death. Her breath stilled, mouth open in horror. It was like watching shadow puppets fall upon one another in a mockery of battle, for her husband moved as gracefully as a wraith.

The first one fell from his horse and startled the creature, sending it bolting past Rosa, the corpse bouncing behind as it was tangled with the reins. The others roared in fury, drowned out by the crash of waves over the hill. They dived from their horses, brandishing their weapons: daggers, swords, axes. Shields were raised.

Grimulf did not balk when they surrounded him. He hunched over, wolf-like, lips pulled into a snarl. He faced the smallest of the men. The group hesitated, not knowing who would first strike, none wanting to be caught by an ally's blade.

The sword was nothing to Grimulf. It might as well be made of mist. He jerked his weapon behind him, catching the tallest warrior behind in the jaw—there was the crunch of teeth and a choked, bloodied cry—and then thrusting forward to sever the hand of the one he faced. He heaved the sword and swung in a frenzy. The scream tearing from him was wild and animal, but of no creature from this world. It was somewhere far below in the depths, where the spirits and dead roamed.

Rosa trembled. Her flesh was so frigid there might as well be a layer of frost. This was the berserker Grimulf had warned her about. The monster he kept tightly contained within, which frightened even him.

Two more men fell. There was a flick in the air, like the dashing of raven's feathers, but she knew it was blood. A great pool formed, inching closer, coming for her. The marriage returned, the spilling of the sow's blood. She covered her mouth to stop the lurching of nausea and tasted copper. She spat, terrified the men's blood had reached her, but it was the thorns of the bush, biting her from how tightly she had clung on.

This man was not her husband. It was another creature wearing his skin. A demon. He grinned brutally as he took down another one. Kicked the man aside as one would flotsam.

And yet... When the remaining man backed off, Grimulf looked behind. Towards her. He did not see Rosa, but he was looking in the distance, thinking she had escaped. His smile was now relieved.

No matter the beast her husband turned into at the taste of blood, Rosa remained at the foremost of his thoughts. Even wild, he protected her. Did that not make him worthy of redemption, so long as he clung to his love?

The last man was running now. Grimulf laughed at his retreating back, harsh like the cracking of the earth. Rosa released her own choked sigh of astonishment. Their pursuers were gone. Once Grimulf calmed, she could leave her hiding place and tend to his wounds, kiss every new scar. He would be furious at her for remaining, but he would surely appreciate her loyalty.

More horses appeared, double what had come before. There were men she recognised, those Grimulf would have known as a boy and sworn to protect as chieftain. His sword became a thing of rigid steel, gripped too tightly as though its weight was keenly felt.

Grimulf disarmed two of the men who went for him. There were too many. They piled in, beating him down with their staves. One cracked against his wrist and the sword broke free from his grasp.

A moan of misery escaped Rosa and they mistook it for the winds. They kicked and jabbed at him until he was on the ground. Grimulf was bound as he kicked and thrashed, an animal biting at its bonds.

Then all the fight blew out, the candle snuffed. He bowed his head as he was dragged to his feet, much smaller than the man he was. The men reclaimed their horses, Grimulf forced to walk behind.

She could do nothing. It would have been better if she had kept running, as at least she could pretend Grimulf had managed to escape. Now she was alone. Rosa wiped her eyes, smearing her blood over her face without realising.

They would surely kill Grimulf once he was brought before Olaf. Her husband was lost.

All she could do was obey his final command. Rosa ran, heaving with sobs. The monastery was a blurred giant looming over her, fragments of the round tower and spires rearing in her vision. She flung herself against the door, banging her fists.

"Sanctuary!" she cried. "Let me in!"

The door opened. She fell and many hands held and steadied her.

Monks brought her inside, petting wet hair from her face, taking her sopping cloak, chafing her frigid fingers. Their eyes flicked down, taking in her heavy belly then the ring upon her finger.

"What has befallen you, poor child?"

The fire, starting to curl inwards in preparation for sleep, was stoked anew. They dragged a chair in front. One of the younger monks rushed off, returning with a cup of warmed ale. Ripples shuddered over the surface as she clutched it. Someone tried tipping the bottom to get her to drink.

She might not have full control of her body, yet the lie came easily. "My husband and I were travelling to visit family when we were attacked by Vikings." The horrors of the battle flashed over her eyes as shadows and she covered her face, groaning. The cup was quickly taken from her, a sliver of foam rolling over the back of her hand. "There were too many of them. He told me to run while he held them off."

Sharp pains tugged at her belly. She clutched the heavy mound in terror. Had their flight been too much? After having Grimulf taken, would she lose their child as well? Her fingers massaged the underside of her stomach, willing the child to settle. Tears stung the corners of her eyes.

Please little one, she prayed, holding her breath, *you will see this world soon. Hold on.*

"Thank God you were able to reach us. It is no longer safe to travel. The truces do not matter, it seems. Last year the Vikings sacked one of our nunneries. Such a tragedy. We will find you somewhere to rest. All of us will pray for your husband's soul."

"Thank you." As she was led further in the rest of what was said made sense. "A nunnery was sacked? Were there any survivors?"

"Unfortunately, there were a great many deaths. There has been word some of the nuns found shelter in nearby churches. We have offered a roof to the novices who managed to reach here. Ah, there is one. My child, will you assist this traveller? She needs bath and broth."

The young nun turned, arms laden with bedsheets. She smiled kindly.

Rosa recognised her first. Mildritha had not changed at all, whereas Rosa was rain drenched, haggard from lack of sleep and laden with her extra passenger. She realised in time, though. Her eyes widened. Joy flushed her freckled cheeks as she almost called her name.

Rosa quickly shook her head, slightly so the men would not notice. Mildritha understood.

"This way," she told her, indicating to one of the bedrooms.

Once they were away from the others, Mildritha lunged. She engulfed her friend in an embrace and Rosa, so surprised, so relieved, sobbed and held her tightly.

"I thought you were dead," the younger woman said, wiping her tears. "When I saw that beast carry you off, I feared the worst." She took in her pregnant stomach. "Oh, Rosamund, I'm sorry. You're safe now. I won't let him harm you ever again."

"No, this is not... I did get away, Milly, months ago. This child is very much wanted."

Rosa told her the entirety of her story, the truth of it, once the bathtub was brought in. Mildritha knelt next to her, pouring pitchers of hot water over her head. It was a great relief having someone take care of her.

A tendril writhed in her chest. As much as she loved her friend, all she wanted was Grimulf in her place instead.

She was hesitant as she revealed who her husband was and that she had willingly relinquished her nun's habit. Her encounter with the priests had made her wary.

Mildritha cupped her cheek. "You did what was needed. God must have a hand in this, else there would have been no point in it happening."

"You are not disgusted with me?"

"I am glad you found happiness with this man, even if he

is a…" She glanced at the door, then whispered, "Pagan. If only your joy could have lasted. He might escape if he is as strong as you say."

"I pray he will."

"There is the child as well."

Rosa managed a smile. "You will not tell anyone about this?"

"I promise. Once the child is born, I'll help you find a suitable situation or return you to your father."

Mildritha helped Rosa heave herself out of the bath. As she dried herself, she asked, "How did you fare in the escape? Were you able to avoid Olaf's men?"

Mildritha turned from her. She busied with pouring out a cup of wine and plating up some of the bread and cheese.

"Milly… You were not harmed?"

"No, thankfully." This time the nun was hesitant. She brought the tray over while Rosa settled before the fire. "In the darkness I somehow managed to stumble into Sisters Mary and Eawynn."

"They still live?"

"Not anymore. And I do not mourn them. We were attempting to reach this place when the Vikings caught up with us. I cannot believe this, even when I know it is the truth, but the sisters offered me to them in exchange for their lives."

"That is—curse them!" Rosa spluttered, sickened.

"The Vikings slayed them and I kept running. As they chased me, the ground crumbled and I fell into a barrow. My leg was badly twisted. I thought it the end of me. Then I was saved."

Her fingers went to her throat, where her crucifix should have been, the necklace there instead hidden beneath her collar. All Rosa could see was a gold chain. Mildritha sucked at her lip.

"I was so feverish I thought the man was the angel

Gabriel. He looked just like the Lichfield sculpture. He is a knight, Rosa, and…" She could not finish what she meant to say. "I blessed him, then he brought me here and tended to me until my leg healed. He left and I have had no word since."

Rosa took her hand. "Then I hope he will come for you."

She took the goblet, about to drink. The pain in her stomach returned and she jolted, wine splashing on the stones. She curled in on herself, drawing her legs up. It was as if she was the sky and had summoned the rains.

Rosa did not even realise, only felt a release as if a weight had been lifted. Mildritha's gasp was what alerted her to something being wrong.

She looked down. Slowly spilling across was a clear pool. She saw her own hazy shape in its reflection.

She had witnessed all her mother's labours. She knew what took place in the confinement chamber. And yet, as it happened to her, suddenly all her knowledge fled. She stared, stunned, fingers lightly gripping her skirt.

She had stopped breathing. In her mind was her own voice telling her what must be done, but it was muffled and her body seemed unable to respond.

"Rosa, let us get you to bed." Mildritha gripped her shoulder and Rosa was thrust back into herself.

Her child was coming.

"I need—" And she was rattling off everything, probably repeating herself. Mildritha nodded distractedly as she led her to the bed.

There was a pinching sensation at the base of her, when she knew all she should be doing was forcing herself open. When Mildritha tried to nudge her on the bed, she shoved her off and hobbled around. Her back was curved, hovering over the swollen stomach she cradled. She should lie down, like any other common beast giving birth, she ached to, but something else told her to keep moving.

Behind her was a flurry of movement as Mildritha got what was needed. Female servants, travellers, nuns followed the noises and suddenly Rosa was besieged with suggestions. The women argued over whose own birth stories were more shocking.

Rosa gripped the bed, squatting. She was losing track of time, uncertain what should be happening next.

She would see her child soon. Finally know whether it was a son or daughter. See if the child had some of its father's red hair tufting the top of its head.

All thoughts of Grimulf caused a fracture to cut her heart. He should be here to welcome his first child.

Rosa sprawled half-over the bed, sobbing, then screaming in agony. This was death itself. To bring new life, must she die instead?

She crawled to the top, strange women helping her, touching and undressing her. No longer were they strangers, they were bound together in this task. Mildritha fretted in the background.

Her face was bathed, dress pulled so she was left in her shift. An old crone leapt behind as support, another folded her knees against her chest.

"Push!"

The room was spinning. Sweat stung her eyes. A woman was babbling. It sounded almost like her; she wanted Grimulf here, she wanted her mother, even though she was dead. She was praying and begging pagan gods to spare her child. The Christian women pretended not to hear.

Ringing sounded in her ears. In her blurring vision she saw the priestess again, standing over like a carrion bird waiting for its meal to die. She had threatened her child. Rosa tried to lunge for the apparition, but hands held her down from all sides.

There was agony and thrashing and tears. Outside the moon was full and poised in the night, like a bauble someone could carry away. The clouds were thick and edged with dusky grey, the same as leaves yellowed in autumn.

Windblown trees were bent painfully like old women. Lights came on in the monastery, candlelight flickering and awakening. A figure raised a tiny creature that flailed and tipped its head to shriek.

Rosa's eyes were half shut. She ached all over and felt no longer a woman, only an emptied husk. She managed to lift her arms to demand her child. One of the serving women brought the baby to the top of the bed, while below a carving knife sliced the cord that had provided nourishment and had begun to shrivel as it left her.

Rosa used the bedsheet to carefully wipe the blood and membrane coating the child. It squirmed, red, wrinkled face puckered, but beautiful and hers. The child she thought she would never have when she first joined the nunnery.

"My daughter. Mildred."

She marvelled over the tiny fingers. When she rubbed her thumb over the tear drop sized nail, it was as gently as one would touch a snowflake, for fear it would melt in the heat of her palm. The baby did not vanish. She was here in her arms, incomprehensibly small, face emerging from the blankets.

Rosa looked up. Her hope had been brittle and soon fragmented. Grimulf did not stand there in the doorway. It was her and Mildred now, together and yet alone.

Her happy, breathy laughs choked. Tears throbbed down her cheeks and suddenly she was howling.

The tranquillity of the nunnery, the sensation time had stopped, cocooned and safe, was gone. Not even the hazy memories remained. Her husband had been captured and was most certainly dead.

She had her beautiful daughter, she was immensely grateful, yet she knew they would always be in flight. None would welcome a disgraced nun and her Viking child. She wondered over the state of her soul, as she had relinquished the innocence she had promised when wedding herself to God.

What sort of life could she promise her child? Mildred began to wail as well.

The women stepped back. It was Mildritha who held her. She brushed aside her tears. Soothingly made nonsense noises, either to the baby or Rosa.

"Let me have the child now," she urged.

At the brush of fingers on her arm, Rosa tightened her grip. She would not give her daughter up. She had won against the priestess' promise, yet something could easily creep in like smoke and steal her from her in the last minute.

"No one is going to harm the darling creature," an old woman told her. A cot was brought in from another room. "You must rest."

The cot, a trail of spider webs clinging to the bottom, was pushed to Rosa's side of the bed. Blankets and pillows were piled on, then Rosa let go and Mildred was placed upon them. Her blanket was swaddled tight around her, but she pried a fist free, waving it as though to capture the stars outside.

Rosa slid down until she was beneath the covers, curling her knees into her sagging, emptied stomach. She watched her child with wide, startled eyes.

She came from me, she thought with frightened wonderment. *And I must protect her.*

The candles were blown out. Mildritha was the last to leave. She looked upon the woman and child and did not quite recognise her friend. Then she shut the door.

Rosa waited until she could make out the outlines of the cot and the small creature within. She smiled, finally shutting her eyes.

CHAPTER 9

R osa watched Mildred lay in her cot, gently snoring. It seemed impossible, as if the child was nothing more than a piece of artwork she had created.

Once the tiny eyes opened and then screwed up to wail, she would be real and in need of attention. That was what frightened her. Asleep and nothing could harm her.

Rosa's appetite had departed, but she forced herself to eat. She needed to be strong. While she wavered over the cot, wishing she could hide Mildred from the rest of the world, a horrible choice loomed.

Grimulf had not returned. Rosa needed to find out the truth.

The baby settled at her breast, nosing out where her nipple was and sucking almost to the point of pain. At least she showed no sign of weakness. She had her father's strength. Rosa stroked the few strands of wispy red hair already on her crown.

There were many travellers who had come to the monastery. One of them was a woman with five children, the youngest only a few months old. She had agreed to take Mildred on until Rosa's return. Her own husband had gone missing, drowned while fishing. She knew the need to go searching.

"You must recover for a little longer," Mildritha impressed upon her. "I cannot understand why you want to go running across the dunes again. If I had done what you did, I think I would simply curl up and die."

Rosa smiled, thinking to herself there had been a slightly haunted look on her friend's face since witnessing her labour.

"It is not so bad once you have the child. You still want to die, but you know you cannot more than ever."

"Surely you want to be near Mildred?"

"I do, but I also need Grimulf."

"And if he is dead?"

Rosa turned aside her head. "While I am unable to watch over my daughter, will you do it in my stead? You are the only person I would consider making her Godmother."

Mildritha hugged her. Rosa returned the embrace, keeping in check her flinch or else her friend would demand she remain in bed. She had almost cleaved in two to bring her daughter into this world and knew she could withstand any blow dealt to her.

Mildritha helped Rosa with obtaining one of the horses from the stables. This time she had a saddle to keep her thighs from being hurt too badly.

"I'll be praying for you," her friend told her as Rosa looked down from her horse.

"I'll return for Mildred."

Then Rosa dug her legs into the horse's sides and the beast shot out of the stable, pounding over the lands. Winds streamed into her face, rain slithering through her hair.

She risked a glance at the monastery as it turned into a blob of shadows, then nothing as it was consumed by the night. Her stomach twisted, hating herself for leaving her daughter. The Vikings might capture Rosa and then her life would be forfeit. She would be making her child an orphan through her headstrong foolishness.

When the horse began to slow, Rosa led it down to the beaches, where she knew she could rest without fear of discovery. The herring had swum elsewhere, the farmers now tending to their cabbage patches. She found dry flotsam, striking her flints to spark off a fire.

The memory of when she had run from Grimulf returned. Her eyes stung, wishing he would come up from behind and tease her. That he would lead her to their home and all of this was nothing but a hallucination, a warning of how badly things could turn out. The warmth of the fire cupping her cheeks and the ache in her belly told her otherwise.

She touched her stomach, mourning the child she should be cradling. Grimulf could be dead after suffering Olaf's tortures. If that was the case, if her love had been stolen, what then? Her heart pounded in the base of her throat, tears stinging needle sharp.

They would come for her next. Olaf was crazed. He would not let her slink away, not when she had angered him.

Their daughter should be her priority. Mildred must survive. She would be all she had left of her husband to love. Her knife felt cool and hard against the bone of her ankle, tucked in her boot.

She needed help. God had not answered her since she had left the nunnery. The only way she had survived was through her own cunning and Grimulf's strength. It pained her, like a spider's bite, to consider He might not be watching over her. Instead, alone in this darkness.

Might Grimulf's Gods answer her call?

Rosa held out her hand. The flames lapped around the air, her skin turning rosy from the threat of heat. She took out her blade.

A single slice to her hand, from the tip of her longest finger to the bottom. Blood welled, droplets streaming. The wind caught upon them just as they were about to fall, dashing them into the flames. Red burst and was consumed by the orange flicker.

"I am not one of your people, Freyja," she called.

There were others, Odin, Thor, Sif, but she knew little of them and did not know if they would be willing to lend their ear. She remembered Grimulf's tale of Freyja, whose husband had departed one day and not returned. She hoped this deity would feel some sympathy with her.

"I do not pretend to be your follower. I offer myself as another woman. One whose husband has been cruelly taken. I do not know whether he lives or has perished. I might never find out. If he lives, lead him back to me. If…" Her throat lurched. She forced herself to go on, "If he does not, lend me your strength so I may bring his child to safety and shelter, then you may return me to my God."

She would have to lie about the child's parentage or else she would be thrown out on the streets. They might even take the child from her. She had her wedding ring at least, that was enough proof the child was not born out of wedlock.

Yet she had not been married in church. Did that not invalidate their vows?

Not in my heart, Rosa reasoned, which was what mattered most. A tear dribbled down her cheek at the thought of denying Grimulf. This would be his child, yet she would have to bundle the truth away and lock it within. A secret between herself and her daughter.

"He isn't coming, is he?" she whispered to the sky, empty of any stars. Her teeth dragged over her lip, her breathing faltered.

My bed will remain empty, she thought, *no more being held protectively, having stories whispered in my ear*. Mildred was all that remained of her time with him. If she wasn't there, then it all might have been a dream...

A sob rattled in her chest. Her face burned. She kept staring at the night sky, rather than hunch over and let her misery overtake her.

The stars might have deserted her, but the moon watched. It was as round as a shield, bright as a cup of cream. The clouds cleaved around it, curling. An aura surrounded the moon, almost as if its glow was the same as the sun, wisps of light swirling.

It was so bright it lit the beach. Rosa held herself, soaking in the warmth of the fire one last time. The bonfire would crumble in on itself soon or the sea would come to claim it.

"Give me strength, Freyja."

It would be a long, perilous night, but she would see tomorrow's sunrise.

Grimulf had given up on pacing. It brought no good, only made him wearier. It did not distract him from the ache of his split knuckles. Moonlight came in from between the bars of his cell, catching the smear of his blood on the wall and making it shine.

Without his sword, he might as well be naked. It had been his father's blade, never had he been parted from it for this long. His uncle certainly knew where to hit him. But it was not this which left him with dread pooling like a live eel in his gut.

Rosa was out there, alone, while he was constrained in this box. All he wanted to do was roar and charge, rather than feel icy horror shivering down his neck.

Might Olaf have helped his brother Ragnar to his death by poisoning his mead, and then waited for Grimulf's return to be rid of him as well? The man must be mad if he thought he could take control through trickery. This was not the way it was done.

For some reason he had not killed him yet. It made him hope some of his uncle's sanity remained. Any lingering fondness for Grimulf would give him the opening to strike.

Grimulf scratched at the stitches in his face, a sloppy job done by a stammering old woman who had been forced into the cell. She'd quickly jabbed the needle in and out to be away from him. Nothing like Rosa's perfect, tiny stitches. At the thought of his wife, he lunged for the door again. It shuddered under his onslaught but held.

There was an intake of breath from the guard, but no other sounds came. Grimulf growled, sloping off, until he sat slumped on the stone bench carved out of the wall.

The cord of his muscles stood thick in his neck. A berserker should not be immobile, he was a constant motion of furious limbs, a whirl just the same as one in the seas. It burned in his blood. No matter how old he became, the anger remained as sharp shards in his veins.

If Rosa was dead—! Grimulf covered his face. At the sound of a wailing howl, he thought it was himself, turned into a pitiful beast. It was only one of the hall dogs carousing at the sight of the full moon. He wished Shuck was with him.

"So much for the mighty warrior," he laughed hopelessly under his breath.

This was not the time for his fists. All he would get from that was his own spilt blood. A great weariness curled around, like bonfire smoke. He needed to be even more cunning than Olaf. Raging would not rescue Rosa from whatever fate hunted her in the night.

His own people had betrayed him. He felt sick. Had he really been such a rowdy brat before his departure that none were loyal when he needed them? He wanted to call for Odin and ask for his wisdom, but his tongue remained still.

Desperation turned him towards another. Grimulf slowly

sank down until he was on his knees. His back was to the moon, for seeing it his thoughts would only think of how the bright orb had tortured him in the past.

Grimulf bowed his head, clasped his hands, and prayed just as he had seen Rosa do. A sense of weightlessness came over him as he shut his eyes, but all he heard was the tumult of his own thoughts. He quietened them, just as he did before the ritual of the wild, but he did not call for Thor.

"God," he said, voice rasping in his throat, "I am not a Christian man. I am a pagan and considered a heathen by you and your people. I do not speak to you for my own gain, but for one of your… lambs." That was what he'd called Rosa upon their first meeting, hadn't he? It seemed so long ago now. "She is alone and in danger. She carries my child. A pagan child, but half of it is also Christian. Spare them from my uncle's wrath. If you need something in exchange—a sacrifice—then take me. Do what you must."

Silence crowded around him. All he felt was the heat of his wound knitting together, the cold pricking his back, the dampness of wind dried seawater coating his trousers. He had no idea if the bargain he had struck had been agreed on.

Slowly, groaning gently, he arose. A pair of eyes watched him between the bars. They were wide and curious, without the darkness and narrowing of age.

"What are you doing?"

Grimulf knew the voice. It belonged to Björn, the young grandson of Gunhild, and the boy Rosa had saved from losing a limb. Grimulf's heart hammered, knowing this chance could easily be wasted.

"I was praying," he gruffly answered, turning his head aside, as though he wanted to be left alone.

"To who? Odin?"

"To the one and only."

The boy's face screwed up in confusion. "Thor?"

"God."

"You—" The boy leaned away and he saw his face entirely. Pale, thick eyebrows and a meagre wisp of a moustache attempting to grow on his top lip. "Do not say that. They'll slit your belly open."

"Do you deny His power? You yourself have had need of it. When the cart turned your arm to pus and bile, my wife, my *Christian* wife, saved you, ungrateful brat!"

"She only used a few herbs," the youth argued. "Any northwoman could have done the same."

"Aye, and it would have turned black and fallen off. You can hold that spear because of Rosa and God."

"Still your tongue!"

Grimulf did not. He tilted his head and what roared next was a prayer. It was a mockery of one, different passages strung together from Rosa's whispers. He might have been asking for God to strike them down for all he knew. The words spilled out, almost musical in the way he spoke them.

Björn staggered back. He covered his ears, as if the words might turn him into something else if he heard them. The spear tumbled from the awkward hold between his arm and body, hitting the ground.

"Grimulf has gone mad! The Mercians have turned him into a fool!" the stupid boy shouted. Men came over, most drunk, thinking it another merriment. They laughed at him. One spat to the side in disgust.

"The Lord has chosen me to speak of your destruction," Grimulf shouted, his voice carrying through the crowd as powerfully as any preacher. "Bring me to Olaf. Let him see if he is mightier than God."

Men fell upon him, binding his hands, striking him around his head. He did not fight, only preached louder. They dragged him through the village.

They were doing exactly what he wanted to shut him up. Grimulf grinned, catching his breath. As the mead hall doors were pulled open, Grimulf became silent. His uncle sat at the head of the table, where his father and brothers had once been, where Grimulf should have been seated.

"Why is he here?" Olaf commanded. His cheeks were flushed, the colour of them almost purple with pain from the voracity of his drinking. Strings of bright liquid crawled down his drinking horn, making it appear as if it might suddenly shatter in his grip, but it was only the spilling of his favoured beer. "I did not ask for him!"

Since Grimulf's capture, they had been celebrating. The priestess Grimulf had thrown out soon returned. She now stood by the throne, bending to pour more of the violently hued drink into the horn, as though she was not respected and feared but as lowly as a common thrall.

The villagers had quickly grasped on an opportunity to be merry. They were celebrating the return of their fish, the stability of the dunes for years to come, thinking they had rid themselves of the miserable curse plaguing Grimulf and his brothers.

The traitors from Grimulf's fellowship were not as loud. They sat there, pleased as foxes come across an unguarded nest of hens. There was more than taking over the settlement in play.

"He's been speaking in tongues, Chieftain," Björn called by Grimulf's side. "It's the moon's fault, I say. Shall it be cut out?" For all his brave words, the boy shrank at the stare Grimulf gave him.

Grimulf was not truly bothered. He was looking for another. It pained him to do this, he knew his mind must be clear, yet he searched for Rudolf amongst the swarm. There he was, standing distant from the others. His arms were tightly crossed, watching Olaf but not once looking upon the old friend he had betrayed.

Grimulf recognised the jewels upon the sheath at his side as belonging to the hoard. At least he now knew why he had been betrayed—the simple hunger of greed. He wanted to believe there was another reason why he turned, something he could have done differently to keep his friend, but he would never know now.

"I speak only the truth," Grimulf answered, eyeing Olaf as the old man strode to meet him.

Even intoxicated, bent under the rigours of age, Olaf was still rigid and able to command himself. The people respected that. Olaf had been quick to speak of his battles and honours, whereas Grimulf had seen only shame in his exploits and hidden them.

Some honesty might have saved Grimulf from taking this path. Instead, he had given his uncle the chance to slyly twist things to his advantage.

Grimulf straightened, his hands bound before him. He did not flinch as Olaf brought out his sword and sliced his bonds in one swift motion, though the sword descended too quickly, clanging jarringly against the stones. The old man tilted his head to look in his eyes, wrinkled face puckered with disdain yet humoured with triumph.

"Truth is a very delicate thing, and is soon revealed as the lie it is," his uncle told him quietly. Then he turned from his nephew, unafraid, and called, "This creature would have you believe we are too weak to attack the Lady of the Mercians. That is what *she* would have you believe, to keep you here tending to your farms. Upon Thor's day we will march!"

Grimulf's eyebrows thrust upwards. "This madness?" He had thought his uncle's only desire was to claim the lands denied to him, given to the elder brother. "The Mercians would slaughter us. None of the other chieftains would agree to this. Life has been made easier with the truce and trading opportunities."

"A simple, bloodless life? You might be happy to be welcomed to Hel, but I would rather be taken to the great hall of Valhalla, knowing we fought with our blade in hand and a roar upon our tongue."

232

Was this what had led to all this misery and death? An old man desperate for one last grab at honour and riches, deluded by a prophecy that fit in with what he desired! Grimulf grimaced. The man he once knew, his rough and ready uncle, was long dead, replaced by a snake poisoned by madness.

And he must entice the snake into snapping, so its neck would stretch out and he could sever it from its body.

"A mighty task indeed," Grimulf said. "You might have once been a great warrior, but that time is long past."

"I have life in me yet, boy."

"Then prove it. I demand the blood feud you denied me when you chased me from this place. Fight me. If you can slay the beast in man's flesh, then it is Thor's proof you are as mighty as the stories once made out. And if I live—"

"There is no chance of that."

"No swords. Only a cord to bind us. I am your nephew. Will you deny your kin his right to die as a warrior might?"

Olaf's bloodshot eyes flicked around carefully, looking at the people. What remained of his teeth gritted together. Even his own men leaned forward in interest. They wanted to see the spilling of blood.

Stiffly jerking his head, Olaf held out his sword and someone came and took it from him. His priestess rushed over, offering what remained in his drinking horn. He snatched it from her, throwing it back, his lips stained yellow at the edges.

He straightened, heaving heavily, eyes beginning to dilate as his mind worked himself up. Grimulf recognised such a sight. His throat tightened, but he would not allow himself to fall into the same mindless rage of the berserker.

Björn tore off his belt, knotting the two men's hands together. A great pounding rhythm thundered across the tables. Now Grimulf could feel Rudolf's eyes on him as he and his uncle turned in a circle, the crowd surging.

If God had answered his prayer, then Grimulf had hurried his own demise for the sake of Rosa's safety.

Rosa allowed herself to rest until the bonfire banked into embers. A noise edged closer, barely registered as she half dozed. It was not the sound of hoofbeats or even another person struggling against the wet sands. Her horse's ears flicked, disturbed but not quite ready to bolt.

Something large and bulbous heaved itself across. Its eyes glistened, reflecting the light of her fire. The mouth gaped and a low droning noise emitted. Rosa stiffened, eyes wide.

The seal was huge, a male protecting his territory. He reared over Rosa. She gripped her knife, fingers drenched in sweat. The creature consisted of flaps upon flaps of fat and she doubted the blade would sink in deep enough, not before he managed to get a bite in.

There came a growl just over her shoulder. It was not a dog. It did not go low but high, a cat's whine of irritation.

Her cat Morgana crouched on the rocks. Her body shifted, tail taut and upright. The seal barked in warning. What could a cat do, even one as big as this one, against this beast?

Morgana leapt. The cat shrieked, as crazed as the winds. Her claws flashed across the seal's snout, teeth biting into his nose. One scratch caught the side of his eye and there was a pained grunt.

The cat crawled onto the seal's back when he tried to bite her, never relenting. Tiny smears of blood coated the speckled flesh.

The seal rolled, throwing Morgana off. She landed on her paws, hissing. Rosa watched, stunned, but now she scrambled to swipe out with her knife.

"Go!" she shouted. "We're more trouble than we're worth!"

The seal agreed. He thrust himself into the sea, vanishing amongst the waves. Rosa buried her fingers in Morgana's matted fur as the cat licked at her wounds.

"You little hell beast," she whispered, panting, relieved and grateful.

She left the horse and cat, Morgana resuming stalking the birds that roosted thereabouts. The mead hall soon appeared. It was just the same as when she had first arrived, but rather than running from something she now ran towards the danger. A storm was building, knitting misty, grey peppered clouds, the clicking of bone needles the rumble of thunder. There was a pale flicker in the distance, a blink of lightning.

She had come to claim her husband.

Her cloak and shawl were pulled over to conceal her face, creeping as the cat might do when returning from a hunt. There were no guards. She was not pleased with this luck. Something must be wrong.

Rain kissed the ground, turning the earth to mud, drenching Rosa within moments. Animals were out in the fields, shivering and letting out plaintive grunts. No one had come to lead them into the byres. There was the bitter tinge of burning stew drifting outside one hut, quickly swallowed by the winds.

No songs boomed in the mead hall. Dogs were not scrapping over tossed bones. All the warmth and happiness she had grown to love was gone. There were dark stains on one wall; the blood of those who had remained loyal to Grimulf, few though they had been.

Overhead, lightning struck its whip soundlessly. Light flashed over her, her shadow leaping in front.

She had been cloven in childbirth. Blood wept from her if she moved too quickly. She should be abed, but any bed except her marriage one would be too lonely.

Rosa crept inside. Amongst the crowd mead had spilt, golden puddles dully glistening. Their backs were to her and she slunk in as a rat would, water dripping from her ragged short hair.

A dog crouched under the table, eyeing her. Rosa remained still, wishing it was Shuck. This one was vaguely familiar, a long wiry thing like a fox, brown furred and missing an eye. It sniffed the hem of her dress, wet nose scraping her bare ankle.

The dog butted its head against her leg, weakly wagging its tail. Relieved, she scratched its ear and it loped off, going on its hind legs to snatch a chicken leg from the table and drag it into its hideaway. At least Rosa had the loyalty of the dogs, if not the men.

The high table was bare of any guests. Trenchers had crashed to the ground, scattering bones and offal. It looked just the same as when the priestess had come, only their roles had been reversed.

Rosa crept behind the throne, peering around the snarling bear's head carving. A gasp of horror rushed out of her, quickly hushed by her hand.

Grimulf grappled with Olaf. Blood streaked his rigid, straining face, one eye squinting shut. His clothes were ragged. The muscles in his thighs rippled as he strained to keep within the circle.

Olaf was faring no better. His teeth were gritted, showing all the ones knocked out, the gums black, bloodied. The fingers of the hand bound to Grimulf were bent back. His still usable hand clenched a rope around Grimulf's throat. Gouges had been ripped through his pouchy cheek. Spittle frothed down his chin alongside his sweat.

Grimulf only remained standing through sheer force of rage, a lesser man would have collapsed. He was younger, stronger, yet Olaf would win. He had turned everything to his favour.

Tears spilled down her face. Her skin prickled, hair standing taut.

Would she be forced to watch her husband die like a baited bear? She wiped her face. No, she would not stand for this. She withdrew her knife.

There was a great anger raging along with her tears. How dare this man try to take everything from her again! Her arms lifted, the knife clutched in her shaking hands. Her hair streamed over her face.

"Olaf!" she roared, and there was her distraction. All looked upon her. Olaf's grip on the rope slackened. "You sacked my nunnery and stole me away, and now you plan to take my husband from me? *Never.*"

She was not human anymore, voice roaring along with the thunder that had caught up with the lightning. It was another's voice coming from her, a sorceress, an enraged Goddess.

"Those you slaughtered have been waiting for you beyond the veil. They come to claim you. I do not offer my God's forgiveness or shrink in fear of Thor's rage. I offer their damnation!"

Rosa threw the knife. Thinking it was meant for them, men sharply parted. It landed at Grimulf's feet. He jerked down for it, slicing the rope off from around his neck.

The Viking raider had not reacted. He stared at Rosa, mouth slack. The sickening sight of one side of his face caving in slowly crawled across.

Olaf teetered. His hand blindly reached for something just above Rosa's head. He went stiff, flesh waxy and yellowing.

Now he fell, slumping to the ground as carelessly as tossed aside pig slops. His eyes rolled into his head, tongue lolling. Staining his lips was a vivid blotch patterned red with blood and the bitter gruit beer he had once loved.

Thunder crashed and lightning danced. A great stillness descended while outside the elements cheered.

None dared approach the corpse that had once been Olaf.

Rosa had called for her God and Thor to strike him down. Which one had been the one to do the deed?

"Both of them," Rosa whispered to herself.

No matter the differences in their faiths, Olaf had been a threat to both of their people. He might have started another war through his madness.

It was Gunhild who dared approach, emerging from the crowd. She stood next to Grimulf, peering curiously at the body. She mouthed something someone might have sworn was "good riddance". The old woman knelt and felt the man from his throat to his chest, the wrinkles on her face stark and twisted with distaste.

"This false man has been tested and punished."

Grimulf severed the bond keeping him tied to the corpse and kissed the old woman upon her forehead in gratitude. He turned to meet the eye of every man who moments before had been baying for his death.

"I am Grimulf, son of Heimer. I came here in good faith to lead you, to ensure the easy life you led under my brothers continued. I am no beast. I have walked beneath the full moon and I walked as a man, not a wolf."

This might be difficult to believe, considering he stood there with blood over his cheeks and his uncle dead at his feet. Some glanced at the open doors, perhaps planning on taking flight, but Rosa loomed over and she frightened them. She could kill a man without need of a blade.

"You do not believe me? The full moon is still here tonight. I will stand beneath it and you will see for yourselves."

A few gripped their blades. His eyes narrowed and their hands fell limp, not quite daring to test him.

"I am tired of this endless death. Never would I turn against my own people, but I will cut down any who think to harm what I protect. Those of you who do not agree are free to leave us, yet I do not want to catch sight of you again."

Rosa approached. He wrapped his arm around her, hand resting upon her stomach, expecting the fullness of their child within. At the dipping of the mound, he stiffened, yet he had to keep speaking.

"This is my wife. I claimed her. She is my mate, my counsel, my witch. All who follow me must follow her—"

"And our daughter!" Rosa cried.

"And our daughter," Grimulf whispered, relieved. The child lived. He spoke again, louder, roaring in joy, "Any God may walk among us, you may choose to be Christian or pagan. All that we demand is your loyalty. For I might not have the fur and teeth of a wolf, but I will defend any who ally themselves to me as the wolf does."

A great pounding started at one of the tables. Thorstein, one armed and chained in preparation for the trial, crashed his remaining fist into the wood like a drumbeat. Others joined in. A woman cheered, clinging to the arm of her man.

They twisted their loyalties as easily as leaves in the winds did. However, all leaves fell in the winter and did not stir. Now they had made their final choice.

Grimulf had won. The hall was his again.

The night pulsed thick and dark in the sky, the stars drowned. Wisps remained of the clouds, but they had been shouldered aside by the bright eye of the moon.

Grimulf strode out of the hall, the people following behind. Rudolf was not amongst them. He had slipped off with a handful of others when Grimulf had given them the choice. As promised, the chieftain would not hunt them down. This night had already glutted itself on blood, he did not hunger to keep watering the soil.

Rosa and Gunhild stood either side of him. The old woman unclasped the ragged remains of his cloak, revealing his bare shoulder rearing through the tears.

Moonlight placed her hand upon the bare flesh. It had paled slightly from his time here, no longer darkened by the sun. A streak of white scar curled around the blue stem of a tattoo of thorns.

No change came about. He still possessed his human flesh.

Grimulf raised his hands, almost grasping the light. He did not grit his teeth in pain. He shut his eyes, tilting his head.

"See?" he murmured lowly, and as he spoke even he believed what he said, "There was no curse. I was turned mad by the poisons I took as a berserker in the East, but now I am free of them. I am a man once more."

"Tell us your stories of the East, my lord," Björn called. "Tell us the magic you saw there."

Grimulf's mouth twisted into a rough smile. "I could have sworn you were considering having my tongue cut out, boy." Gunhild turned, scowling at her grandson.

"That…That," the boy stammered. "We were all tricked by your uncle's lies."

"Come in, then, and I will tell you of the monsters that roam across the sand lands."

They returned to the hall, where the dogs cared little who sat at the tables, so long as there was food to be snatched. It was quieter, almost ashamed, for the people knew only moments before they had been hungry for their chieftain's death.

Someone stood at the entrance, clutching herself. Adelina

remained while others fled. She glanced over her shoulder, at the corpse of the man she had once served. Kohl smeared her face, but it was not from the shedding of tears.

Rosa whispered in her husband's ear, "What do you plan for her?"

Grimulf considered the thrall, then said, "I give her fate to you."

Rosa paused while the others went ahead to deal with Olaf's corpse. She offered her no smile, knowing that although she was not a true priestess she had threatened her child.

"Where is your baby?" Rosa demanded. The thrall had been heavily pregnant when she left her.

Adelina flinched. Her hand pressed into her flat stomach and Rosa felt herself begin to waver too quickly.

"The child lives. A boy. Orm that man demanded I call him." Her eyes flicked to where the body was. "I have not seen my son since I brought him into this world."

Rosa wondered why Olaf would want to name the child, but soon realised. "He was the father?"

A sharp jerk of her head in assent. Rosa doubted there had been any tenderness in that union.

"He would have killed a daughter," Adelina told her. "Instead, he took my son from me and all I could do was obey in the hopes of seeing him again."

When Rosa thought of her own child, she knew she would do anything to keep her close.

"If the boy remains in the camp, Grimulf will bring him to you. Only, tell me why Olaf did all this. Was it simply madness?"

If Adelina had shared his bed, then she might know some of what the man had been. Rosa no longer flinched or tasted something foul as she spoke his name. He did not frighten her.

"He was old. Every morning he would moan about his

pains and go hunting for a glorious death. No one would offer him that. The men here are all farmers and none of the chieftains would bother with him. They were too busy strengthening their trading ties with the Mercians.

"Then a priestess of Freyja, a true one, arrived at the camp. She had journeyed from Denmark, sent by her Jarl to give this message. She spoke of a new war against the Mercians, of complete Viking control of these lands, honour and riches, and O... Olaf eagerly believed this."

So, someone had been stirring trouble from further afield, where they could not feel the ramifications of the discord they had caused.

Adelina went on, "But the priestess had been angered by Olaf, for he tried to lay hands upon her. She told him he might start the war against the Mercians, but he would not live to see glory. His death would come when he saw his blood upon the face of his kin. He killed her for this."

And the priestess had got her revenge. Rosa pulled her cloak tighter around herself, looking out at the dark, still sea.

"Come with me," she told the thrall. "We'll reunite you with your child. I understand the depths us mothers will go."

They went inside. The great doors closed behind them, cradling the warmth of the fires and the rumble of stories.

Olaf was not given the honour of a proper burial. There would be no longboat to carry his body, no fires or mourning. Some of the men carried the body to the dunes, then flung him into the hightide to be swept away.

They found Rudolf in the morning. He lay face down in the marshes, sunken in peat and pathetically drowned in a small stream. From the tracks surrounding him, he had run as though something wild and ferocious had chased him to his death.

Mildritha rode across the beach with Mildred tucked under her cloak. The steed was a familiar one to Rosa—the white stallion she had first ridden with. Somehow the horse had found his way home. The man riding with the nun was one Rosa might not know by face but knew from deeds. Mildritha's Gabriel.

The knight helped the nun down, mindful of her precious load. His touch lingered on her arm, which Rosa quickly noticed with a smile. Mildritha had a chance, if she was able to read her men right.

Gabriel spoke little. He remained by the horse, eyeing Rosa and Grimulf as a hawk might a pair of snakes if they came too close to its chick. It was Mildritha who ran over to them, grinning, and told them all what had happened. Rosa held her daughter close, relieving the panging ache in her breast as she fed her.

The horse had been running across the marshland when he stamped upon a fallen Gabriel. He was returning to the monastery when his fellow knights attacked and left him for dead. He might not have survived had the horse not come upon him, even if he near shattered his shoulder. It was how he was able to be reunited with Mildritha.

Grimulf barely heard. Instead, he peered in wonder at his daughter, unable to quite believe she came from them.

"It is like how a seed turns into a tree," he murmured. "One moment a mere sapling, then a great beast laden with fruits."

"I'm sure your mother thought the same thing. A mere cub suddenly turned into a great grizzly bear," Rosa teased, and received a nip on her ear as he kissed her from behind.

Mildritha watched them, cheeks slightly pink in embarrassment. "Is this how a husband and wife are with one another?" she wondered aloud without even realising.

Grimulf grinned at her, knowing not to take to heart her slight flinch. "Aye, a happy one. Thank you for caring for my wife and daughter when I was unable to. Stay with us for however long you wish."

The nun bowed her head, then leaned over to kiss Rosa's cheek. She whispered in her ear.

"I am glad things have turned out all right, but I cannot stay. Gabriel and I must be off quickly."

"What...?" And yet Rosa had a sneaking suspicion what Mildritha spoke of.

"I am no longer a nun. Gabriel came back for me, Rosa. He offered me his hand. My father has had dealings with his brother and forbidden this union. He commanded the monks to keep me prisoner, so he could bring his own suitable husband! The monks are my friends. They sent word to Gabriel and he came to free me."

"Then I wish you good luck." She watched as the young woman was helped to mount by her soon to be husband. "Take the horse and get as far as you can."

Grimulf and Rosa watched the pair ride off, the twilight sky a hazy gold soon about to swirl with night. Mildred nestled close to her mother, seeking out her breast even in sleep.

Finally, they were complete.

EPILOGUE

Mildred ran ahead, weaving in and out the dune grasses. Daylight made her hair glow as bright as an orange flame. Shuck, old though he was, ran alongside, tongue lolling from his white peppered snout.

"Not too far!" Rosa called but made no move to chase her.

She knew she would never stray; her man and girl never did. Morgana was somewhere nearby, stalking after rats. She'd be fine on her own, as always, and Gunhild was fond of the cat.

From where she stood on the edges of the Gernemuth settlement, she could see the seas from here. The endless blue of warm waves, seafoam scraping over the sands. The boat was anchored just below and the men were nailing shut barrels of water, carrying boxes of salted herring, leading on livestock. On the beaches were the remnants of a bonfire, where burned their sacrifices to Thor to give them good weather.

It would be a long journey. They might decide never to return to these lands, but Rosa knew she could not forget this place. They would always have ties here. The villagers spoke of their story as if it was another legend.

Thorstein had been tasked as overseer of their village, until Orm was of age to take over and continue the family legacy. The young boy would not go the way of his father, not with Adelina to watch over him.

Hands came up from behind to wrap around Rosa, tugging her against a broad chest. She laughed as kisses were marked along her throat and shoulder.

"I thought you were busy preparing?"

"I'll always have time for my mate and pup," Grimulf said.

"Then best catch her before she gets stuck down a rabbit hole."

Grimulf brushed past, roaring as a bear might. There came giggles and squeals in the bushes. Grimulf re-emerged, Mildred squirming in his grip, beating at him with her small fists and laughing.

"You are needed for a very important task, girl," he said, and held his hand out to Rosa. She took it and was surprised when they began walking away from the boats.

"Where are we going?"

"We have been wedded in Freyja's eyes. I think it only right we are joined in church as well."

Up ahead was the monastery Rosa had found shelter in, where Mildritha had once been but had now run off with her knight Gabriel. The priests welcomed them, even if their smiles dimmed slightly at the sight of Grimulf stooping under their doorway.

However, they were good men. They blessed the water in their font and anointed Grimulf's forehead. Rosa remained by his side, Mildred sitting in one of the pews with Shuck's head on her lap.

"Admit all your sins, my son."

Haltingly, Grimulf spoke, "I have killed men and loved women. I have worked for those who have commanded evil things. Always, I have followed what I thought was right and then later regretted it. I have been mad. I will sin again, I am certain, but I wish to be good."

Grimulf's rumbling voice filled the church with tales of bloodshed and dark magic it had never heard before. The priest before him paled. Mildred continued fussing the dog, too innocent to mind what she heard. Rosa's eyebrows rose slightly, but she showed no distress.

This was his confession. He would shake off his sins from the past. Now he was no longer the bloodthirsty warrior but the man she loved, who had given her a daughter and protected them. Her wolf in man's flesh. Her tame wolf.

She rode to his village desperate for his protection, yet she had come to crave his love instead.

Grimulf was baptised. The couple knelt before the altar, the ceremony commencing. Their vows were exchanged. As Rosa spoke them, she silently thought the pagan vows she had spoken held a stronger meaning.

This time, with Olaf dead, there were no other claims upon her. The marriage would truly be binding. They kissed and arose, holding hands. All three and the dog left the church. Some sparrows shot off from the roof. The gulls were flying out to sea, the best of signs.

Rosa paused by a small cluster of shrubs that had a sweet, entrancing scent she could not quite name. She stroked the pinkish catkins sprouting from the crown then plucked some of the teardrop yellow fruits and leaves, crushing one between her thumb and finger. She sniffed, frowning.

"Grimulf?" she called, and her husband paused, their daughter dangling from his arm. "What are these?"

He approached. "I thought you knew all that grows here. That is bog-myrtle. We use it to brew gruit beer."

It was the drink Olaf had favoured so much, before their Gods struck him down. Berserkers often mixed it with the other substances they quaffed. Rosa coated the tip of her tongue in the juice. She spat, dashing the rest of the bittersweet leaves aside.

"I think there are better ways of getting drunk. Promise me you'll not drink anything as disgusting as this."

"As always, I'll obey your counsel, my witch," he told her fondly.

The journey to Scandinavia would be long and arduous. There was promise of excitement and new lands to explore, and a fresh start to raise their family.

The burning in Grimulf's blood had passed into her veins. Rosa wanted to see what was beyond.

THE END

Don't miss out on your next favorite book!

Join the Satin Romance mailing list
www.satinromance.com/mail.html

THANK YOU FOR READING

Did you enjoy this book?

We invite you to leave a review at your favorite book site, such as Goodreads, Amazon, Barnes & Noble, etc.

DID YOU KNOW THAT LEAVING A REVIEW...

- Helps other readers find books they may enjoy.
- Gives you a chance to let your voice be heard.
- Gives authors recognition for their hard work.
- Doesn't have to be long. A sentence or two about why you liked the book will do.

ABOUT THE AUTHOR

Kitty-Lydia Dye wanders the beaches for inspiration with her little Viking warrior, Bramble the dog. Her historical fiction has been influenced by local myths roaming the haunting landscape of the Norfolk marshes. The idea for her romance novel, The Bride Who Rode in With the Storm, came about after her recent move from the beautiful cathedral city of Norwich to the coast. Hemsby, the 'by' suffix meaning settlement in Old Norse, is believed to have been founded by Viking settlers.

Many of her short stories have appeared in The People's Friend magazine. She has also released a collection inspired by Gaston Leroux's The Phantom of the Opera.

She enjoys knitting dog jumpers, gazing at the waves at night, exploring church ruins as well as taking part in amateur dramatics (and played the part of an evil flying monkey!)

kittylydiadye.blogspot.com

facebook.com/inkspiders

twitter.com/KittyLydiaDye

instagram.com/kittylydiadye

Lightning Source UK Ltd.
Milton Keynes UK
UKHW012035121021
392103UK00001B/43